A GOODNIGHT KISS

Alex had intended a simple goodnight kiss, until he saw his own desire mirrored in Samantha's eyes. His mouth settled on hers and he pulled her closer.

His tongue outlined her lips, coaxing her to open up to him. One hand moved lower, pressing her hips into closer contact with the hard muscles of his body. His other hand caressed the silky skin just above the fabric of her dress, sending shivers up and down her spine.

He raised his head and planted a few more light kisses on her face. He could feel her heart racing in time with his own as he held her close, her head resting against his chest. After a few moments he loosened his hold, tipping her face up to his.

"Well, sweetheart," he said softly, his voice still thick with desire. "I can't say I'm totally surprised by what we just experienced."

Samantha was disquieted by his words and the look in his eyes, but she was even more disturbed by her own reactions. "Alex," she said shakily, "I have too much pride and too much to lose to get involved in a casual affair."

He sighed. "I don't expect you to, that's not what I want either, and that's not what I think of you. All I'm asking is that you give us a chance. Our friendship means a lot to me. I have to admit I want more than that, though. I won't rush you, but I want us to be honest with each other."

Samantha felt a twinge of guilt. She hadn't been entirely honest, but she couldn't bring herself to make any confessions of her own. Unable to speak, she just nodded.

BOOK YOUR PLACE ON OUR WEBSITE AND MAKE THE ARABESQUE ROMANCE CONNECTION!

We've created a customized website just for our very special Arabesque readers, where you can get the inside scoop on everything that's going on with Arabesque romance novels.

When you come online, you'll have the exciting opportunity to:

- View covers of upcoming books
- Read sample chapters
- Learn about our future publishing schedule (listed by publication month *and author*)
- Find out when your favorite authors will be visiting a city near you
- Search for and order backlist books from our online catalog
- Check out author bios and background information
- Send e-mail to your favorite authors
- Meet the Kensington staff online
- Join us in weekly chats with authors, readers and other guests
- Get writing guidelines
- AND MUCH MORE!

**Visit our website at
http://www.arabesquebooks.com**

SECRETS

Marilyn Tyner

Pinnacle Books
Kensington Publishing Corp.
http://www.arabesquebooks.com

PINNACLE BOOKS are published by

Kensington Publishing Corp.
850 Third Avenue
New York, NY 10022

Pinnacle, the P logo and Arabesque, the Arabesque logo are Reg. U.S. Pat. & TM Off.

First Printing: December, 1998
10 9 8 7 6 5 4 3 2 1

Printed in the United States of America

ACKNOWLEDGMENTS

First and foremost I am grateful to God. Although I admit that there are certain logistics involved in writing that can be learned, I believe that the ability to write is a God-given talent. It is one which I did not discover until midlife, and it still amazes me when readers compliment me and express their enjoyment of my stories.

There are a number of people to whom I am grateful for their encouragement, enthusiasm, and help. My friends and family, as well as the readers with whom I have had contact who expressed their enjoyment of my first novel, *Step By Step*.

For the most part, I will refrain from naming specific persons to avoid the possibility of overlooking someone. There are a few people that I must mention, however.

To my sister, Alice Wootson, who was initially responsible for my decision to attempt writing. Her encouragement has meant a lot to me.

To my friend, Kathy Johnson, whom I refer to as my unofficial publicist. Her contacts and publicity efforts on my behalf have been helpful and are greatly appreciated.

To my former editor, Monica Harris, whose enthusiasm and encouragement gave my ego a boost when I was unsure of my ability. Her specific comments with my first novel were very helpful to me in writing this novel.

To my current editor, Karen Thomas, who, in the short time that I have worked with her, has been very helpful. Her personal concern has shown me that a business arrangement does not preclude a caring attitude.

To my agent, Linda Hyatt, who always finds time to answer my questions or listen to my comments, whether business or personal. Her enthusiasm and encouragement have helped make me feel confident in my ability.

Prologue

The car traveled slowly down the tree-lined suburban street, almost coming to a complete stop as it passed the stone house with the wraparound porch. The driver looked longingly at the comfortable old structure, reluctant to say the final good-bye. She'd had to have one last look before leaving it behind forever. The house held so many memories, good and bad.

She didn't delude herself into thinking she would leave the memories behind. Unfortunately memories were not something you could pack up and store away—you carried them with you, wherever you went. All she could hope was that it would be a little easier to live with them without the daily reminders, like the chair.

She had kept most of the furniture, but her father's favorite armchair was one of the pieces she had donated to a local shelter. That had been a difficult decision, although she had known it was for the best. Every time she had looked at it, this past year, she expected to see him sitting there, reading his newspaper.

She had tried rearranging the furniture, but, no matter where the chair was placed, her eyes were drawn to it. In the back of her mind was the knowledge that she should dispose of it. When she started packing and listing items for the move, she had finally found the courage to do so.

Strangely enough, it had taken more courage to get rid of the chair than it had for the decision to move. Her concern for Jessica's welfare overrode any hesitation she had about moving.

After she had taken the first few steps toward relocation, she tried to convince herself that making a fresh start was always a good idea. It was time to close this chapter of her life and put it behind her. She kept telling herself that this change would be good for both of them, even though she had been forced into it.

She glanced in the rear-view mirror at the toddler playing happily in her car seat, chattering unintelligibly to herself. She smiled at the child's gibberish. Jessica had always been such a pleasant, happy child. It was up to Samantha to see that she stayed that way.

There was a very real likelihood that the child's happy, pleasant disposition would soon disappear if she was put in a foster home, or sent to live with that woman who barely knew her. It was so unfair. But then, so many things in her young life had seemed unfair.

Until recently Mrs. Thomas had never shown any interest in getting to know Jessica. Samantha had no idea what had prompted her sudden concern. She didn't really care what had prompted it. She could not afford to ignore the woman's veiled threats.

Just thinking about Mrs. Thomas was enough to wipe the smile from Samantha's face. She sighed. Although she had been telling herself, over and over, that making a fresh start would be good for them, she could not help feeling resentful. It was only one of the many decisions she'd had to make in the past year. She'd had some doubts about the other decisions, but they had all been proven to be beneficial. She prayed that this move would also work in their favor.

Fortunately Jessica was too young to be greatly affected by the move. Samantha was the one on whom the weight rested. Uprooting them from the home she had known since childhood had hurt, but she was caught up in a situation that left her little choice. A situation in which running away appeared to be the only solution to the problem.

She had made a promise, and this was the only way she could be sure of being allowed to keep her promise. This past year had been difficult, but whenever self-pity threatened to engulf her, she reminded herself that she was in a much better position than most young women faced with raising a child alone.

Even before he became ill, her father had voiced his confidence in her ability to take care of Jessica. Both he and Martha had expressed pride in the way she had managed the previous year, during Martha's illness. At the time Samantha had not been quite as confident, but she had been determined not to let them down.

After he'd had the first heart attack, her father had given her a brief explanation of the arrangements he had made to take care of her financial needs. It was as though he had known he would not recover. She had tried to stop him—she had not wanted to consider that possibility. But her father had never been one to shrink from reality, and he had insisted that she needed to be prepared for any eventuality.

As he had explained, she was financially secure, thanks to the money from the insurance and the sale of the house. It would have to take care of them until she could find a job.

When she thought about the insurance, the memories of that difficult time flooded her mind. She would never forget that awful day that had thrust her into this situation. Insurance and finances had been the last thing on her mind when she made that last visit to the hospital.

She had walked quickly through the hospital corridors, oblivious of her surroundings, intent on reaching the room. She had come in response to the doctor's telephone call informing her that her father had had another heart attack. When he gave her some of the details of her father's condition, she realized that he was slipping away, although the doctor never actually said that. She had left home immediately after the call—she had to see him, be with him.

The room had been quiet, except for the subdued hum of machinery and the soft but constant beeps coming from the monitor. There was a strange, distasteful odor that pervaded her nostrils, one she had come to regard as a typical hospital odor.

Samantha had sat there for hours, watching the still figure in the bed, her eyes reflecting a world of grief that any observer would find heartbreaking in one so young. She glanced down at the once strong brown hand that she held cradled in both of hers. A hand now feeble and tinged a sickly gray.

Finally her father stirred and opened his eyes, trying to focus on her. She smiled weakly and squeezed his hand, fighting back the tears. When he spoke, she had to lean over to hear his words.

"I'm sorry, sweetheart. You're so young to have such a heavy burden, but you're a strong, intelligent woman, like your mother and grandmother. I know you'll manage. Take care of Jessica, and take care of yourself. God bless you."

A few minutes later he was gone, that awful whine of the machine signaling his passage. Almost immediately the room had been filled with people, one of them ushering her out to the waiting room. They need not have bothered. She knew what was happening. And she knew there was nothing they could do to change it.

Samantha peered in the mirror again, at the child who was now sleeping peacefully in the backseat. Her promise to take good care of the baby was always in the back of her mind. Her decisions were always based on that vow and her determination to live up to it. Her father and Martha had put their trust in her, and she would do whatever was necessary to ensure Jessica's well-being and happiness.

She admitted some anxiety concerning the fact that she did not have a job yet, but she was confident that she could find a part-time job, at least. She was more worried about finding a good baby-sitter for Jessica. She anticipated that might take a while, and she had been afraid to wait that long to get away. She had also considered that the matter of child care was not easy to arrange from a distance.

Mrs. Cummings's questions and suggestions had put her on guard, even before Mrs. Thomas visited her. That visit had made her realize that it would be foolish to just sit there and wait for a social worker to show up on her doorstep one day. By that time it would be too late to prevent some nameless bureaucrat from exercising what he considered his responsibility. She was afraid such an action would be disastrous to Jessica—and she was the only one who could prevent it.

One

Samantha poured her second cup of coffee and walked over to the window, gazing out at the dreary sky and steady stream of rain. It was unfortunate that today appeared to be one of those times the weatherman would be proven right in his prediction. The sun was unlikely to make an appearance that day. She sighed. For a brief moment she considered canceling the trip to the library, but she hated to disappoint Jessica. The toddler looked forward to the story hours.

Samantha had mentioned it to her earlier, and there was no way to back out of it without a long session of trying to explain the reason. Using the rain seemed like a weak excuse, even in her own mind, and it would never appease the child. Besides, when she thought about it realistically, a little rain wouldn't hurt.

She suspected she was just feeling a little dejected. No matter how she tried to fight it, late spring always had that effect on her. It was the same time of year that she had lost both of her parents, and Martha. She had always thought it was strange that they had each died in early June.

Samantha shook off her dark mood. Instead of moping around, she should be having a small celebration. She had just received her final grades for the semester with nothing under a "B" and, if all went well, she should have her degree by January. She realized that this was a small accomplishment by most standards, but it was an important step for her.

She had come a long way in two years. After relocating to Yardley, she'd had little trouble finding part-time work. Her first job had been as a clerk in a doctor's office, but before long she had left there for her current part-time job at one of the hospitals in the area.

Jessica's voice broke into Samantha's thoughts. "All done, Mommy. We go now?" she asked eagerly, her thick braids bobbing, as she nodded her head.

Samantha came away from the window. "In a few minutes, sweetheart."

As she wiped the ring of milk from the child's face, she reflected on Jessica's deep bronze complexion and thick black braids that were such a contrast to her own lighter skin and red hair that it had drawn stares more than once. A few people had even been bold enough to comment on the contrast. Samantha had dismissed their curiosity with the explanation that the child resembled her father.

"Let Mommy wash the dishes first," she explained, "then we'll go."

The following week Samantha took advantage of the brief recess before the start of summer classes. She had given careful consideration to the feasibility of squeezing summer courses into her schedule. When she had enrolled for summer courses the previous year, her foremost concern had been the possibility that Jessica might suffer from her absence. It did not take long for her to realize that the child was quite content to stay with Mrs. Elliott through the summer, along with most of her playmates. With that concern settled, she had decided that the advantages outweighed the extra work involved.

Her advisor had tried to talk her out of taking summer classes, voicing her concern that Samantha might find the load too stressful. Samantha assured her that she could handle it. She was determined to get her degree as soon as possible. It was hectic sometimes, but it was worth it.

Limiting herself to part-time work had given her time to finish school, without neglecting Jessica. The pay wasn't much, but it kept her from having to deplete her savings. Having her degree would increase her chances of getting full-time employment with decent pay. She was already thinking ahead to starting her job search in the fall.

She had thought it all out carefully. Her plan was to have her degree by the time Jessica turned four. Then she could put the child in nursery school, and they could both settle into a more normal routine.

Along with her break from school, Samantha decided to take the week off from work too. She had planned a number of activities and, luckily, the weather had cooperated beautifully. She and Jessica had been out almost every day, starting with feeding the ducks at the pond in the picturesque town.

The small town in the suburbs of Philadelphia suited her well. The town itself was quiet and neighborly, but close enough to available jobs and school. It was also easily accessible to such activities as visiting the zoo, the aquarium, and the Please Touch Museum in the city, all of which had been squeezed into that one week.

They had just returned from one of their outings on Friday when her friend, Amy, called to invite them to a cookout on the Fourth of July.

"I thought I'd catch you early," her friend explained, "before you made other plans."

Samantha laughed. "You definitely caught me early enough. I haven't even considered making plans for the holiday. I didn't really want to think about it because I know how fast the summer goes after the Fourth. We'll be there. Can I bring anything?"

"Just yourself and Jessica. We'll see you then."

The morning of the Fourth of July dawned gray and cloudy. Samantha had not heard the weather forecast, but she was hoping the clouds would disappear before the time for Amy's cook-out. She was glad to see the sun make its appearance before they had finished their breakfast. After all, an indoor barbecue wasn't much fun.

"I have a surprise for you," she said to Jessica as she cleared away the dishes. "We're going to see Cassandra today. Her mommy invited us to a cookout."

"We go see Sanda?" she asked excitedly. Then she frowned. "What's a cookout?"

Samantha smiled. "Well, we play games and eat all kinds of good things, like potato salad and burgers and hot dogs."

When Samantha pulled into Amy's driveway, Jessica was practically jumping up and down in her car seat. She had spied Cassandra and, as soon as Samantha had helped her out of the car, she was running toward the teenager, calling her name. Cassandra turned and smiled, holding out her arms to the child.

Samantha had known Amy, a child psychologist, for almost a year. Her friend worked in the office of a local psychiatrist, but they had actually met through her daughter when Cassandra had been recommended as a baby-sitter.

Samantha had run into a problem with one of her courses that she could fit it into her schedule only as an evening class. Mrs. Elliott took care of Jessica during the day, and normally Samantha was able to schedule her classes on the days she wasn't working. Cassandra had sat for one of Mrs. Elliott's other charges, and the child's mother had suggested she give the teenager a call.

Jessica had taken to Cassandra immediately. That alone had been a big plus. Aside from that, though, Samantha had been impressed with the teenager's patience and the fact that she appeared to actually enjoy the time she spent with the toddler. Her sense of responsibility gave Samantha peace of mind, knowing Jessica was in capable hands.

She watched the teenager now, as she hugged Jessica. She

always made the child feel special, without spoiling her. At first, Samantha had wondered if that special knack was a result of having a psychologist as a mother. After she had known the teenager for a while, she decided it was just a natural part of her personality. She was outgoing and friendly toward everyone.

Samantha greeted her hostess, and they chatted for a few minutes before Amy's duties called her away.

"Is there anything I can do to help?" Samantha asked.

"Not today. I noticed that Cassandra has taken charge of Jessica, so just relax."

Samantha wandered around for a while. She chatted with a few of the other guests and then strolled over to greet her host. A short time later she was manning the grill. Amy spied her and shook her head as she approached.

"I told you to relax, but I see Rob put you to work," her friend said.

Samantha smiled. "He didn't put me to work. I offered to watch the chicken and ribs, while he went to get the steaks and some more burgers."

"I want you to meet my employer, who also happens to be a good friend. Eloise, this is Samantha Desmond, Jessica's mother. Samantha, this is Dr. Simon.

"She's already met Jessica, thanks to Cassandra's off-target Frisbee. Jessica was running after it and almost collided with Eloise."

Eloise Simon was a tall, slender woman with short mixed gray hair. Her smooth mahogany-colored complexion belied her age, which, according to Amy, was somewhere in her midfifties.

"I'm glad it was just a near collision," Samantha said, extending her hand. "It's nice to meet you."

Eloise chuckled. "You have to be prepared for things like children running after Frisbees when you come to a cookout," she replied, as they briefly shook hands.

"Amy's told me a lot about you, Samantha. I understand you're in college and working too."

Samantha explained that she was working only part-time at

one of the hospitals and expected to finish school the following semester. The two women chatted for a while. When she learned that Samantha's degree would be in business and accounting, the older woman agreed that it was a wise choice. It would give her a good background for a career in a number of fields.

"I'll find out soon enough," Samantha informed her. "I plan to start looking for full-time work this fall."

Eloise gestured to Jessica and Cassandra, playing on the lawn. "It must be especially difficult, though, caring for a young child while going to school and working."

Samantha shrugged. "I admit she's a handful sometimes, but in many ways I've been more fortunate than a lot of people in my position. I have a very good baby-sitter—actually two sitters. Cassandra filled in for my regular sitter last semester, while I was at my evening class."

Eloise smiled. "Judging from what I saw earlier, the two of them get along quite well."

"Yes, they do." Just then the two subjects of their conversation came running over. Jessica started chattering and Samantha gently stopped her.

"Excuse yourself, Jessica. Mommy's talking."

" 'Scuse me, Mommy."

"I'll let you tend to your little whirlwind, Samantha," Eloise said. "It was nice talking to you. I'll keep my ears open for full-time jobs that might interest you."

"Thank you, Eloise. I'd appreciate that."

Samantha turned her attention to Cassandra as Eloise moved away. "I think Jessica's ready to eat, Samantha. I am too. Do you want me to fix her a plate?" Cassandra asked.

Before Samantha could reply, Rob approached with a platter of steaks and hamburgers, ready for the grill.

"Sorry it took so long, Samantha," Rob apologized. "One of our guests called. He'd gotten lost, and I had to give him directions."

"That's okay." She stepped away from the grill, motioning to the girls.

"Since your father's here to resume his duties, Cassandra, why don't we all get something to eat?"

Hours later Samantha tucked a happily exhausted Jessica into bed. After the cookout she and a few other parents had taken the children across the river to watch the fireworks. Cassandra and her sister, Jennifer, had ridden along with Samantha and Jessica.

She'd had some reservations as to whether Jessica would be so frightened by the noise that she wouldn't appreciate the beauty. It was the first time the child had seen fireworks, and she had shrieked and clapped her hands in appreciation throughout the entire display. Samantha derived as much pleasure from watching the child as she did from the show itself.

Jessica was so wound up from the excitement that Samantha was afraid she would be awake for hours afterward. Instead, she had worn herself out and had fallen asleep in the car on the way home. Samantha had carried her upstairs and roused her just long enough to get her into pajamas. She'd fallen back to sleep almost as soon as her head touched the pillow.

Two

Just as Samantha had predicted, the summer sped by and, all too soon, she was preparing for her fall classes. She had also started writing her resume. Even when it was finished, she couldn't actually mail it to any prospective employers yet, but barring some unexpected disaster, completing the last two courses shouldn't be a problem.

She had been perusing the classified ads for weeks, trying to get a realistic idea of the jobs available. She had also composed a list of possible nursery schools for Jessica, but before making arrangements to visit them, she discussed her plans with Mrs. Elliott. She didn't want the older woman to get the impression that she was dissatisfied with the care she had given the child.

"I'd like to start her with just three days in preschool until next fall. It will be an entirely new environment for her, and I think it might be best to let her become accustomed to it gradually. I'd like for her to continue with you for the other two days. Hopefully, by September of next year, she'll be ready for a full day at nursery school," Samantha explained.

"Fortunately I've never had a problem with her getting along with other children, but I think socializing with more children her own age will be to her advantage."

"I agree, Samantha. The idea of starting her on a part-time basis makes sense too. Although I'll miss her when she goes to nursery school full-time, I understand how important it is for her to have that experience before she starts kindergarten."

Within a few weeks Samantha had narrowed her choices of schools for Jessica and submitted her name for the waiting lists. She had also finished her resume, based on the assumption that she would pass her final two courses. Her advisor had assured her there were no other barriers to her anticipated graduation.

With those two projects well under way, she started scanning the real estate sections of the newspapers. When she had relocated, Samantha had settled for renting an apartment. At that time she had wanted to move as soon as possible and could not wait until the house was actually sold. As soon as the agent had given her a date for the settlement on the house, she had found an apartment and signed the lease.

She had even arranged the move and had actually settled most of their belongings in their new home beforehand. It had made the final move much easier. The apartment was comfortable, but now she was ready for a house.

She had looked at several houses by mid-October and had found one that she thought would be perfect. It was a three-bedroom town house with a family room adjacent to the eat-in kitchen. The living room, situated to the right of the foyer, had a fireplace and a bay window. The spacious master bedroom had its own bath with a whirlpool tub. The room that would be Jessica's had built-in shelves on either side of the window seat in front of the bay window.

Samantha was tempted to put a deposit on it but had restrained herself. It was unlikely that she could get a mortgage without a full-time job. Even if she could qualify for a mortgage, she felt uncomfortable making that great a commitment without a more substantial income.

When she inherited her father's house, she had originally planned to live there. When she was forced to relocate, she had sold the property. With the money from that, and the insurance, she could almost afford to pay for a new house in cash, but she was unwilling to deplete her resources to that extent. Using a portion of it for a large down payment would enable her to manage the payments comfortably and still have a substantial nest egg.

Near the end of October, she attended a job fair. Although she had been uncomfortable with the idea of mailing resumes to prospective employers, meeting their representatives in person gave her the opportunity to better explain her situation. Almost two weeks later she was waiting for responses from the job fair when she received a telephone call from Eloise.

"I asked Amy for your telephone number. I don't know if you're aware that I opened a second office in Trenton a few months ago. My main office has been in Newtown for years. Unfortunately, my office manager recently informed me that she won't be returning to work after she has her baby in February.

"I recalled your telling me that you would be applying for full-time employment in the fall and, although I've been on the lookout for you, nothing has come to my attention. It occurred to me that you might be interested in the position. I believe it would suit you, and the timing would be perfect. If so, I'd like to see your resume and schedule an interview."

"I'm glad you thought of me, Eloise, and I would like to find out more about it," Samantha replied, trying to contain her excitement.

"I've completed a tentative resume. I'll mail you a copy. Of course, this is all provided nothing happens to throw a wrench into my graduation in January."

They set a date for the interview, and Samantha hung up. She recalled the older woman's promise to keep her ears open for her, but she had never expected that the job offer might come directly from her. Samantha picked up the phone again and dialed Amy's number.

"Eloise just called," she told her friend. "Maybe I shouldn't be talking about it—I might jinx myself. I'm so excited, though, I have to tell you. She may be interested in hiring me as her office manager. I have an interview with her next week."

"That's great, Samantha, although it doesn't come as a big surprise. I knew Betty was leaving and when Eloise asked for your number, it wasn't hard to guess what she had in mind. I don't think you have to worry about a jinx, but I'll save my congratulations until after the interview."

"There's one more thing, Amy. I have to ask you a question," Samantha said hesitantly.

"You didn't have anything to do with this, did you? I mean, like giving Eloise a push in my direction?"

"I assure you, Samantha, my only involvement was in giving Eloise your phone number," she assured her. "Eloise has good instincts about people, which isn't surprising. Personally I think she'd be lucky to have you working for her. I know how conscientious you are about everything you do."

As she finished her statement, Amy chuckled. "Besides, once you get to know Eloise, you'll realize that no one pushes her into doing anything."

Samantha laughed too. "I don't really know her, but I think I already understand what you mean. I had to ask, though. Maybe I just needed that little boost to my ego. Thanks, Amy."

"Anytime. By the way, how are you coming along with the nursery school search?"

Samantha brought her friend up to date. "I've started on my next project too. I'm looking for a house. Actually I found one I really like. I haven't put a deposit on it yet. If all goes well at my interview with Eloise, or if I get a response from one of the resumes, I'll call the agent. Hopefully it won't be sold before then."

"Good luck, and don't be upset if you don't get it. My mother always said that if you don't get something you really want, you just have to believe that something better will come along."

"I'll keep that in mind. Thanks again, Amy."

Samantha hung up the phone, smiling to herself. Amy was probably right. After all, there were plenty of houses on the market and, thanks to her father's foresight, another one was bound to come along that would suit her just as well.

The following Monday Samantha had her interview with Eloise, and within a week she was hired. Samantha need not have worried that Eloise Simon's decision was based on a snap judgment or that she had been influenced by anyone else's opinion. As Amy had suggested, her years of professional experience had made her a very good judge of people, and she had learned to trust that judgment.

They agreed that Samantha would start her new job after the holidays, which would give Betty, the current manager, a few weeks to show her the ropes. Eloise's practice consisted of individual therapy and family counseling, as well as group sessions. Aside from her practice, the doctor also served on the board of two mental health centers and a hospital.

The day after Eloise informed her she was hired, Samantha called the real estate agent. The house she had mentioned to Amy was still on the market. She made arrangements to look at it again and called Amy.

"Hi, Amy. I called to tell you I got the job."

"That's great, Samantha. Congratulations!"

"That's not the only good news. The house I told you about is still available. I just talked to the agent, and I have an appointment to see it Saturday. If you're not busy, I'd like for you to come with me.

"Since you've been through this before, you know what to look for," Samantha explained. "I'm so excited, I'm sure I won't be looking as closely as I should."

"What time Saturday?"

"Noon. I wanted to talk to Cassandra, too, about watching Jessica. I'd rather not take her with me."

"Noon sounds fine. Hold on a minute, and I'll check with Cassandra," she offered.

A moment later Amy returned to the phone. "Cassandra says she'll be free to baby-sit. Why don't I meet you at your house and bring Cassandra with me?"

"That'll be great. I'll see you Saturday."

Samantha had just put in a load of laundry when Amy and Cassandra arrived at eleven-thirty on Saturday. Jessica came running out of her room as soon as she heard the knock on the door.

"Sanda!" she squealed, running toward the teenager. She had been a little disappointed when Samantha started her fall classes and she was told that Cassandra would no longer be baby-sitting in the evenings. Jessica had missed the teenager.

Cassandra caught the youngster, lifting her into her arms.

"Hi, Jessie, I've missed you."

"Me, too," Jessica murmured, hugging the teenager's neck.

Samantha smiled as Cassandra put Jessica down, and the toddler began tugging her hand. "Come see what I made."

Samantha called after them, as they headed toward the child's bedroom. "You can help yourself to lunch, whenever you're ready. There are cold cuts and tuna salad in the fridge."

When they were out of sight, Amy said, "She meant it, you know. She really has missed Jessica, although I think she took herself by surprise when she admitted it. It's not a cool thing for a teenager to admit."

On their way home, after looking at the house, Samantha asked, "What do you think, honestly?"

"I think it's perfect for you. I hadn't mentioned it earlier, but I'm glad it's been raining for two days. When Rob and I were looking for a house, I happened to visit one house just after a heavy rainfall. There were three inches of water in the basement.

"If we hadn't seen this basement for ourselves, I was going to suggest that you insist on a written guarantee that there's no problem."

"Now you know why I wanted you to come with me," Samantha reminded her. "I was so busy looking at the living space that the possibility of water problems in the basement never occurred to me."

"Well, all you have to do now is wait and see if your offer is accepted."

"Oh sure," Samantha said, laughing, "that's all. That and start preparing to move. Have you looked around my apartment lately? It's amazing the amount of stuff one accumulates. I'll just have to try to hold on to the excitement of moving, and maybe I won't think of the work involved."

"If there's anything I can do to help, just let me know. I'm sure Cassandra would be happy to take Jessica off your hands for a few hours on the weekends while you pack."

"I'll keep that in mind."

The following week the agent notified Samantha that she was well on her way to becoming a homeowner. Settlement was scheduled for the end of January, which wasn't the best time for moving.

Samantha didn't care if she had to move in the middle of a blizzard. As long as the movers didn't cancel, nothing would stop her from moving into her very own home. She'd heard that old cliche, 'Home is where the heart is,' many times, but there was nothing like owning your own house.

Along with the usual activities involved with the Christmas holidays, Samantha spent her time packing and making decorating plans for the new house. Fortunately the house was in move-in condition, which meant she wouldn't have to worry about painting or even any major cleaning.

She ordered the appliances she would need and scheduled their delivery for the day after her expected move. Although she would not make any major decorating changes until spring, by the end of the holidays, she had mapped out plans for exactly what she wanted to do in each room.

As the new year approached, Samantha contemplated the changes that were taking place in her life. She reflected on the years that had passed since she had been left alone with a child just out of infancy. She was always mindful of her good fortune—not just the financial aspects, although she didn't downplay that part of it. After all, it was what would enable her to move into her new home within a few weeks.

Her friendship with Amy was high on her list, whenever she counted her blessings, as well as the immense assistance she received from Mrs. Elliott. Some people might think that Mrs. Elliott was only doing what Samantha paid her to do, but Samantha knew that no amount of money could pay for the love and care Jessica received.

In less than a month, she would have her degree and one of her main objectives would have been accomplished. In some ways Samantha felt as though she had been marking time for the last few years. She never really thought of it as dull—although her social life was lacking, she had been too busy for it to be dull. After all the turmoil she had been through in her young life, she had welcomed what some would have considered a humdrum routine. Those years had served their purpose. Now she was ready for something more, and she would soon have it in the form of a new house and an interesting and challenging new job.

She was not disappointed in her expectations of the job. It did, indeed, prove to be a challenge. Her basic duties consisted of supervising two clerks, managing the accounts, and overseeing the appointment schedule. In addition to this, it was her responsibility to coordinate Eloise's conference trips and board meetings.

Along with the job and the house, her plans for Jessica had been realized. The week after placing the deposit on the house, she had received a call from one of the schools informing her that there was an opening available immediately. Samantha had decided that there was no reason to wait the extra weeks until she started her new job.

Jessica had more than adapted to school—she thrived there. She came home each day excited about some new discovery. Even Mrs. Elliott had remarked on the changes in her.

She had always had an agreeable, easygoing disposition, but in just a few weeks, Samantha noticed that she was becoming more independent. She would play alone for hours, moving from one toy to the next, or just looking at her books.

Samantha was surprised when she realized that there was a marked improvement in her speech. There were very few times now that Samantha could not understand the child's words. Of course, the fact that she was almost four years old accounted for some of the improvement.

When Samantha had begun considering nursery schools, she had been taken aback by the sudden realization that Jessica would be four years old in a few months. It was hard to believe it had been that long. She was reminded of all that had happened in that time: the loss of her father, as well as the stepmother who had been an important part of her life for such a short time.

She recalled her father telling her so many times how much she resembled her grandmother. He had been so sure she could manage and, largely because of his provisions, she had.

Three

Five years later

"Can she, Mommy, please, can she?" the child pleaded, her chocolate-brown eyes as big as saucers.

Samantha was preoccupied and had been only half listening to the little girl. She was cleaning out closets and mentally estimating the expense of replacing the clothes the child had outgrown in just a few short months.

She'd been postponing this chore for weeks, but when school started, she knew she could put it off no longer. Jessica's spring and summer clothes were fine for now, but with the opening of school, the cool weather could not be far behind. Judging from the clothes she had purchased during the summer, she knew the majority of the fall and winter clothes from the previous year would no longer fit her. She had not realized just how many of them would need to be replaced until she had actually started sorting through the clothes.

The child repeated her question, finally getting Samantha's attention.

"I'm sorry, honey," she apologized, her hand absently smoothing the child's braids. "What did you ask me?"

"Can Melanie sleep over tomorrow? We won't be any trouble, I promise."

"Who is Melanie?" Samantha questioned, her attention now

focused on the child. "I don't remember any friend of yours named Melanie."

"She just came to our school, and she's my best friend," the child insisted. "I think she's shy."

Samantha smiled. Being shy had never been part of Jessica's personality. It didn't surprise her that Jessica had not only befriended the newcomer, but had instantly decided that they would be best friends.

"I don't think so, honey, it's rather short notice," she explained. "I'll have to talk to her mother first. Maybe we can plan it for some other time."

"She don't have a mother."

"She doesn't have a mother," Samantha automatically corrected, her mind reverting to her task. "Who does she live with?"

Jessica looked exasperated. "She has a father," she explained.

Samantha was chagrined at her own chauvinism, overlooking all of the single fathers raising children. When she thought about that, another question occurred to her.

"Jessica, how do you know she doesn't have a mother?"

"She has a angel, like mine."

"An angel?" Samantha asked, looking puzzled. Then she nodded, remembering. "You mean the little pin I gave you?"

"Uh-huh. She has one too. She said her daddy gave it to her because her mommy is in heaven. He told her it would remind her that there was always a angel watching over her. Just like you told me. Remember?"

"Yes, I remember," Samantha said quietly.

"Anyway, can't you ask her daddy?"

"Yes, I can ask him, sweetheart, but it's still short notice now, to arrange it for tomorrow. I'll try to get in touch with her father, and maybe we can arrange for her to stay over sometime in the next few weeks. Okay?"

Seeing the look of disappointment on the little girl's face, she attempted to soften the blow. "I'll tell you what. Maybe her father will let her come to the movies with us next Saturday."

Jessica brightened a little. "Okay," she agreed reluctantly.

* * *

On Monday, when Samantha picked up Jessica at school, she recalled the child's request. She had her point out her new best friend among the children waiting to board the school bus and introduced herself to Melanie. They waited while Melanie boarded the school bus, then Samantha took Jessica back to the office with her.

She had been careful not to mention the invitation to the movies. She had on occasion been placed in that uncomfortable position herself by other parents. It would never do to issue the invitation without first discussing it with the child's father.

The arrangement of taking Jessica to the office with her had started as a result of Mrs. Elliott being hospitalized due to an emergency. Jessica had been just four years old at the time, and Samantha had been faced with the dilemma of arranging child care with very short notice. The nursery school she attended three days a week had been unable to accommodate her for the other two days.

Eloise had actually been the one to suggest the solution. She had proposed bringing Jessica to the office for the two days of the week that the baby-sitter usually took care of her.

It had worked so well the first few weeks that Eloise assured her there was no reason for her to look for another baby-sitter. The arrangement had continued through the months of Mrs. Elliott's recuperation.

Jessica's independence, and the fact that Samantha's duties involved mostly paperwork, had been responsible for the arrangement being successful. From the beginning the child had been quite content to keep busy with her toys and books.

When Jessica started kindergarten, Samantha brought her to the office for the second half of the day. And later, when she went on to elementary school, Samantha had arranged to pick her up at school and bring her back to the office until the end of the workday.

In the early stages of their acquaintance, she had seen examples of Eloise's generosity, so she hadn't been very surprised. Even so, Samantha was well aware that Eloise's latitude with this arrangement was unusual and extremely generous.

Thursday evening Samantha attempted to contact Melanie's father. She was informed that he was out of town and was not expected to return until the following Wednesday.

When she hung up the telephone, she explained to Jessica.

"I'm afraid we'll have to postpone Melanie's visit a little longer. Her father is away until next week. All I can do is try to contact him then."

As Samantha expected, Jessica was disappointed with this delay. On Monday she reminded her mother that she said she would try again. Samantha then explained that Dr. MacKenzie would not return until Wednesday.

Even if Samantha had forgotten the expected day of his return, she need not have worried. Wednesday evening the child reminded her. Samantha tried once again to contact the elusive Dr. MacKenzie.

She identified herself to the housekeeper, Mrs. Henderson. "I hope I'm not making a nuisance of myself. My daughter has been pleading with me for weeks to contact Melanie's father for permission for her to visit."

"It's no bother," Mrs. Henderson assured her, "but I'm afraid Dr. MacKenzie has not returned. I originally expected him back today, but his business took longer than he expected. If you'll give me a number where you can be reached, I'll be sure to give him your message and ask him to contact you when he returns."

Samantha thanked her and explained. "The girls exchanged numbers a couple of weeks ago. However, Melanie may or may not still have it." She gave Mrs. Henderson her home telephone number, as well as the office number.

After she hung up, she explained the situation to Jessica. "There's nothing else we can do now, honey. You'll just have to be patient."

The following day was hectic for Samantha. Her entire morning was spent meeting with the programmer, discussing the new software for the computer system.

Although it would be a few weeks before the system was actually installed, she had scheduled a preliminary meeting to explain the specific needs of the office. Once she explained this to the programmer, he was able to suggest the software that should be purchased to suit their purposes. Eloise had left everything in her hands, explaining that it made perfect sense, since Samantha would be the one responsible for its use.

Fortunately there were only a few patients that day—unfortunately they were all scheduled that morning. It was long past lunchtime and the clerk had left for a dental appointment. Amy volunteered to go out for sandwiches, leaving Samantha alone in the office.

Amy had been gone only a few minutes when Samantha heard the door in the front of the office close. Knowing Amy could not have returned in such a short time, she went to see who had come in.

When she emerged from her office, there was a man standing in the center of the room, casually looking around as if appraising the subdued but comfortable surroundings. She had a brief view of a broad back and narrow hips encased in a navy-blue suit that looked expensive, judging by its perfect fit.

When he turned, her breath caught in her throat and she thought of the romance novels Amy was forever reading. He was handsome, but that one-word description was an understatement. Amy was always talking about the men in her novels who exuded pure masculinity, but Samantha would never have believed such men really existed until now.

His skin was a deep bronze, and his face already showed the beginnings of five-o'clock shadow. His black hair was thick and short cropped, as if in an effort to tame its curls. It hadn't been a total success—she had already seen how it lay in waves at the back of his head, stopping just short of the top of his collar.

His eyelashes would have put any woman to shame, but what drew her attention more than anything were his eyes, as black as his hair, with a penetrating quality that was quite disturbing. Shaking herself out of her daze, she managed to find her voice.

"May I help you?"

She had been so intent on her scrutiny that she was unaware she had also been the subject of a thorough examination. The first thing he had noticed was her hair. It was probably the first thing any man would notice, a rich coppery red. He fleetingly wondered how many times, as a child, she had been called "carrot top."

His initial thought was that it was a crime the way she had pulled it back into a tight French twist, but the stark style drew his attention to eyes the color of dark amber. Closer observation convinced him that those long lashes were too dark for the hair color to be natural.

Her complexion, too, belied the color of her hair. Not deathly pale, like most redheads he had ever seen. He might have had difficulty describing it until the term peaches and cream came to mind. He had heard that description, but never pictured it until now. It was a perfect blend of ivory, soft gold, and the palest pink, with not a hint of freckles.

In spite of these observations, he found it hard to believe that glorious hair color was something out of a bottle. His eyes traveled the length of her body, and he decided that the question of her natural hair color was not the only incentive for seeing what lay beneath that prim tailored suit.

She would never have succeeded as a model—her body was much too generously curved for that. But then he had never been greatly attracted to women who were built like young boys. Her voice brought him abruptly out of his reverie.

"I'm looking for Samantha Desmond," he said, still smiling.

As she approached him, Samantha realized that he towered over her five foot five inches. Even with her usual three-inch heels, she felt dwarfed by him. She would not have thought it possible, but his attraction increased when he smiled. She then watched his smile fade with her reply.

"I'm Miss Desmond. What can I do for you?"

"You're Miss Desmond?" he echoed, stressing the "Miss."

His emphasis on her title and the slight change in his demeanor did not escape Samantha, and her own smile rapidly disappeared.

In all the years she had known them, neither Eloise nor Amy had ever questioned Samantha about Jessica's father, and she was grateful to them for that. Of course, in this day and age it was no longer an uncommon situation, and Samantha had decided that under the circumstances it was better for people to believe that she was an unwed mother.

She knew from some of their conversations that Eloise suspected she had never been married, but she had respected her privacy. Evidently she considered her employee's personal life irrelevant. Apparently he was not one of those people who agreed with that attitude.

Suddenly she realized where she had seen those eyes and that smile. "You're Melanie's father." It was more a statement than a question.

"Yes, Alex MacKenzie. I received a message that you had called."

"How did you know where to find me? I left this number, but not the address."

"We have a mutual acquaintance. Eloise is an old friend of my mother's. She also happens to be my godmother." He shrugged and explained. "I recognized the telephone number. As the saying goes, 'It's a small world.'"

"Yes, I suppose it is," she said hesitantly. "Anyway, I called because, ever since they met, Jessica has been begging to have Melanie sleep over. I explained that I would have to discuss it with you. I thought perhaps we could start with her coming to the movies with us on Saturday."

He paused, as though weighing some momentous decision.

Finally he replied. "The trip to the movies will be fine, but an overnight visit is out of the question. What time will she need to be dropped off, and what time shall I come for her afterward?"

Samantha bit back the retort that was on the tip of her tongue and clasped her hands together to avoid balling them into fists. She had planned to include chauffeur duties in her invitation, but he did not appear to be open to any discussion on the subject. It would serve no purpose to have a disagreement over it.

"I plan to take them to dinner after the movie, unless you have some objection."

"I have no objection, Miss Desmond. What time?"

They settled on a time, and he turned to leave. Samantha stood watching as he crossed the office and opened the door, holding it open for Amy, who was just returning with their lunch.

"Who was that hunk?" Amy asked excitedly, after he had closed the door behind him.

"Have you been holding out on me? I have to tell you, girl, he's quite an improvement over Martin. I mean, Martin's attractive in his own way, but nothing like him," she said, gesturing toward the door Alex had just exited. "By the way, does Martin know about him?"

Samantha shook her head. She had met Martin, an insurance broker, when Eloise introduced them a little over two years ago. He handled all of the office's insurance, as well as some of Eloise's personal investments.

"Slow down, Amy, you're babbling. Besides, there's no reason for Martin to know anything about him. You know Martin and I are only friends."

Samantha peered at her friend, smiling. "I think you're also starting to drool."

Amy laughed. "You're probably right, but I can't help it, girlfriend. He's almost too good to be real. Who is he?"

"He's the father of one of Jessica's friends," she replied in answer to Amy's question. "He just came by to settle the arrangements for Melanie to come to the movies with us on Saturday."

Amy heaved an exaggerated sigh. "I should have expected that some sister had already snatched up a man like that."

Ever since they had become friends, Amy had been badgering her about her social life—or more precisely, the lack thereof. In spite of those urgings, Amy had never seemed overly excited about the few dates Samantha had had with Martin.

Samantha kept to herself the information that Melanie didn't have a mother. As long as Amy thought he was taken, she would refrain from throwing any hints about him. They settled down to lunch, and Samantha determinedly put aside disturbing thoughts of Dr. MacKenzie.

As he drove away, Alex realized one of the questions that had come to mind earlier had been answered. When he had asked Eloise about her practice, she had given him a glowing report on her wonderful office manager, a young African-American woman. That helped to explain the fact that her complexion was not what one would normally have expected with that red hair.

He did wonder though about the source of that unusual hair. After a closer observation, he would have been quite surprised if the color proved to be anything but natural.

As he pondered their conversation, he became a little angry with himself at his initial reaction to her marital status. He was also surprised—he had never considered himself judgmental.

He had certainly known his share of single mothers and had never given their status a second thought. But then he had never felt toward them the immediate physical attraction he had felt toward Samantha. It was amazing how quickly objectivity flew out the window when there was a possibility of personal feelings becoming involved.

Four

Saturday morning Samantha was up early, as usual. Eight-year-olds didn't understand the concept of sleeping in on week-ends. After giving Jessica her breakfast, she started her usual weekend chores and had just finished cleaning up after lunch when the doorbell rang. A quick glance at the clock told her it was probably Alex and Melanie.

She opened the door to them, reminding herself to hold her tongue in check. She managed to smile only by focusing her attention on the innocent little girl in front of her.

"Hello, Melanie. I'm glad you could join us. Let me take your jacket. We're not quite ready to leave yet."

Samantha turned to Jessica and added, "Go and put your books away, sweetheart. We'll be ready to leave in a little while."

Alex watched Samantha during this exchange, aware that she was attempting to ignore him. He noticed that the smile she had pasted on her face as she opened the door seemed to change to the genuine article when she addressed his daughter. As these thoughts flickered through his mind, she turned to him once again with that smile that did not reach her eyes.

"If you have no further instructions, Dr. MacKenzie, Melanie should be back by six-thirty for you to pick her up."

Alex didn't respond immediately, but his black eyes bored into hers. Samantha held his gaze, determined not to flinch or waver.

Finally he replied, "I have no further instructions, Miss Desmond. I'll return at seven for Melanie."

After he left, Samantha took a few minutes to calm herself before calling the girls to prepare to leave. What was it about him that infuriated her so? There was an arrogance about him, but she had encountered that particular trait many times before and had never allowed it to affect her composure.

She had been fighting her temper since she was a child, but since reaching adulthood, she had been very successful in keeping it under control. For some reason, though, Alex MacKenzie simply rubbed her the wrong way. His attitude toward the fact that she was a single mother was part of it, but it was not the first time she had encountered that attitude. It did not entirely explain her reaction to what she perceived as his disapproval.

The afternoon was a great success. Samantha was a little surprised at how well-behaved the girls had been. She had always been proud of Jessica for her generosity and unselfishness, which sometimes surprised others when they learned that she was an only child. Watching the two of them together, she was aware of that same trait in Melanie. No doubt it was the main reason they got along so well with each other.

When Alex returned for his daughter, his stay was very brief, and Samantha made no offer or invitation that would delay his departure.

"Can Jessica spend the night, Daddy?" Melanie asked, as her father helped her into her jacket.

Samantha held her breath and glanced covertly at Alex. No parent would appreciate being put on the spot without having discussed the invitation first, in private. He remained passive, however, showing no signs of embarrassment or anger.

"Not tonight, honey. Maybe we can arrange it for next weekend, when you'll have more time to spend together."

"Can she?" the child asked, looking at Samantha.

Samantha considered declining, but she was not a spiteful person by nature. Besides, to refuse would be childish and would hurt no one but the children. She agreed to the visit, although she resented Alex's insistence on taking the part of chauffeur again.

Samantha would arrange for Jessica to ride the school bus with Melanie on Friday, and Alex would bring her home on Saturday. Samantha bit her tongue and didn't argue the issue. It would save her from having to interrupt her day at the office.

From then on the pattern seemed to be set. The girls became so attached to each other that hardly a day went by without one or the other phoning or visiting. Jessica was invited to spend the night twice and, although Melanie continued to visit, her father refused a second invitation for an overnight stay.

Samantha's anger over this issue continued to grow. She issued no more invitations after the second refusal, but it was becoming more and more difficult to hold her tongue.

As time passed, Samantha's anger grew, along with Amy's curiosity about her relationship with Alex. She was aware of the girls' growing friendship and Samantha had finally reluctantly confessed that Alex was unmarried. Even though she reminded her friend that this did not necessarily mean he was unattached, her revelation opened the door to Amy's unbridled speculation.

Samantha's answers to her friend's questions were always vague, insisting she knew little about his personal life. After all, her contact with him was limited only to whatever was necessary for the girls' friendship. This explanation did not stop her friend's questions. She could not understand why Samantha had not gleaned more information from Alex by now.

Early in October Amy was in the midst of one of her inquisitions when the telephone rang. Samantha was grateful for the interruption.

"Hello, Sam," Martin greeted her cheerfully. "How are you?"

Samantha stiffened slightly at his shortened version of her name. She had tried unsuccessfully to get him to refrain from using it. He always apologized when she reminded him, but he never seemed to remember not to do it in the first place. She had finally given up, telling herself that she might be overly sensitive about it.

"I'm fine, Martin," she replied. "Busy as usual. How's everything with you? How are the kids?"

"They're fine. As a matter of fact, I'm taking them to the aquarium Saturday. Believe it or not, they haven't been there yet."

"Well, I'm sure they'll enjoy it."

They chatted for a few more minutes and, before he hung up, he reminded her of their date to attend a charity ball that month. She had accepted his invitation weeks earlier, although they both understood that it wasn't a date in the real sense of the word.

They had dated a few times, shortly after their first meeting. Those few dates were all she had needed to realize that she was not interested in anything more than friendship.

It didn't really surprise her that he expressed no disappointment when she explained her feelings. Although he had been divorced for almost two years, there had been little clues that made Samantha believe he was still in love with his former wife.

He had never discussed the reason for his divorce, unlike some men who felt the need to explain how their wives just didn't understand them. Samantha suspected part of the problem was that Martin was a workaholic. She had experienced it firsthand, when he had broken several of their dates because there was some work that, according to him, absolutely had to be done that evening.

It was merely an inconvenience for her, but she could understand how it could become a major problem in a marriage. She hoped that the divorce had finally opened his eyes. Even if he and Joanne never got back together, at least his children could benefit from a change in his priorities. Maybe this proposed trip to the aquarium was the beginning, if he didn't cancel that at the last minute.

That afternoon she had a meeting with Eloise. She brought her employer up to date on the status of the new software. Then they discussed Eloise's conference schedule. A few months earlier Samantha had accompanied Eloise to one of her medical conferences. Samantha had had some misgivings about it at first.

She had been uncertain about leaving Jessica for four days, since the child had never been away from home for more than one night. The problem had been solved when Amy offered to keep Jessica for the weekend.

Samantha discussed it with the child, who was excited about the chance to spend a whole weekend with Cassandra and her sister, Jennifer. They both doted on the child and, as far as Jessica was concerned, the arrangement was a great idea.

Samantha was still feeling a little guilty and uncertain, until she spoke with the child on the telephone the second evening of her absence. Jessica had shown no indication that she was homesick, or that she even missed Samantha. In fact, she sounded as though she was having the time of her young life.

Samantha's feelings had been hurt at first. Then she reminded herself that this was part of what growing up was all about. She was determined that she would not be one of those parents who clung to their children, stifling them.

After they completed their business, the conversation turned to personal topics. In the years that Samantha had worked for Eloise, their relationship had grown into more than just an employee-employer association.

As Eloise prepared to leave, she asked, "How is Jessica? I haven't seen her for a few weeks."

"She's fine. In fact, I believe you're familiar with the new friend she's made at school, Melanie MacKenzie. Even though she just recently moved here, the two of them are practically inseparable already."

"Melanie MacKenzie? Are you referring to Alex MacKenzie's daughter?"

"One and the same. I understand you're a good friend of the family. He told me you're his godmother."

Eloise nodded and smiled. "That's right. His mother and I have known each other since we were children. When I spoke with her a few months ago, his mother mentioned that he was planning to move back to this area. As a matter of fact, he called me himself a few weeks ago, just after he moved here."

"I had some difficulty getting in touch with him. Jessica had been begging to have Melanie sleep over. His housekeeper told me he was out of town when I called."

"I believe he was winding up his practice in Chicago," Eloise explained. "He's a pediatrician, although I seem to remember his mother telling me had taken a position with a medical research company in New Jersey."

"I left a message for him, and he came by here to give his permission for Melanie to go to the movies with us. I suppose he wanted to meet me in person, before making his decision. Especially since he refused the sleep-over invitation—and I think permission for the movies was given reluctantly."

"What do you mean, reluctantly?" Eloise asked. Samantha's tone of voice led her to believe the encounter with Alex had not been altogether pleasant.

"Well," Samantha said, trying to sound nonchalant, "I don't think he approved of me. Especially when I introduce myself as Miss Desmond. I guess your acceptance of my situation made me forget how judgmental people can be, even in this day and age."

"I don't understand, Samantha. What did he say to make you think he was reluctant to have Melanie visit Jessica?" her employer questioned.

"Basically the fact that he immediately vetoed the sleep-over, but that he supposed that going out to a movie would be all right. I guess he had visions of streams of men coming in and out of my house all night."

When she saw the hurt expression in Samantha's eyes, Eloise started to speak. She suspected the reason for Alex's reluctance. Unfortunately she couldn't reveal her opinions to Samantha.

She observed the young woman closely and soon noticed that her expression changed. She had learned, early in their relationship, that the subtle darkening of those amber eyes signaled anger.

"What are you planning, Samantha?"

"Planning?" Samantha repeated innocently. "I'm not planning anything. I just think he needs to learn that he shouldn't go around making assumptions about people he doesn't know."

A few minutes later Eloise left, and Samantha thought about their conversation. She had not really planned to reveal her displeasure with Alex. The anger she still felt from their encounter had not abated, and she had spoken before thinking.

It brought to mind the many admonitions she had received from her father when she was growing up. They had clashed more than a few times as a result of her temper. Although he admitted that it was an inherent part of her makeup, he refused to condone it.

He had assured her that it was a trait she could overcome, in spite of her red hair. He had insisted that simply because it was a natural inclination, it was not uncontrollable—she would just have to work harder at it.

She wanted to believe that she had learned to control it. On the other hand, she had to admit that until recently nothing had happened to really put it to the test.

Five

The evening of the charity ball, Samantha was putting the finishing touches on her makeup when Jessica came skipping into the room. As she spritzed herself with Opium, the child pleaded, "Can I have some too?"

Samantha smiled. "Hold out your arm," she instructed.

In between sniffing her arm every few minutes to take in the heady fragrance, Jessica watched with interest as Samantha finished dressing.

Her gown was black velvet with a wide square neckline and long fitted sleeves, its simple flowing lines and slightly flared skirt a perfect foil for her lush curves. The stark color provided just the right backdrop for her creamy skin and bright hair, which was arranged in a twisted coil, extending from the top of her head to the nape of her neck.

She clipped on pearl drop earrings that matched the pendant nestling just above the cleavage of her full breasts. Slipping on the black peau-de-soie pumps, she picked up her evening bag, holding her hand out to Jessica.

"Shall we go downstairs? Cassandra should be here soon."

As they reached the bottom step, the doorbell rang. Samantha greeted the baby-sitter and gave her instructions for the evening. Cassandra took Jessica into the kitchen to fix a snack, just as the doorbell rang again.

Samantha opened the door to Martin and felt a twinge of

guilt when she realized that she was comparing him with another man who had entered her life just a few short weeks ago.
Martin was an attractive man, charming and entertaining—and
he left her absolutely cold.

She couldn't say the same for her new acquaintance. She hated
to admit it, considering the annoyance she sometimes felt toward
Alex. He certainly had never gone out of his way to be charming.
In spite of this, she was aware of an undeniable attraction. She'd
heard the word "chemistry" bandied about a number of times,
but she considered it an overworked term that had no real meaning.

Samantha said her good-byes to Jessica and Cassandra and
moments later they were on their way. When they were settled
in the car, Martin turned to her.

"I'm glad you agreed to come with me tonight. I have a
confession to make. I'm expecting Joanne, my ex-wife, to be
at this affair, and I needed a friendly companion by my side. I
hope you don't mind," he said with a guilty smile.

Samantha couldn't resist making a point. "It's a little late to
be asking me that, isn't it?" she asked, her face serious.

Martin, looking sheepish, opened his mouth to apologize, but
she stopped him.

This time Samantha smiled, as she replied, "It's all right,
Martin, I don't mind. Although I'm sure there are other women
who would have been happy to accept your invitation, I think
I understand why you chose me. I'm safe and you're still in
love with Joanne. Am I right?"

He smiled weakly and asked, "Is it that obvious?"

She shrugged. "I wouldn't say it's obvious. There were little
clues that led me to believe that it was a very distinct possibility.
Don't worry about it. If my presence will help you get through a
difficult evening, I'm glad to do it. After all, what are friends for?"

The first part of the evening went well, despite the fact that
Joanne was, indeed, present and Martin spent the first hour

following her every move with his eyes. Samantha couldn't begin to understand what he was feeling, but that didn't keep her from being able to sympathize with him.

Later in the evening Samantha noticed that Martin's eyes had once again strayed to where Joanne stood. She was engaged in conversation with a man who appeared to be her escort for the evening.

Samantha leaned slightly toward Martin and suggested, "Why don't you ask her to dance?"

He shook his head, looking down at his hands. "Her date might not appreciate that."

Samantha replied, "It's only a dance, Martin. Besides, maybe her date is just a friend, too, like yours."

Martin made no reply, but his eyes had returned to his ex-wife. The possible reason for his reluctance occurred to her.

"From what you've told me, your separation and divorce were amicable. Is there some other reason you think she might refuse?" Samantha asked.

He shrugged and Samantha placed her hand over his, adding, "Well, as long as you can handle the possibility of rejection, what do you have to lose?"

After a while Martin summoned the courage to follow Samantha's suggestion. Once he had taken the step, it appeared he could not tear himself away from Joanne. Finally they parted, and he returned to the table, smiling guiltily.

"I think I owe you an apology for being gone so long," he murmured.

She returned his smile. "No problem. It was my idea, remember."

Later that evening, when Samantha returned from the powder room, Martin was standing near their table, talking with two other couples. She recognized two of the people as an older couple she had met earlier in the evening. The other man seemed familiar and as she came closer, her pulse accelerated. Even with his back to her, there was no mistaking his identity. Martin spied her out of the corner of his eye and held out his hand, drawing her into the group to introduce her.

As the introductions were performed, Alex informed him, "Samantha and I have met. Our daughters have become practically inseparable."

Mrs. Cosgrove, the older woman, looked startled. "You have a daughter Melanie's age? Why, you couldn't have been much more than a child yourself when she was born."

Samantha was saved from having to reply when Martin deftly changed the subject. "Has Melanie adjusted to the move?" he asked Alex.

"She didn't cope very well at first," he replied, "but she's coming along now. I was concerned about her having to leave her friends in Chicago. I'm convinced that part of her improvement is due to the way Jessica immediately befriended her."

Samantha was a little surprised to hear him give so much credit to Jessica for his daughter's adjustment to her new environment. She was almost ready to concede that he might not be as unfair as she had thought.

As the men continued their conversation, Samantha took the opportunity to appraise Alex's companion. Allison was exactly the type of woman she would have pictured on his arm. Tall, glamorous, and sophisticated, she was wearing a blue silk dress that clung to every curve of her slim figure. Samantha felt an unwelcome knot in the pit of her stomach when she envisioned this beautiful woman being held in those strong arms.

She had purposely avoided looking at Alex, but before long her eyes were drawn to him against her will. She could not find words to describe Alex MacKenzie in evening clothes. His muscular build was not in the least subdued by the austere tuxedo.

Once again she was reminded of Amy's novels, her mind conjuring up an image of strong arms sweeping some woman off her feet and carrying her away. She shook her head slightly, forcing herself to look away from him. She made a mental note to tell Amy to refrain from reading any more of her favorite passages aloud. If she wasn't careful, she would be in danger of drooling, herself.

Her gaze returned to him once again to find those disturbing black eyes staring into hers. It was almost as if he was aware of the scene she had just played in her mind, and she felt the color creeping up her neck.

Fortunately his gaze was broken when his companion drew him off to the dance floor. Seconds later she and Martin joined the crowd, and the spell was broken. Samantha was just a little disgusted with herself for her reactions to Alex. She didn't even like the man!

Mentally searching for an explanation for these feelings, she decided she was probably just uneasy because he was so overbearing and arrogant and irritating. At least that was what she told herself.

Later that evening her theory was put to the test, after Alex and Allison had chosen to sit at their table, much to Samantha's dismay. Allison excused herself to go and powder her nose, just as the band started playing a slow romantic number. Martin was a few tables away, chatting with a business associate, and she could come up with no acceptable excuse to refuse when Alex asked her to dance.

When they reached the dance floor, he drew her immediately into a close embrace. She stiffened slightly and he urged, softly, "Relax, there's not much I can do to you here on the dance floor."

She could hear the amusement in his voice and willed the tension from her body. "That's better," he murmured.

A moment later he asked, "How long have you known Martin?"

"A little over two years. And you?"

"We were in school together," he informed her. "We kept in touch at first, but after a while we just never seemed to find time to keep up with each other. I didn't realize he was divorced until my visit here a few months ago."

He leaned back and waited until she looked up at him before inquiring, "Did you know his wife is here this evening?"

Samantha was determined not to let him get her hackles up, but she could not resist one shot. "His ex-wife," she corrected him. "Yes, I know."

"He's dancing with her now," he continued. "Doesn't that bother you?"

"No," she replied innocently. "Should it?"

There was a slight pause before his response and, when it came, his voice dripped with sarcasm. "Are you that sure of yourself—or of him?"

"As a matter of fact, Dr. MacKenzie . . ." she began.

"Alex," he corrected smoothly.

"As I said, Dr. MacKenzie," she persisted, "it's not the first time they've danced this evening. As a matter of fact, you evidently missed the rather long conversation he had with her earlier. Furthermore, for your information, not that it's really any of your business, I was the one who suggested that he ask her to dance."

Trying to pull away from him, she went on. "And now I'd like to return to the table."

"Why?" he asked, tightening his hold on her.

"Because," she said through clenched teeth. "I don't want to dance with you."

He chuckled softly, infuriating her even more. "That's too bad," he responded, looking around at the other couples on the dance floor.

"It would be rude for us to push our way through the crowd in the middle of the dance—and quite unnecessary. So you might as well calm down and resign yourself to suffering my unwanted attentions for a few more minutes."

Samantha was seething, but there was nothing she could do about it without causing an embarrassing scene. She was aware that he was taking full advantage of her predicament as his hand slid to just below the curve of her back, pressing her more closely to the disturbing hardness of his body. His other hand clasped hers, holding it against his solid chest. He was careful to keep his actions just within the bounds of propriety.

Samantha became even more frustrated when her own body began to react to his nearness, his body pressed intimately to hers and the heady masculine scent that emanated from him. Her pulse raced, and she was sure he was aware of it when he lifted her hand to his lips, planting a kiss on the pulse at her wrist.

After what seemed an eternity, the dance ended and she returned to her seat on somewhat unsteady legs. Her efforts to regain her composure were not helped by the fact that Alex's eyes were on her, whenever she happened to glance his way, which occurred much too frequently. What would Allison think if she noticed her absorption? She redoubled her efforts to focus on something other than the man across the table.

He felt no compunction about the attention he had paid to Samantha. Allison was an old friend whose fiancé had been called out of town on business at the last minute.

He had been preoccupied with Samantha since he had first seen her that evening. In truth, his preoccupation had started long before that. Seeing her with Martin had come as a surprise and, somewhere in the back of his mind, he wondered if she might be one of the reasons for the breakup of his friend's marriage. His opinion had changed after watching the two of them for a while—they certainly did not behave as lovers.

His curiosity concerning that relationship had originally prompted his invitation to dance. He had reasoned that he could question her subtly in the course of a private conversation. Of course, as it turned out, he had not been very subtle with his questions. He knew he'd angered her, even before the amber lights in her eyes had darkened in warning.

He had no reason to doubt her statement that she had encouraged Martin's actions. In spite of her anger, her obvious indifference toward the amount of time Martin spent with Joanne convinced him that they were no more than friends. It was this last revelation that pleased him the most.

He smiled to himself. Although it hadn't been his intention to antagonize her, he was not the least repentant. She reminded him of a feisty kitten baring her claws at a huge German shepherd.

His other reason for asking her to dance was very simple. It gave him an excuse to take her in his arms. He wondered what it would be like to be on the receiving end of all that energy, if it were channeled into passion rather than anger. The more he thought about it, the more fascinating the prospects seemed.

The rest of the evening passed slowly and rather hazily for Samantha. She was angry with herself for allowing Alex to fluster her. Unfortunately Martin was in no hurry to leave. He seemed content to pass the time watching Joanne. When the affair finally ended, she mentally breathed a sigh of relief.

Less than one week later, Samantha had reason to recall that evening. Having previously hinted to her employer that her association with Alex was somewhat strained, she should have expected that the subject would eventually resurface.

The new software had been installed, and she had scheduled a meeting with Eloise to give her a demonstration. Afterward, the conversation turned to personal matters.

"So how are Melanie and Jessica getting along?" Eloise asked.

"Still as inseparable as ever. As a matter of fact, she's coming over Saturday to bake cookies. It's a practice run for my usual Christmas cookie baking marathon."

"And how are the parents getting along?"

"All right," Samantha replied, rising from her desk to return a stack of folders to the file cabinet.

"Have you taken Alex down a peg or two yet?" Eloise asked, smiling.

Samantha abruptly turned back to her employer. "I never said—" she blurted out. She saw the smile on Eloise's face and smiled herself.

"Well, I didn't say anything about taking him down a peg," she insisted.

"You know," Eloise continued, "I've been considering possible reasons for the antagonism between you two, ever since our conversation weeks ago. I haven't reached any conclusions, but I do have my suspicions. I think for now though, I'll keep them to myself.

"I understand why you would be reluctant to discuss him with me, considering our relationship. I suppose, because of that relationship, I feel compelled to speak up in his defense. I've known Alex all his life and, unless he's changed a great deal since his younger days, you're wrong about the reasons for his refusal to let Melanie stay with you overnight."

"Eloise, it really isn't necessary to defend him. I don't know him well enough to make any judgments on his basic personality, I . . ." Samantha stopped in midsentence, realizing she had been making judgments.

Eloise's voice brought her back to the conversation. "Samantha?"

"I'm sorry, Eloise, I lost my train of thought for a moment," she continued. "I was just saying that I can speak only of his attitude toward me personally."

"As I said, I have my own theory about that," Eloise reiterated.

"Maybe now that your daughters are such good friends, it's time for the two of you to try following their example."

She rose to leave, adding, "Well, now that I've had my say, I won't press the issue. I think I've had more than my share of butting in to your personal life."

"I never think of your advice as butting in, Eloise," Samantha assured her. "I'm grateful for the help you've given me over the years, and I never turn up my nose at advice that's offered in the right spirit. After all, I still have to make the final decision."

"It's good to hear you say that, but as far as our arrangement is concerned, it's been as beneficial to me as it has to you, maybe more so. Having an office manager who keeps everything running smoothly makes a big difference in my ability to fulfill my commitments."

Samantha laughed softly. "We're starting to sound like a mutual admiration society."

"You're right," Eloise said, smiling, "enough is enough. I'd better be on my way," she added, looking at her watch. "I have a meeting in a half hour."

Six

Early Saturday morning Samantha was awakened by a small, impatient voice. "Wake up, Mom. We have to get ready to make the cookies."

Samantha opened one eye slowly. "Jessica, we have plenty of time. I have other things to do before we start the cookies."

"I know. That's why we have to start now. I'll help. I can dust real good, you know."

Samantha smiled and dragged herself into a sitting position. "Yes, I know, but do you think we could have breakfast first?"

"Okay," the child agreed. "I'll go set the table."

"Wash up first," Samantha reminded her, as she ran off.

By eleven o'clock she had finished the laundry and was setting out the ingredients for the cookies when the doorbell rang. She opened the door, as usual attempting to focus her attention on Melanie. However, it was impossible to ignore the man standing just behind the child. He was wearing blue jeans that fit like a glove and a thick white sweater that made his shoulders seem even broader.

When his eyes raked over her own jeans-clad figure, she took a deep breath. She told herself the quickening of her heartbeat was due only to her temper—it had nothing to do with his frank appraisal. Nevertheless she was thankful that she was wearing an oversized sweatshirt which came almost to her knees.

"Hi, Melanie. Hello, Dr. MacKenzie," she said with that

same pasted-on smile that was transformed when turned on Melanie.

She stood aside as they entered. Taking the child's coat, she turned to hang it in the closet, while Alex said his good-byes to his daughter.

He seemed in no hurry to leave. He watched, smiling at Samantha's outfit, as she instructed the children to go upstairs and play for a few minutes. Did she really think she could hide those curves with a baggy sweatshirt?

Her preoccupation with the girls had also given him time to take in his surroundings. The foyer displayed a number of African and African-American prints. Most of them, he noticed, were a variation on a "Mother and Child" theme. In addition to the prints, there was a beautiful piece of needlework, also an African "Mother and Child."

What he glimpsed of the living room was furnished with a large overstuffed sofa, chair, and ottoman in navy blue, with throw pillows in an Oriental print fabric. The walls were painted a soft gold with medium oak stained woodwork. The entire arrangement was offset by a beautiful Oriental carpet.

When she turned her attention back to him, he commented, "You have a nice home. It looks very comfortable, and this artwork is beautiful. Eloise is probably one of the few people I know who appreciates her employees' hard work, and pays them accordingly."

As soon as the words left his mouth, Alex regretted it. He was also a little appalled at his choice of words. Her salary was none of his business, and that wasn't really what he had meant. He would have attempted to take back his words and explain, but she gave him no such opportunity.

After making certain that the children were out of sight, she turned to him with eyes flashing.

"Dr. MacKenzie . . ." she began.

"Alex," he corrected.

"Dr. MacKenzie," she continued stubbornly. "As a matter of fact, Eloise pays me very well to manage two offices and I, in turn, work very hard for every cent. Not that it's any of your business.

"Furthermore, in case you're insinuating that someone else contributes to this household, let me set you straight. Jessica and I are the only people who live here or sleep here. Perhaps you'd care to search the closets or look under the bed for traces of men's clothing.

"I understand your concern for your daughter and the possibility of her being exposed to a situation of which you don't approve, but I care just as much about Jessica's morals."

Alex was fascinated by her as she stood there with her hands on her hips, her eyes now the color of whiskey. He could barely concentrate on her words, not that the actual words were necessary to grasp the gist of her tirade.

Receiving no response from him, she went on. "Eloise said that she and your mother were good friends. Knowing that, I find it hard to believe that your mother never taught you about making snap judgments about people you don't know. But then you're probably one of those people who was born so stubborn and opinionated that she gave up on you."

"Are you finished?" he asked quietly.

"Yes," she replied, slowly regaining her composure.

He paused and his gaze traveled from her hair, down her body, and back up once again. "You know, when I first met you, I wondered if that hair was real or from a bottle. After seeing another of those little demonstrations of your temper, I believe I have my answer."

Samantha's cheeks were burning partly from his brazen appraisal and partly from her humiliation at her loss of temper. She had intended to give him a piece of her mind, but she planned to do it with a bit more control. She should have known that losing her temper was only a matter of time. There was something about this man that always managed to shatter her poise, with what appeared to be very little effort on his part.

Alex realized that he had just seen a perfect demonstration

of her contradictory behavior. One minute she was giving him hell and the next minute she was blushing. He was even more determined to explore all the facets of her personality, but it would have to wait until another time.

His black eyes held hers as he continued. "You're probably justified in your anger, and I apologize for my choice of words, but I didn't mean to imply what you think. For one thing, making a home comfortable involves more than money.

"Also, I know that this county, and this area in particular, is not the most economical place to live—and many employers couldn't care less about whether or not they pay their employees a decent salary, no matter how hard they work.

"I do admit that you're correct about my concern for Melanie, and I don't need to explain my reasons for wanting her at home at night, but they have nothing to do with your lifestyle."

Before she could find her voice to reply, he asked, "What time will the baking session be over?"

Samantha took a deep breath, forcing her temper under control before replying. "If you have no objections, I had planned to make a day of it and order pizza for dinner after we finish the cookies. I'll be sure to have her home whenever you wish, or at least no later than seven-thirty."

"Seven-thirty will be fine," he agreed. "If you have paper and pencil handy, I'll write down the directions."

She was a little surprised that he did not again insist on coming to pick up his daughter. She walked over to the telephone and retrieved the items he requested.

"The directions are fairly simple, but you have the telephone number, just in case there's a problem."

She was still staring at the slip of paper, as he let himself out. Samantha thought about his apology and her own tirade. Maybe she had taken his words the wrong way. She still considered him arrogant and opinionated, but maybe he wasn't as bad as she had originally thought.

* * *

As he drove away, Alex replayed in his mind their verbal exchange. He was more upset with himself than with her. Why did he always manage to say the wrong thing?

His discovery, at their first meeting, that she was unmarried with a child had conjured up unpleasant memories, and he had instinctively reacted to them. He had been unaware that those thoughts showed on his face, until he noticed the change in her expression, and then it was too late.

He realized afterward that he had been so intent on his appreciation of her physical attributes, he had been caught off-guard when she introduced herself. The physical attraction had been there from the beginning, and the contact he had with her as a result of the children's friendship increased his interest.

The contradictions in her personality fascinated him. In spite of what he was certain would be a formidable temper if ever let loose completely, there was a certain shyness and naivete about her.

He had long since regretted his hasty assumptions at their first encounter. His ex-wife's betrayal could explain his distrust, to a certain extent, but it didn't justify or excuse his behavior. It was unfair to put her in the same category as Marci.

Eventually he might be able to make her understand the reasons for his actions concerning his daughter. It was important to him that she understand that, and a few other things. He would like to have an opportunity to explain, if he could manage to keep from antagonizing her long enough for them to have a decent conversation.

It was just after seven when Samantha pulled up in front of the MacKenzie house. She double-checked the number on the stone wall with the number written on the slip of paper Alex had given her. There was no mistake—the huge English Tudor house she glimpsed through the trees was Melanie's home.

She pulled into the circular driveway, muttering under her

breath, "And he had the nerve to wonder how I could live so well."

"What did you say, Mommy?"

"Nothing, dear. I was just reading the paper to make sure we have the right address."

"This my house," Melanie piped up. "There's my daddy."

Samantha looked toward the garage and saw Alex getting out of a navy-blue Mercedes. She stopped the car, got out, and was opening the back door for Melanie as he walked over to them.

"I see you found it. Did you have any trouble?"

"No," Samantha assured him. "The development is familiar to me, and your directions were very good."

"Hi, munchkin," he greeted his daughter. "Did you have fun?"

Melanie nodded excitedly. "We made tons of cookies and Mrs. Desmond let me bring some home." As she finished, Samantha handed him two large tins.

"She said I have to share them and not eat them all myself. Do you want some, Daddy?"

"Of course. I'll even make some hot chocolate to go with them." He turned to Samantha. "Would you care to join us?"

Samantha hesitated, and Jessica chimed in, "Can we, Mom? Please."

"Well, maybe for just a little while," she agreed.

After hanging their coats, Alex led the way to the kitchen. He made the hot chocolate, and they sat around the kitchen talking and munching cookies. The girls giggled and talked excitedly about the coming holidays. Halloween was less than two weeks away with Thanksgiving and Christmas not far behind.

"How long have you worked for Eloise?" Alex asked.

"About five years. Her previous office manager quit soon after she opened the Trenton office," she explained. "It was one of the best things that ever happened to me."

"Contrary to what you may think, I am aware how hard you work. From what Eloise has told me, she was the lucky one.

It's not always easy finding someone dependable to manage two offices, especially with her busy schedule.

"She's an excellent doctor and a very compassionate person, but even she admits that, when it comes to the business end of her practice, she's not the most organized person in the world."

Samantha was taken off-guard by his compliment. Before she could reply, they were joined by a plump, gray-haired woman who entered through the back door.

"How was the church meeting?" Alex asked.

"Good, I was glad to hear they've started a scholarship fund. It's not much, but at least we're making an effort to help the young people."

"Samantha, this is my aunt, Sarah Henderson," he explained. "She takes very good care of us. I don't think I could manage without her."

"So you're Jessica's mother," she said, taking Samantha's hand. "I'm glad to finally meet you. Those two sure have become great friends."

She turned to the girls and added, "I guess I don't have to ask if you had a good time. It looks like you're still having a party."

"It's not really a party," Melanie said. "Do you want a cookie?"

"Not tonight, sugar," Sarah replied. "I just stopped in to take the roast out of the freezer for tomorrow's dinner. Fred rushed me out of here so fast, I forgot."

"You didn't have to bother, Sarah. You could have just called me."

"Oh, it's no bother. It's not like it was out of my way."

She started toward the pantry, with Melanie and Jessica tagging along, still filling her in on the day's activities. Samantha watched them go and, when she turned her attention back to Alex, he was staring at her with a strange look in his eyes. She couldn't seem to tear her eyes away from his gaze, until the girls' chatter signaled their return.

Samantha looked away and murmured, "I think it's time for us to be going."

Moments later Sarah had left and Samantha was helping Jessica into her coat. The girls said their good-byes while Alex helped her on with her coat, his hand brushing the side of her neck. She felt a small shock of awareness and had to steel herself to keep from jumping away from him.

"Thank you for the hot chocolate," she murmured, avoiding his eyes.

"You're welcome. And thank you for giving Melanie such an enjoyable day."

He walked them to the car, holding both doors open while they settled themselves. Moments later they were pulling out of the driveway and on their way home.

After Jessica was in bed, Samantha recalled that short but pleasant interlude in the MacKenzie's kitchen. When he was not being judgmental and opinionated, Alex was quite charming—perhaps too charming.

She could no longer overlook the physical attraction she felt. It had actually started with that first meeting in the office. In spite of the antagonism, she had felt it. At the time she had tried to ignore it, but then that brief moment in his arms on the dance floor had forced her to acknowledge it.

She recalled the jolt she had felt at his slight accidental touch. With that kind of reaction from such an innocuous touch, what reaction would result from a more deliberate, prolonged contact?

"Cool it, Samantha," she muttered to herself. "Don't even think about. Just limit your contact with him to whatever is necessary as far as the girls are concerned. That's probably all he's interested in anyway. Be content that you've overcome your antagonism, and let that be the end of it."

Seven

Samantha should have guessed that it would not take long for the antagonism to reassert itself. Little more than a week had passed since that enjoyable evening in Alex's kitchen before the pleasant feelings were set aside and she was once again angrily confronting him. This time it was on behalf of his own daughter.

She had arrived at school to pick up Jessica a little later than her usual time, and the buses had already left. The last of the office personnel left as she and Jessica exited the building.

She was pulling out of the parking lot when she noticed Melanie standing at one of the side doors. She immediately stopped the car and approached the child.

"What are you doing here, Melanie?" she asked. "You've missed your bus. In fact, all of the buses have left."

"I'm not supposed to take the bus today. Today's my piano lesson, and I have to wait for Miss Lawson."

"Miss Lawson is picking you up here? Didn't they tell you to wait inside?"

"I was inside, but I had to go to the bathroom and then I decided to wait out here," the child explained. "Uncle Fred always takes me, but he had to take Aunt Sarah to the doctor. Aunt Sarah said Miss Lawson will come and get me today."

"Well, why don't we wait with you? You girls get in the car, it's cold out here. I'll watch for Miss Lawson."

By this time the school was empty, except for the janitor, and a half hour later, they were still waiting. Samantha was slowly losing the battle to keep her temper under control. She called Alex's home from her cell phone, but there was no answer.

She explained to Melanie that Miss Lawson must have run into a problem, and she would take her home. She picked up the phone and dialed the office.

"Hi, Alice, it's Samantha. Are there any messages for me?"

"Just your dentist's office. They called to remind you of your appointment on Monday."

"Okay, thanks. Is Amy with a patient?"

"No, she just left . . . the patient, that is."

"Good, let me speak to Amy, please."

She waited a moment, still watching for Miss Lawson, and getting angrier by the second. Finally a voice came on the other end of the line.

"Hi, Amy. I need a favor. I've run into a problem, and I probably won't be able to get back to the office. Would you lock up for me?"

"Sure, Samantha. Are you and Jessica all right? You didn't have an accident, did you?"

"No, no. It's nothing serious—we're fine," she assured her.

"Okay, I'll take care of everything here. I'll see you on Monday."

She tried once more to contact Alex, but with no luck, and contented herself with leaving a message on the answering machine.

When she arrived at the MacKenzie home, the door was answered by Mrs. Henderson. "Hello, Samantha. I got your message. I can't imagine what happened to Miss Lawson. I hope you haven't been put to too much trouble."

"It was no trouble for me, Mrs. Henderson. I would like to speak to Dr. MacKenzie though."

"I'm sorry, Alex isn't home yet. He should be here any minute, if you'd like to wait, or I can ask him to give you a call."

"That won't be necessary," a deep voice responded from the doorway to the kitchen. "Dr. MacKenzie is right here. What seems to be the problem?"

"I'd like to speak with you," Samantha snapped. "In private."

His eyes narrowed, but he spoke quietly. "Sarah, why don't you take the girls into the kitchen. Maybe they'd like a snack or some hot chocolate."

He set down his briefcase on a small credenza and hung his jacket in the closet next to it. He then turned his gaze to Samantha and gestured to a door on the other side of the hall.

"In here."

He had barely closed the door when Samantha let loose with all the fury that had been building inside her since she had found his child alone—and, in her eyes, abandoned.

"You make such a show of being so particular about the company your daughter keeps. I would think that you would be more careful about the people you select to fulfill your obligations to her.

"That child would still be standing out there on the curb if I hadn't decided to wait until Miss Lawson put in an appearance. There wouldn't even have been anyone left at the school for her to go in and call, which is another matter that you need to address.

"Anything could have happened to her. She could have wandered off and gotten lost out there in freezing weather. Or someone could have picked her up and carried her off to who knows where."

Halfway through her outpouring of anger, the tears had started to sting the backs of her eyes, but she blinked them back. As the possibilities she had voiced began to sink in, the tears could no longer be held back. She turned away to hide them and tried to gain control of her emotions.

She was trying to discreetly wipe away the tears when Alex came up behind her. Turning her to face him, he took a large snow-white handkerchief from his pocket and began mopping up the tears. When he had finished, he removed her coat and urged her to have a seat.

"Are you all right now?" he asked softly.

"I . . . I'm fine," she stammered.

Before he could say any more, the phone rang. He excused himself and went to answer it. Samantha caught the beginning of his side of the conversation.

"I have it, Sarah." He paused a moment and sighed, before replying, "Yes, she's here. A friend brought her home."

There was another pause and Samantha didn't hear any more, except a word now and then. Her mind was occupied with all the things she had just said. She now felt terrible about her accusations.

She knew what it was like as a single parent trying to arrange for your child's care when you had to work all day. From what she had seen, his care and concern for his child were unquestionable. It wasn't his fault that the arrangements had fallen through. How could she have said those awful things to him?

He returned to her, explaining. "That was Miss Lawson. She had a minor car accident on her way to pick up Melanie. Nothing serious, but the other driver insisted on calling the police. By the time the police arrived and the reports were done, well . . .

"She said she called here—but, of course, there was no answer. Fred had taken Sarah to the doctor. She apologized, but I told her that in the future if one of us is not available to bring Melanie she'll have to skip her lesson.

"First of all, I don't understand why Melanie was outside waiting."

Samantha repeated his daughter's explanation. He shook his head.

"Miss Lawson was to have been at the school before the buses left. You're right, I should have made contingent plans and given the school instructions to notify me if she failed to show. I'll also be sure to remind Melanie that she's not to go outside of the school alone, for any reason." Samantha appeared puzzled, and he stopped abruptly.

"My telling you this must seem out of character, but under the circumstances, I feel the least I can do is to explain how the situation came about and assure you that it will not happen again."

"I'm sorry. It seems that you haven't cornered the market on snap judgments. I guess I was just so scared for her, I got a little carried away."

"Don't worry about it. I'm happy to see such concern on my child's behalf."

He smiled and Samantha was mesmerized by it. She vaguely wondered how many women he had bowled over by that lethal smile.

He fingered a wisp of hair that had escaped, brushing it back behind her ear. "Besides," he murmured, "I think I mentioned it before—with that hair I have a feeling that getting carried away is a way of life for you."

Samantha blushed but managed to come to her own defense. "That's not really true. I'm usually in very good control of my emotions and my temper." *Except around you*, she added silently.

Aloud she said, "I think I'd better get Jessica. We should be leaving."

"Why don't you join us for dinner? I'm sure the girls would enjoy spending more time together. Besides it's Friday, so there's no rush to get homework done or get to bed early."

The words had barely left his lips when they conjured up a disturbing image. Along with the image, the thought flitted through his mind that he might be in a hurry to get to bed early, if she was sharing that bed.

The invitation to dinner had been a spur of the moment idea, inspired by a desire to keep her there a little longer. Maybe a little more time together would give them an opportunity to have a normal conversation. Hopefully this time he could manage not to put his foot in his mouth.

Samantha voiced her doubts about accepting his invitation.

"I don't want to cause a problem for Mrs. Henderson. I'm sure she's made her plans already. There's nothing worse than having a certain number of chops, or whatever, and having last-minute dinner guests thrust on you."

"I'm sure it won't be a problem. If there isn't enough of whatever she planned for dinner, I think we both know the girls will be more than satisfied with hamburgers." He held out his hand, giving her no choice but to take it. "Shall we go and find out what's for dinner?"

Alex sniffed the air as they entered the kitchen. "Ah, chili," he informed her. "I told you there wouldn't be a problem. When she makes chili, Sarah thinks she's feeding the neighborhood."

Sarah smiled and looked up from where she was slicing cucumbers for a salad. "You always say that, but none of it ever goes to waste," she replied.

"Of course not," he said. "Everyone knows it's even better the second day, sometimes even the third day."

He led Samantha to a chair, informed Sarah that he had invited her and Jessica to stay for dinner, and turned to Samantha. "You can keep Sarah company while I change clothes." On his way out the door, he added, "I'll tell the girls the good news."

"Is there anything I can do to help?" Samantha asked after Alex had left.

"As a matter of fact, yes. If you don't mind, you can finish the salad while I slice the bread to go in the oven," she said, gesturing toward the counter where a loaf of crisp French bread sat waiting.

The two women chatted as they worked. "How do you like Bucks County?" Samantha asked.

"It's a nice area," Sarah admitted. "When Alex told us he was relocating, I could tell he wanted to ask us to come with them, but I guess he thought it was too much to expect. I asked him outright what he planned to do about Melanie. When he hesitated, I suggested we might be willing to relocate, too, if that was what he wanted.

"I've been taking care of Melanie since she was a baby. Even when her mother was alive and she and Alex were together, she never had much time for the child, and no patience. But then Marci never had much time for anyone but herself. After all that child's been through, I couldn't see her having to get used to strangers taking care of her.

"I stopped working about ten years ago, and Fred retired last year. We talked it over and decided there wasn't really anything to keep us in Chicago.

"Alex has been very good to us, better than our own niece, Melanie's mother. When he bought this house, he insisted on fixing up the space over the garage so Fred and I would have our own apartment."

She slid the foil-wrapped bread into the oven and walked over to where Samantha was now tossing the salad. Until that moment Sarah had been talking almost nonstop. Samantha looked up, wondering at the sudden silence.

"Is something wrong?" she asked.

"Oh no, honey. I was just thinking about how kind you've been to Melanie, including her in so many of your activities with Jessica."

"Actually it's been a help to me in some ways. The two girls get along so well when they're together, it keeps Jessica occupied too."

Gathering up the bits and pieces from the salad vegetables for the garbage disposal, she continued. "Part of me still feels that I should be apologizing for imposing on you. Even before he knew what you had planned for dinner, Alex insisted you wouldn't mind two extra mouths for dinner."

Sarah waved away her apology. "Don't give it a second thought, child. It's no problem at all. Alex will just have fewer leftovers waiting for him when he raids my kitchen."

"I'll just have to look a little harder when I'm raiding," Alex said from the doorway.

He looked at Samantha and winked. "I want you to know, she means it when she refers to this as her kitchen. Don't get me wrong, though. I'm perfectly satisfied to let her have the kitchen. The meals that come out of it are worth it."

At that moment Sarah's husband joined them. Alex had just completed the introductions, when Melanie and Jessica burst into the kitchen. "We washed our hands like you said, Daddy," Melanie informed him.

"Good girls. Go sit down now. Dinner's ready."

After dinner the children went upstairs to play. Sarah and Fred said their good nights and went to their own apartment. At Alex's suggestion, he and Samantha adjourned to the living room.

Even considering the children's friendship, there had been only a few times when she had been left alone with Alex. It was always a bit unnerving.

The physical attraction she felt for him was disturbing in its intensity. Neither Martin, nor any other of the few men she'd dated, had held any great physical appeal. Consequently she'd never had any trouble keeping them at a distance.

With Alex she had discovered what people meant when they talked about hearts fluttering. It was how she felt sometimes when he looked at her and, when he touched her, she turned into a marshmallow.

Until now their initial antagonism had served to keep the physical attraction under control, but she was aware of the intense feelings simmering just below the surface, and they hadn't even had a real date. Keeping this in mind, Samantha settled into the comfortable wing chair near the fire.

Her reason for choosing a single chair was obvious to Alex. He smiled and sat in the matching chair, directly across from her. Perhaps he was aware of her reactions to him because the spark of attraction was mutual.

He was amused by her actions. If she were thinking straight, she'd realize that he wasn't likely to initiate a romantic interlude with both of their children at play just one flight of stairs away.

As soon as that fact occurred to him, he realized that they both needed a diversion.

"Do you play chess?" he inquired.

"I haven't played in years. I'm not sure I even remember the proper moves for the men," she told him.

"Actually it's probably more important to remember the improper moves," he quipped.

His meaning didn't escape her, and she turned her head to keep him from seeing the color staining her cheeks. He stood up, took the few steps separating them, and lifted her hand from its resting place on the arm of the chair, pulling her from the safety of her seat.

"Come on, let's see how much you remember," he urged. Her flush deepened when it occurred to her that his second statement, whether intended or not, was also a double entendre.

She was painfully aware that he had guessed her thoughts when he chuckled and leaned over to whisper, "About chess." Her hand still locked in his grasp, he led her into his study.

He had just put her into "check" for the third time when she glared at him and he chuckled. "You realize that this is grossly unfair," she accused. "I don't know why I let you talk me into this."

"Don't feel bad. We'll consider this a practice run. I'll even allow you a few more practices before I get tough. Let me just show you a few moves that might get you out of the corner you've worked yourself into, and we'll consider your first lesson ended."

She was barely able to concentrate on what he was trying to tell her. She was convinced that chess was not a game to be playing with this man. She was continually reading other meanings into every statement he made.

They were setting the pieces back in their original places when he suddenly looked up and asked, "Will you have dinner with me Saturday?"

"Dinner?" she echoed.

"Dinner," he repeated. "At a restaurant, just the two of us.

In fact, I know of a very nice restaurant north of here. It even has a small band, for dancing."

"I don't know. Saturday's a busy night for sitters. It might be short notice to find one. I'll see what I can arrange."

"All right, but if you have a problem finding a sitter and, if you don't mind, Jessica can spend the night with Melanie. I'm sure, since she'll already be baby-sitting Melanie, Sarah won't mind having Jessica included. So what other excuse are you going to come up with?"

"That's not an excuse, it's a valid concern," she insisted.

Samantha appreciated his offer, and she did not doubt that Sarah would be agreeable to the arrangement. She would probably consider it acceptable if they were better acquainted. Having met Sarah for the first time that evening, she felt it would be taking advantage of the older woman.

"Yes, I agree, it is a valid concern. And I've just given you a valid solution to the problem, so I guess that means your answer is yes."

"Why do I get the feeling that in some way you're still playing chess?" *Or "cat and mouse,"* she thought.

Alex didn't respond immediately, but his eyes held hers, waiting for her reply. She remained silent a little too long to suit him and finally he declared, "Good, that's settled. I'll pick you up at seven."

Eight

That was how a simple little chess game was responsible for her current predicament: standing in front of her open closet, trying to decide what to wear. Cassandra had arrived a few minutes earlier and was keeping Jessica occupied, which was fortunate since Samantha was already a bundle of nerves.

She finally chose a cream-colored wool crepe dress that had a softly swirling skirt and a fitted long-sleeved bodice with matching cream-colored satin collar and cuffs. The large round malachite pendant and earrings had been a gift from Eloise.

She was just slipping her feet into the emerald snakeskin pumps when the doorbell rang. She grabbed the matching clutch bag from her bed, took a deep breath, and murmured to herself, "You're being ridiculous, you know. It's only a simple dinner date."

It was easy enough to tell herself that, but deep down she knew that nothing that involved being alone with Alexander MacKenzie was simple.

Until they entered the restaurant and she noticed the small band in the corner, Samantha had forgotten that he had mentioned dancing in his invitation. Alex hadn't forgotten—it was one of the reasons he had selected that particular restaurant. The feel of her in his arms when he danced with her at the charity ball was still fresh in his mind.

Since that time he had learned more about her from Eloise,

who was impressed with her intelligence and self-confidence in managing the two offices. He had decided that this same self-confidence probably accounted in part for her outspokenness, which he had already observed for himself.

After they'd been seated and placed their orders, Samantha relaxed, her earlier nervousness slowly dissipating.

"I like this place," she said, looking around. "How did you discover it?"

"Martin told me about it. Having been out of the area for a while, I asked him for suggestions." He watched her closely, adding, "He brought his wife—excuse me, his ex-wife—here a couple of weeks ago."

Samantha looked him in the eye and was careful to show no reaction, other than to respond, "That's nice."

Her message was clear. She was not going to discuss her relationship with Martin. Alex smiled—she didn't know that her words and actions at the charity ball had already given him the answer he wanted.

As she finished her statement, the waiter approached. The next few minutes were spent perusing and discussing the menu. Alex selected a Cajun shrimp dish, and Samantha settled on the chicken marsala.

"I take it you like spicy food," Samantha commented.

"The spicier and hotter, the better," he admitted. "And you?"

"I can't say, the hotter, the better, but I guess medium spicy is okay."

She chided herself for allowing her mind to stray into dangerous territory again. This talk about liking things hot and spicy could get out of hand. She wondered briefly if that particular preference carried over into his taste in women.

Alex had no general preference. He was attracted to her—hot and spicy or mild and innocent . . . it didn't really matter. However, he'd had enough contact with her to know firsthand that her calm, somewhat shy exterior covered a fiery temper and probably an equally fiery passion. He was also beginning to realize that what he felt was no fleeting, superficial fascination.

Midway through their meal, Alex asked, "Do you like jazz?"

"For the most part, yes," she replied. "Why do you ask?"

"There are a couple of clubs in Philly that Martin also recommended. I thought we might try one of them in the future."

"One of those clubs wouldn't happen to be Zanzibar Blue, would it?"

"As a matter of fact, yes. Have you been there?"

"No, but I've heard of it."

"What other types of music do you like?"

"Well, it really depends on the mood I'm in at any given time. When I want to relax and not think, I usually prefer classical music. It's very soothing."

She laughed softly and added, "Unless, of course, you're listening to Wagner. Although I find I get my housework done faster listening to Wagner. How about you? What do you like?"

"Basically the same. There aren't many types of music that I actually dislike, except some of the louder versions of rock music. I guess I'm showing my age when I say this, but in my opinion it's questionable whether it should even be called music."

"I know what you mean. I think that's the kind only a teenager can love. Although sometimes I wonder if they really love it or listen to it only because they know it annoys their parents. Personally I'm not looking forward to the time when I'll have to cope with the typical teenager's idea of music."

Alex laughed. "You may have a point about their reasons for listening to it. I've already had a taste of it. My sister has two teenagers, and I'm hoping that by the time Melanie reaches that age, I'll be used to it."

"Speaking of music," Alex said, as he stood and held out his hand. "I think it's time we took full advantage of the music at our disposal right now."

Placing her hand in his, Samantha rose from her seat and he led her to the dance floor. Before he had taken her in his arms, Samantha recalled the way her body had reacted to him when they danced at the charity ball, in spite of the anger she had felt at the time. Now, without even the doubtful protection of anger, it was fortunate that there was no conversation between them.

Although it might have served to distract her from the physical sensations, her powers of concentration were somewhat limited. His hand rested just below her waist, and his thighs brushed hers with almost every movement.

As he took her in his arms, Alex smiled and gave himself over to the pure enjoyment of having her within his embrace once again. She was where he had wanted her since that first dance, and he was unwilling to let her go.

They danced through several numbers before Alex finally led her back to the table. After ordering fresh coffee, they talked quietly for a while, the topic eventually turning to their daughters.

"They've known each other such a short time, and they've become so close, it amazes me," Alex commented, "but I guess that's not so unusual for children."

"It sometimes surprises me too," Samantha agreed. "I think there's one thing that we're forgetting though. I think we should both prepare ourselves for that first major disagreement. That's not unusual for children either. It's bound to come sooner or later, and they'll probably be devastated when it happens."

She paused briefly then added, "On the other hand, let's not borrow trouble."

The evening passed quickly after that and, much too soon, they were on the road again. There was little conversation on the ride home, both of them still wrapped in the cocoon of the simple pleasure derived from each other's company.

When they arrived at her home, Samantha looked in on Jessica and Cassandra. They were both sound asleep. Alex took his leave after a brief kiss on her cheek, leaving her feeling strangely disappointed.

Halloween was only a few days away when Samantha and Jessica received surprise visitors. They had just finished cleaning up after dinner when the doorbell rang. She answered the door to find Alex and Melanie on her doorstep.

"Surprise! Happy birthday!" the little girl exclaimed and started giggling.

"I took a chance on finding you home. I know I should have called first, but I wanted to surprise you," he explained.

"How did you know?"

"Melanie saw Jessica making a card for you in school yesterday. She told her that it was for your birthday today. Melanie mentioned it to me last night and, well, here we are."

As they entered, Melanie handed her a box. "It's a birthday cake," she said excitedly. "My daddy said we could have a party, if it's all right with you."

Samantha looked at him, and he shrugged apologetically.

"It's fine with me," she assured the child, "but I'm afraid we might get sick. I already have a cake." She glanced up at Alex and added, "Jessica insisted on it."

She set the cake on the hall table and turned back to them to take their coats. Her surprise and delight shone in her eyes as Alex handed her a bouquet of flowers he had been hiding behind his back.

"Thank you," she murmured, "they're beautiful."

"You're welcome. Maybe you can put one of the cakes in the freezer for another time," Alex suggested.

"I guess I'll save the one I bought. Jessica was a little disappointed in it anyway. I didn't have time to get a real birthday cake."

"Actually this one started out as a regular cake. I simply waited while the baker added the decorations to it."

"I guess my mistake was in thinking it wouldn't matter," she explained.

Samantha led the way to the kitchen and began setting out dishes. She took the ice cream from the freezer and, as she lifted the cake from the box, Alex asked, "So how many candles do we need?"

Samantha laughed. "Is that what you consider a subtle way of asking my age?"

Alex shook his head, chuckling. "I guess it wasn't very subtle, was it? So . . . ?"

"Twenty-six. Satisfied?" she asked, placing the requisite number of candles on the cake.

Alex nodded, still smiling.

"Okay. What about you?"

"I'll be thirty-four in January."

"Thirty-four, hmm. You'll be over the hill, soon."

Alex laughed. "Thanks a lot."

"Well, let's get this party started," she said, smiling.

As enjoyable as the "party" was, unfortunately, it ended early because the next day was a school day. As she saw them to the door, Alex turned to her.

"I'd like to take you out to dinner, Saturday, for a real celebration, just the two of us. Will you come? I've already asked Sarah, and she assured me that it won't be a problem for Jessica to spend the night with Melanie."

Even before she spoke, the look on her face told him that for some reason she was not too pleased with his plans.

"You were that sure I'd accept?"

"No, but I'm quite an optimist. Besides, I thought it would be best to cover all contingencies before issuing the invitation— that way I could eliminate at least one of the reasons you might refuse," he admitted with a smile.

Samantha couldn't resist a smile herself. "In other words, you were actually expecting me to refuse?"

Alex rolled his eyes. Shaking his head, he replied, "I can't win, can I?"

Samantha laughed at his expression. "I'll be happy to have dinner with you, Alex."

Nine

Saturday afternoon Samantha dropped Jessica off at the MacKenzies' home. Her impending date prompted her to consider the changes that were rapidly taking place in her relationship with Alex, since their initial antagonism had eased. She still was not sure where their relationship was headed—well, actually that was not entirely true. She could reasonably guess where it was headed. From the look in Alex's eyes and her own feelings, she could rule out the possibility that it would remain platonic. The question was, where would it end?

Until now she hadn't taken the time to really consider how she felt about the direction it had taken, or where she would like it to end. If her intuition was right, she would eventually have to decide how much she was willing to risk on their relationship.

She enjoyed Alex's company, and there was no question that she was physically attracted to him. The possibility occurred to her that, in spite of some of his cryptic comments, her intuition might be wrong. Maybe she was reading more into those looks than he intended. After all, that peck on the cheek after their last date certainly was no indication of anything more than friendship. Maybe he hadn't shared those sensations she'd felt when he held her in his arms.

He might actually want nothing more than friendship. Maybe he just wanted to put an end to the antagonism. If that was indeed the case, she would have no need to make any decision concerning her own actions. Unfortunately that thought engendered more disappointment than relief.

"This speculation is getting you nowhere, Samantha," she murmured to herself. "You'll know what he has in mind soon enough. There's no need to rush things, just wait and see what develops." Meanwhile she would just enjoy his company and friendship, if that was all there was to be.

While she was musing on the possibilities concerning their relationship, she was also searching through her closet, mentally rejecting one outfit after another. She finally settled on an emerald-green lambswool knit dress. Its cowl neck draped softly and modestly in front but dipped enticingly to the middle of her back. The color brought out the gold flecks in her eyes and the fiery highlights in her hair.

She was on her way down the stairs when the doorbell rang, signaling Alex's arrival. When she opened the door to him, she wondered vaguely if she would ever become inured to the sight of him.

He wore a suit of medium gray with burgundy pinstripes. The burgundy tie and pink shirt did nothing to subdue his blatant masculinity. He seemed to have grown even taller since she had last seen him, and much more threatening to her peace of mind.

Alex was unaware of her appraisal—he was too busy making his own. His fingers itched to loosen the restricting French twist, not because it was unbecoming, but just because it was so restricting. He'd already had many visions of that magnificent hair tumbling around her shoulders.

The soft fabric of her dress fell straight from her shoulders. Or at least it would have been straight, if not for the tempting curves that it failed to hide.

"Hello, Alex," she murmured, when she found her voice.

"Good evening, Samantha," he returned, smiling.

When he smiled, the answers to Samantha's earlier questions became clearer. The look in his eyes gave new meaning to the story of Little Red Riding Hood. He had said that they were having dinner, but she was beginning to wonder just what he had in mind for dessert.

When she turned her back to him to open the closet, Alex had to restrain himself to keep from caressing the appealing expanse of skin from the nape of her neck to the middle of her back. He wondered if it was as soft and smooth as it looked. When his hand brushed against a portion of that skin as he helped her on with her coat, his question was answered. He sighed inwardly. He knew he would never be satisfied until his next question was answered. Was her skin that soft and smooth all over?

Alex had chosen a restaurant across the river in New Jersey. Their table was situated next to the window where they could just glimpse the lights of the small towns across the river. Unlike their previous date, Samantha seemed unable to dispel the butterflies that invaded her stomach. Her earlier speculations had served to heighten her awareness of him—every word, every gesture seemed to be branded into her mind. She was convinced that he could read her thoughts, and she blushed every time their eyes met, which in turn increased her uneasiness.

It took all of her powers of concentration to hold up her end of the conversation, which fortunately involved general topics that didn't require much thought. They had finished their meal and were enjoying their coffee when the conversation turned to their respective careers.

"How do you like working for Eloise?" Alex asked and then smiled and added, "I guess that's not a fair question. Knowing that she's my godmother, what could you say?"

"I don't mind the question, but now you might not believe me when I say I enjoy it very much. She's been very helpful and accommodating—it's not easy making child care arrangements. I'm sure you're aware of that yourself."

"Yes, I've always been thankful for Sarah and Fred. Sarah's

been taking care of Melanie since she was a baby. How did you meet Eloise?"

Samantha told him of her friendship with Amy and subsequent introduction to Eloise. "I was really surprised when she called and asked to see my resume. Within weeks she had hired me. I guess it was one of those cases of being in the right place at the right time."

"You're not originally from this area, are you?" he asked casually.

"It depends on what you mean by 'this area.' I grew up in Media, in Delaware County."

"What led you to move here?"

Samantha was unprepared for his question, and she was not ready to explain the reason for her relocation. She didn't answer immediately, and Alex could see she wasn't pleased at the turn their discussion had taken.

"I'm sorry. I didn't mean to pry," he apologized.

Samantha shrugged away his apology. "I just felt the need for a change. What about you? Did you decide you'd had enough of the big city?"

"Not exactly, although that may have been part of the reason," he replied.

"Eloise said you had a private practice in Chicago. I know you're in research now, but will you eventually set up another practice here?"

He turned to gaze out the window a moment before replying simply, "No."

Samantha didn't notice the change in his expression and went on. "I suppose it's not that easy setting up a practice, but you could go into partnership with another doctor already in practice, couldn't you?"

He turned back to face her, and this time she saw the sadness in his eyes. He looked down at his hands folded on the table. His answer was abrupt, his voice expressionless.

"The remainder of my medical career will be spent in research. I won't go into private practice again."

It was obvious that the topic was not open to further discussion. "It seems it's my turn to apologize for prying," she said, reaching over to touch his hands.

Their eyes met and held, and she found herself blushing when he unfolded his hands to clasp hers. "It's all right. I know all about the impulse to ask questions. In spite of the fact that we haven't known each other long, Samantha, I believe that your questions, like mine, are prompted by a desire for us to get to know each other better."

"I guess it's not as easy for adults as it is for children. We're always concerned that we might appear to be prying."

She went on to qualify her statement. "At least some of us are. Some people don't really care if their questions are too personal, even when they border on outright rudeness."

Her mention of their children brought to mind his ban on overnight visits for Melanie. That along with their conversation about getting better acquainted made him realize that he owed her an explanation. If his relationship with Samantha was to progress, and he was determined that it progress, he had to make it clear that his refusal had nothing to do with her.

"Samantha," he began hesitantly. "You should know by now that our friendship means a great deal to me. Keeping that in mind, my conscience tells me I need to explain something to you. It concerns my refusal to allow Melanie to sleep over with Jessica."

He paused, looking at her intently, then he took a deep breath and went on. "Although you haven't mentioned it since that first tirade, I know that you had taken that refusal to be doubts about having Melanie associate with you, and I think . . . I hope . . . you know by now that that isn't the case. Even if that question is no longer an issue, it's time you were told the real reason behind my decision."

He looked down at his hands, now folded on the table, and continued. "I haven't allowed Melanie to visit overnight with anyone because she sometimes sleepwalks. She's been doing it off and on for years. At one time prior to our move, she had started to show some improvement, but I think the move caused more of an upheaval than I anticipated. Within weeks she started sleepwalking again.

"For that reason I've preferred to have her at home, where I can take precautions for her safety. There haven't been any occurrences lately, and it appears that she's become accustomed to the new surroundings and the household routine. Hopefully the problem has ended once and for all."

A number of questions crowded Samantha's mind, but she held her tongue. She did not want to be one of those prying people she had condemned a few minutes earlier, and her previous question appeared to have already opened a wound.

Since he had seen fit to explain this much, perhaps he would eventually feel comfortable enough with their relationship to confide the reasons behind his decision to give up practicing medicine. The fact that he had offered an explanation for refusing the overnight visits was enough for now.

"I'm sorry, Alex. Under the circumstances I can understand your hesitancy and, if you change your mind in the future, I'll take whatever precautions you feel are necessary. On the other hand, if you're not completely comfortable with that and you don't change your mind, that's okay too. I can accept that."

"I appreciate that, Samantha. As I said, the problem seems to be over, and I have been considering giving it a try. I just want to give it a little more time."

Just then the band returned from a break. Taking her hand, Alex stood up. "Enough serious talk. This is supposed to be a celebration. Let's dance."

For the next two hours they danced and talked and danced some more. Samantha was glad to see the sadness that had been in his eyes earlier had been dispelled. It had been replaced by a look that was less upsetting but even more compelling. It was an expression she had come to recognize as desire, and she had no doubt that the same expression was reflected in her own eyes.

* * *

It was after eleven o'clock when Alex glanced at his watch. "I suppose we should be going," he said reluctantly.

Samantha nodded, also reluctantly. Moments later they were on their way back to Samantha's house. Although there was no conversation, the silence was not uncomfortable, merely an indication that they were both digesting all that had been said earlier that evening.

Shortly after their arrival, she was seated beside Alex on her sofa, sharing a pot of fresh coffee. The coffee had really been an excuse to avoid having the evening end.

Alex waited just long enough for her to finish pouring the coffee before taking her in his arms. Samantha went willingly. It was as if she had been waiting for this the whole evening. The kiss was long and searching. Samantha knew she was in trouble when he finally lifted his head and she realized she wasn't ready for it to end.

He ran his hand along her cheek, smoothing back a wisp of hair that had escaped. His eyes held hers, then traveled to her flaming tresses, as he forced himself to pull back slightly.

"I think we'd better try conversation for a while. As a matter of fact, there is a question that's been floating around in my head for quite some time."

Samantha smiled. "I was wondering when you'd finally get around to it."

Alex looked puzzled. "How do you know what I'm going to ask?"

"It's a question I've been answering all my life. I've learned to recognize the signs."

"All right, Miss Clairvoyant, what's the question?"

Samantha closed her eyes, feigned a serious expression, and put her hands to her temples. "Ah, yes. It's coming to me," she chanted.

She opened her eyes, smiling. "Where on earth did you get that hair?"

Alex laughed. "Okay, I'm convinced of your mind-reading abilities. So what's the answer?"

"My grandmother. She was a Scotswoman and a very unusual lady. She met my grandfather during World War II when she was a nurse. They fell in love and, against the kind of opposition we can imagine they faced, they were married.

"Even considering the problems they faced in their attempts to get approval for the marriage, she wasn't totally prepared for the reactions she encountered when they returned to the 'Good Old U.S.A.' She refused to knuckle under though, even after my grandfather died and she had a small child to raise on her own. She could give as good as she got. My parents always said that although she was always a lady, she had a formidable temper—especially when facing injustice."

She chuckled. "One of my mother's favorite expressions was that Grandma 'didn't take tea for the fever.' "

She paused, nodding her head. "You know, it's funny. Some of the old expressions you hear don't make much sense when you try to dissect them, but you get the message.

"I knew my grandmother for only a short time. She died when I was nine, but I was old enough to know that she didn't stand for any foolishness."

"I think maybe she passed on more than the hair color to her granddaughter," Alex said.

"You wouldn't be referring to my temper, would you? My father used to say the same thing."

"Actually I was referring to strength and determination. Of course, now that you mention it, I suppose the temper is part and parcel of the whole deal."

"You mentioned that before. Actually my temper is under much better control than it used to be, thanks to my father."

"What was he like; was he very strict?"

"Not really. He was quite softhearted in many ways. He was also soft-spoken, but tough. He never raised his voice—he just made it clear that my tantrums were to be restricted to the privacy of my own room."

Alex chuckled. "I'm sorry," he apologized when she frowned. "It's just that I could easily picture you stomping up to your room. You probably had smoke coming from those flames," he said, fingering the lock of hair that had once again escaped.

"So your hair came from your grandmother. What about those sherry-colored eyes? Did they come from her too?"

"No, my father's eyes were this color. It was a rather startling combination, since his eyes were lighter than his complexion. It gave people quite a surprise."

"Probably not nearly as big a surprise as they get when they meet you."

Her facial expression immediately sobered. "I'm sorry," Alex murmured. "Did I say something wrong?"

Samantha gave him a half-smile, touching his arm lightly. "No, Alex. It's just that the surprise was the easy part. What wasn't so easy to take was the attitude of some people who considered that I wasn't 'black enough.' I've never tried to hide my heritage, any part of it, but that wasn't enough for some people. I never understood what that term meant. More than that, I resented it. I still resent it."

His other hand came up to cover hers. "I've heard people use that expression myself. Like you, I never understood what they meant. A few times I've asked them to explain. Of course, they looked at me like I was crazy, but I never have received an explanation."

He raised her hand to his lips, and Samantha forgot about any resentment she had felt toward anyone in the past. "I hope you don't still let it bother you. It's not worth it."

She gave him a real smile this time. "You're right," she admitted. "And I don't usually. I guess when I started talking, it brought back some of those memories. I assure you, I haven't lost any sleep over it since I was a teenager. I'm not about to let that happen again."

"Good, I wouldn't want to be the cause of your losing sleep . . . at least not from worry," he said.

Before she could respond to his implication, he stood up, adding, "Speaking of losing sleep, it's getting late. I think it's time for me to leave."

She walked him to the door. "I enjoyed this evening, Samantha. I especially enjoyed our talk. I like getting to know you, and I'd like for us to spend more time together, without the girls. As much as I love them, I think we owe it to ourselves to allow more time for just the two of us."

He was watching her closely as he finished his statement. "I hope you don't have a problem with this plan."

"I have no problem with that, Alex. In fact, I'd like it very much. I enjoyed this evening too." She looked into his eyes as she spoke.

The expression there made her wonder exactly what else was in his plan. Moments later she had her answer.

"I'm very glad to hear that," he murmured, taking her in his arms.

Alex had intended a simple good-night kiss, until he saw his own desire mirrored in her eyes. His mouth settled on hers, and he pulled her closer.

His tongue outlined her lips, coaxing her to open up to him. One hand moved lower, pressing her hips into closer contact with the hard muscles of his body. His other hand caressed the silky skin just above the fabric of her dress, sending shivers up and down her spine.

She clung to his shoulders at first, but as he deepened the kiss she stretched up on tiptoe and looped her arms around his neck. He leaned his shoulders back against the wall and lifted her off her feet, his hands cupping the soft flesh of her buttocks, both of them oblivious to everything but each other, lost in a storm of sensations.

Samantha trembled as one of Alex's hands moved first to caress the nape of her neck and then to slide down her back. Dipping below the neckline of her dress, his featherlight touch wreaked havoc with her senses. Alex became aware that he was in danger of losing control when she shuddered in his arms. He did not want to let her go—she felt so good, tasted so sweet.

His hands encircled her waist and slowly lowered her, skimming the length of his body, until her toes once again touched the floor. With some effort, he raised his head and planted a few more light kisses on her face. He could feel her heart racing in time with his own as he held her close, her head resting against his chest. His hand continued to stroke her back until their breathing slowed to a normal pace. After a few moments he loosened his hold, tipping her face up to his.

"Well, sweetheart," he said softly, his voice still thick with desire. "I can't say I'm totally surprised by what we just experienced."

Samantha was disquieted by his words and the look in his eyes, but she was even more disturbed by her own reactions. He noted the wary look in her eyes and attempted to ease her apprehension.

"Don't be afraid of me, Samantha," he urged. "I wouldn't do anything to hurt you. It's obvious that there is quite an attraction between us—and I don't think we can, or should, ignore it."

"Alex," she said shakily. "I don't want to have an affair with you. Contrary to what you may think about me, I'm not like that. I have too much pride to do that to myself and too much to lose to get involved in a casual affair."

He sighed. "I don't expect you to. That's not what I want, either, and that's not what I think of you. I suppose in the beginning I gave you that impression and I apologize. There is nothing casual about my feelings for you.

"All I'm asking is that you give us a chance, and that you trust me not to do anything to hurt you. As I've said before, I'm your friend, first, and that friendship means a lot to me. I have to admit I want more than that though. I'm a patient man and I won't rush you, but I want us to be honest with each other."

Samantha felt a twinge of guilt. She hadn't been entirely honest, but she couldn't bring herself to make any confessions of her own. Unable to speak, she just nodded.

"Good. Now I think I'd better leave and let you get some sleep. It is getting late." He opened the door, dropped one last kiss on the tip of her nose, and was gone a moment later.

Ten

Samantha thought about their conversation as she prepared for bed. With the friendship that had developed between Jessica and Melanie, it would be impossible to avoid him. Who was she kidding? She had no desire to avoid him.

She enjoyed being with him, but there was much more to it than that—she wanted him, probably as much as he wanted her. She had known that even before the kiss. She had never felt this way about any other man, had never really believed feelings like this existed. For years she had been making light of Amy's romantic novels, convinced that the sensations described in them were pure fantasy. Alex MacKenzie had made a believer of her.

After dissecting her own feelings, she recalled her speculations earlier that evening, thinking that he might have nothing more in his mind than friendship. She had discarded that idea very early in the evening, just by seeing the look in his eyes when he greeted her at the door.

Any further questions she had in her mind had been answered candidly and completely before he departed. He had left no doubt as to his intentions—eventually he wanted her in his bed. The real dilemma for Samantha was in the fact that she wanted it too. Her fear of having him discover the truth was probably the biggest reason for her restraint.

However, that fear was not the only restraint. She had meant what she said about casual affairs. Even before people had become so concerned with the health dangers, she had never seen the appeal of hopping in bed with one man after another. She would probably never understand women who could sleep with a man simply for the physical pleasures, without becoming emotionally involved.

She had always known that she was not one of those women, which meant she had to be prepared to withstand the emotional upheaval, if the affair came to an end. She had seen enough broken relationships to know that there were no guarantees. No matter what she felt, there was always the possibility that he would eventually grow tired of her.

Contrary to decreasing, Alex's interest was steadily growing, and he could not conceive of ever tiring of her. He was true to his word not to rush her into a physical relationship. However, his promise didn't include denying himself the pleasure of touching her or kissing her. It would have been too much to expect him to resist that temptation, and he was determined that eventually he would satisfy his craving for more . . . much more.

Her usual air of quiet reserve was in total opposition to the temper he had encountered and the passion he could feel rise to the surface every time he kissed her. Although he was careful to keep his desire under control, that control was becoming more and more difficult to maintain.

When he was younger, he would have expected such a reaction. At his age he thought his self-control would be easier to maintain, and that had been true, until a certain redhead had sent his physical urges into overdrive.

He had never experienced feelings this intense for any woman, not even his ex-wife. Marci had taught him one important lesson though—beauty was, indeed, skin-deep. She had been beautiful and glamorous . . . and self-centered and cold. He still sometimes wondered how he could have been so blind.

He was honest enough to admit that his initial attraction to Samantha had been physical: those amber eyes and brilliant hair, to say nothing of the generous, tempting curves of her body. After Marci, however, he had learned his lesson well, and he knew that it was much more than physical beauty that had drawn him to Samantha.

Beyond the physical aspects, she appealed to him for a number of reasons. The one that stood out the most was her genuine concern for the happiness and well-being of those around her. He had seen evidence of that in her encouragement to Martin, her fear for the safety of his daughter, and her sympathy toward his own situation.

Until now he had hesitated to acknowledge the depth of his feelings, but it was difficult to ignore the likelihood that he was falling in love with Samantha Desmond.

Alex kept his plans for them to have more time together without the girls. They were together often—sometimes with the children, but at least one evening a week it was just the two of them. It didn't matter if they went out to dinner, with or without dancing, or just a movie or concert. The only thing that seemed to matter was that they were together.

Although Alex had made clear his physical desires, his revelation in mid-November told her just how serious he was about their relationship.

They had been to a play in Philadelphia and when Alex brought her home, she invited him in. After they were seated comfortably on the sofa, he turned toward her, hesitating only momentarily before taking her in his arms. She was expecting his kiss, but was surprised and a little disappointed when it came. It was more a show of affection than passion.

He lifted his head and looked into her eyes as if searching something, before pulling her into his arms again, just holding her. It was a few moments before he broke the silence. The glimpse she'd had of the expression in his eyes told her he had something serious on his mind.

"For the past couple of weeks, I've been thinking about what you asked me about leaving my practice. I've tried a few times since then to broach the subject, but I couldn't find the courage. I finally decided tonight that I owe it to you to explain.

"A couple of weeks ago, I assured you that I'm not looking for a casual affair, Samantha. I've always felt that honesty is one of the most important factors in any relationship. To tell you the truth, I had that lesson driven home to me the hard way. For that reason I've decided that you deserve to know exactly why I gave up the active practice of medicine."

"I care for you, too, Alex," Samantha confessed. "But you don't owe me any explanations."

"I'm not so sure about that. When I explain, there's a chance it may change your opinion of me. In spite of that, or maybe because of it, I owe you this—before our relationship progresses any further. Aside from that, maybe I owe it to myself. I won't feel completely comfortable until I get it off my chest."

He paused a moment, as though trying to find the right words. It also seemed to Samantha that he seemed to be gathering his courage. He had loosened his embrace but still clung to her hands, as if he derived some strength or comfort from the contact.

He then continued. "I gave up my medical practice because I felt, still feel, responsible for the death of one of my patients, a ten-year-old little girl. Her mother brought her to me because she seemed to be unusually tired and listless. After examining her and questioning her mother, I considered a number of possible diagnoses.

"Her mother was a rather nervous woman, and I decided not to worry her with any of the possibilities until I was sure of the diagnosis. I gave her instructions to notify me if the child showed any other symptoms, or seemed worse, and my general instructions to see that the child ate a balanced diet. I also gave her a referral for further lab tests and instructed her to make an appointment to return the following week."

He closed his eyes for a moment as if he was attempting to blot out the pain his next words recalled. "I couldn't keep track of all my patients to see that they followed my instructions. I'd never had a problem before. I was also going through my own problems with Melanie at that time, although that's no excuse.

"Two weeks later I received a telephone call from the hospital. The child had been admitted in a diabetic coma, and they had been informed that I was her pediatrician. The next day she died."

"I found out later that Lisa had attended a birthday party the day before she was admitted to the hospital: hot dogs, potato chips, cake and ice cream, a smorgasbord of junk food. Aside from ignoring the instructions about the child's diet, her mother hadn't taken the child for the lab tests or made a follow-up appointment. I could understand not restricting the child's diet and indulging her at the birthday party. What I couldn't understand was, why she would ignore something as important as the lab tests?

"I found out that she had just been laid off from her job and had no medical insurance, so she decided the tests would have to wait until she could save at least a portion of the money it would cost to have them completed.

"If she'd had the tests done, I'd have received the results and called her in immediately. I'd have been able to stress the importance of the diet and start treatment for Lisa. I blame myself for not checking the records to see if the test results had been received."

Samantha's heart went out to him. The terrible guilt and pain he carried were obvious in his face. "Alex, it wasn't your fault. You gave the child's mother specific instructions. How could you even suspect that she wouldn't follow them?

"Not only that, personally I wouldn't think that it was your responsibility to keep track of whether or not a patient has followed through once you've ordered the tests. It would seem to me that it would be the parent's responsibility, not only to see that the tests were done, but to find out if your office had received the results."

Alex shook his head. "I should have emphasized the importance of the instructions I gave her. I should have—I don't know. I should have done something more."

"Tell me something," Samantha persisted. "If you had known that there was no medical insurance to pay for the test, what would you have done?"

"I would have done whatever I had to do to see that the child had those tests done. There were agencies that could probably have helped, if I had known." He closed his eyes again, looking drained.

She had learned enough in their short acquaintance to have no doubt about his compassion. "Even to the point of paying for them yourself, if necessary." It was more a statement than a question.

Alex opened his eyes to find her staring at him intently, her own eyes slightly misted with tears. He gently enfolded her in his arms and replied, "I don't know, maybe. I'd like to believe that anyway. In any event it doesn't really matter now. It's in the past, and I can't change it."

Samantha forced herself to pull away from him. It felt so comfortable nestled in his arms, too comfortable. Looking up into his eyes, she murmured, "It does matter. If it keeps you from doing what you were really meant to do, it matters."

She started to say more, but his fingertip on her lips stopped her. "I understand what you're saying, Samantha, but I have to continue with what I'm doing right now. Maybe in time I'll feel differently." He released her and stood up.

"And now," he said reluctantly, "I suppose we'd better call it a night. It's getting late."

She walked him to the door, and he turned to face her. "Whatever I decide about my career in the future, I'm glad I told you about Lisa. I needed to get it out in the open. I've been concerned that this would turn you away from me."

He took her hand and smiled. "I should have known better. I just hope it didn't spoil your evening."

"Of course not. I enjoyed the evening very much."

"I'm glad, because I did too."

The significance of Alex's revelation did not escape Samantha. She was deeply moved that he trusted her enough to reveal a part of himself that he considered a flaw. The fact that she didn't see it as a flaw didn't matter—he couldn't have been certain of her reaction. The necessity of being honest with her had been more important than the possibility of hurting their relationship. As far as he was concerned, hiding it from her would have been even more damaging.

Once again guilt washed over her. She hadn't accorded him that same honesty. She knew she should tell him . . . and she would eventually. Of course, there was a slim possibility that he would guess part of the truth, if their relationship continued on its present course. At least she had some control over the progress of that relationship.

Before the end of the month, however, she had reason to question the amount of control she had over that progress. Until she'd met Alex, she'd begun to think that the hormones she'd heard other women discussing were totally lacking in her. Evidently they had only been asleep. Alex had awakened them with a vengeance. The physical desire was only part of the danger. Add to that the fact that she was falling in love with him, and the danger increased considerably.

She had seriously considered her feelings and reactions to him and, when they started dating regularly, she decided that her only defense was to be careful of the times and places that she was alone with him. Every time they parted after a date, she'd had to consciously force herself to let go when her senses were screaming to cling tighter, to pull him closer.

Well aware of her own susceptibility, Samantha had continued to hire a baby-sitter for their dates. It was safer than leaving Jessica with Sarah. This way they would not be alone when he brought her home.

She should have realized that Alex would eventually catch on to her little strategy. She should also have realized that once he caught on, her would question it. After her most recent refusal to leave Jessica with Sarah, he broached the subject.

They'd been to dinner and then a movie. He had refused her invitation to come in when he deposited her at her door, but before leaving, he turned to her.

"Sarah asked me why you won't bring Jessica to stay overnight with Melanie when we go out. I think she has it in her mind that either you don't want Jessica to stay with her, or she somehow gave you the impression that it's a problem for her."

Samantha felt the color suffuse her cheeks and tried vainly to come up with a plausible answer. Finally she said, "Of course I don't have a problem with Sarah baby-sitting, and she certainly has done nothing to make me think she's unwilling. I just didn't want to take advantage of her." Her reply sounded weak even to her own ears, and she couldn't bring herself to look at him.

Alex, however, would not let her off that easily. Raising her chin with his forefinger, he forced her to look him in the eye.

"It's not necessary, Samantha. You don't need a chaperone to keep me in line. I promised you I wouldn't rush you. Nothing will happen between us unless, and until, you want it to."

Her blush deepened when he added softly, "Maybe that's the real problem. Maybe protecting yourself from me isn't the issue."

He paused, taking her hand in his, his thumb caressing her wrist. "It's your decision, sweetheart. I want you, I've made no secret of that—and I have good reason to believe you feel the same. I won't pressure you. I'm a patient man and, until you decide you're ready to take the next step, I'm content to enjoy your company as much as possible."

Samantha opened her mouth to reply, but Alex decided they had done enough talking. He kissed her thoroughly and a few minutes later he was gone, leaving her to deal with the passion he had aroused.

* * *

The following week was Thanksgiving, and Samantha planned carefully for the holiday feast. She had hesitantly invited Alex and Melanie to dinner, including Sarah and Fred in the invitation. Alex accepted on behalf of the others, with Sarah's insistence that she let her bring the dessert.

By the time the day arrived, Samantha's nerves were on edge. It was her first real dinner party and, having tasted Sarah's excellent cooking on several occasions, she was feeling rather uncertain about her own culinary talents.

After tasting each dish, she was satisfied that everything was not only acceptable but actually quite good. She supposed the years of helping her mother and later cooking for her father had taught her more than she realized.

The turkey was arranged on the platter and, along with the candied yams, set in the oven on a low temperature to keep them warm. The greens and gravy were steaming in their pans on top of the stove.

Her preparations proceeded without any problems, except that they had taken longer than expected. She had just slipped on her dress when she heard the doorbell. Slipping her feet into her shoes, she went to welcome her guests, with Jessica following closely on her heels.

Opening the door to her guests, she offered her apologies as she took their coats and ushered them into the living room. "I'm sorry, I guess I haven't yet mastered the timing for these things. Please excuse me, I'll only be a moment. I just have to do something with my hair."

Captivated by the flaming mass of waves and curls framing her face, Alex could not bear the thought of her consigning them to a French twist or braid. She turned to leave, but he captured her hand to restrain her.

"Your hair looks fine. I like it down."

Sarah reinforced his suggestion. "Don't worry about it, child. You don't need to be formal with us."

She had reason to remember Alex's words all through dinner. It seemed every time she glanced his way, his eyes were on her.

She couldn't say that it made her uncomfortable, only very much aware of the feelings that simmered just below the surface.

After dinner the girls busied themselves with board games, insisting that Sarah join them since Fred had become engrossed in the football game on television. Although Samantha assured Alex that she would not be upset if he indulged in that traditional Thanksgiving Day pasttime, he insisted on helping with the cleanup.

They worked well together and in no time the job was done. Alex watched as she finished wiping the counters and turned on the dishwasher. She turned from that task to find him standing just inches in front of her. She looked up into his eyes, her heart pounding as his hands clasped her waist.

"I've been wanting to do this all day," he murmured, as one hand came up to bury itself in the flaming tresses. At the same time he lowered his mouth to capture hers in a hot, sweet lingering kiss. It was a while before they were both sufficiently composed to join the others.

During their absence the children had naturally turned their thoughts to the rapidly approaching Christmas holidays, and that in turn led to a discussion of the school program. Both children were part of the chorus that would sing the carols for the short play that was planned.

The girls had decided that they should all go to the program together. Samantha questioned the feasibility of this, pointing out to Jessica that Sarah and Fred would also like to see Melanie perform, and there wasn't room for all of them in one car. Alex assured her that there would be plenty of room for everyone in his minivan. The plans were made, and before long the evening had come to an end.

Eleven

The weekend before the school program, Samantha considered once again the problem of the Christmas tree. Every year she went through the quandary of whether or not to get a real tree. She thought about the job of lugging it into and out of the house, cleaning up the needles, and making certain it had enough water.

She invariably decided that none of these drawbacks was sufficient reason to give up and buy a fake one. She knew that a big part of her decision was based on the fact that her father had always insisted on a real tree. So as usual she purchased the tree, set it up, and with Jessica's help decorated it.

That same weekend she had been pleasantly surprised to see Alex and Melanie at the little church located on the banks of the picturesque pond where she had brought Jessica to feed the ducks when she was younger.

After the church service they had stood talking in the parking lot, while he reminisced about the days he had spent ice skating on that same pond when he was growing up. As he talked, she tried to picture Alex as a young boy and was not surprised when he confessed to having been caught more than once sneaking off with his companions, when he should have been doing chores. Samantha had concluded from that revelation that his stubborn streak had probably been there from birth.

* * *

The night of the school Christmas program arrived, and Jessica was so excited, Samantha had her hands full trying to get herself and the child dressed. After combing the child's hair, she hesitated a moment before pinning up her own hair, recalling the look in Alex's eyes on Thanksgiving.

She was tempted to leave it loose, but old habits died hard. She rapidly arranged it in her usual twist and returned to making certain that they were ready when Alex came for them. Finally they were both ready, and Samantha was just slipping into her shoes when the doorbell rang.

When the performance was over, Alex insisting on taking the girls for ice cream to celebrate their grand performance. The girls were engrossed in their sundaes when Alex delivered another surprise invitation.

"I don't know if you've already made other plans, but if not I'd like to have you and Jessica join us for Christmas dinner at my house."

"Actually the past couple of years we've spent Christmas with Eloise, but she mentioned that she had been invited out to dinner this year."

"She has, with us. My mother is arriving tomorrow—she's spent Christmas with us for the last few years. Now that I'm back in Pennsylvania, I thought it would be a nice for her and Eloise to spend the holiday together. Since Melanie and I will be going with her when she returns to Atlanta after Christmas, I decided that this would be a good time for you to meet her."

"Your . . . your mother," Samantha stammered.

"That's right. Melanie has been talking her ear off about Jessica, and she can hardly wait to meet both of you. Since you seem to have no other plans, how about it?" He grinned. "I promise you my mother won't bite, she's really a very nice lady."

Samantha looked sheepish. "I'm sure she is, that's not the point."

In the end she accepted the invitation, but not without misgivings. However, the next few days were so busy she had little time to worry about Christmas dinner or meeting Alex's mother. Although the job of the tree and decorations had been settled, she still had some last-minute shopping to do.

The excitement of the Christmas morning had died down, and they were preparing for dinner at the MacKenzie home, when Samantha's nervousness began returning. Jessica was in the bathtub, her clothes all laid out for her, while Samantha rooted through her closet for something to wear. She had no idea how much Alex had told his mother about her. She tried to compose herself by recalling what she had learned about Mrs. MacKenzie from Eloise. She sounded like a pleasant enough person.

She was showered, made up, her hair was combed, and she was standing in front of her closet still trying to make up her mind about what to wear, when Jessica came into her bedroom. She had finished combing the child's hair a few minutes earlier and sent her off to her room to occupy herself.

"You're not dressed yet?" the child asked impatiently.

"Almost," Samantha replied, finally choosing a plum-colored knit. When she had first seen it in the store, she had loved it but turned away from it because of her red hair. The saleswoman had talked her into trying it on, and she had been pleasantly surprised.

The color was a such a deep rich purple that it enhanced the color of her hair, rather than fighting it for dominance. It had a round neckline and long fitted sleeves. The bodice was fitted to just below the waist, and the skirt was a slightly gathered circle that fell to midcalf.

With it, she wore suede pumps that were dark gray with patches of a lighter gray and purple. The silk scarf that she pinned at the shoulder echoed the same colors as the shoes.

Clipping on silver earrings that matched the scarf pin, she stood back, examined her reflection, and shrugged in resignation as she ushered Jessica out of the room and downstairs.

A short time later at the MacKenzie home, Fred opened the door to them, but Alex was right behind him. "Hello, ladies." He welcomed them with a smile, and Jessica giggled.

"I'll take their coats, Fred."

Just then Melanie appeared, and the two girls greeted each other as though they had been apart for months. As soon as Alex relieved her of her coat, Jessica followed her friend across the hall to the living room.

Alex hung the coats, while Samantha took a deep breath. Taking her hand as they followed the girls, he leaned over and murmured, "You're looking lovely, and there really isn't any reason to be nervous, you know."

Samantha looked up at him in surprise. She could not believe he noticed. She thought she had managed successfully to hide her nervousness. He had greeted her only minutes earlier. How could he have sensed her apprehension in that short time?

He squeezed her hand gently, and she blushed at his next words. "No, it's not very obvious, but I notice everything about you, Samantha. You should know that by now."

When they entered the living room, they discovered that Melanie had already introduced her friend to her grandmother, and the girls proceeded to exchange gifts while Alex introduced her to his mother, Mary.

Samantha greeted Eloise and shook hands with Alex's mother. Mrs. MacKenzie was a tall, full-figured woman whose size was slightly at odds with her soft-spoken demeanor. She had short mixed gray hair, warm brown eyes, and a personality that soon put Samantha at ease.

During the course of their conversation, Samantha learned that she now lived outside of Atlanta, near Alex's older sister, having moved there soon after Alex's father's death.

"How do you like Atlanta?" Samantha asked.

"Being outside of the city, I like it fine. I guess I've never been a city person. At least the weather is a little kinder."

Eloise shook her head at her friend's comment. "But you come north at some point during the winter every year."

"Well, I have to come visit my granddaughter as often as possible. I love Barbara's boys, but the older they get, the more I appreciate being able to escape to my nice quiet apartment."

Her friend chuckled. "That I can believe."

They chatted for a while longer, before Mary excused herself to help Sarah in the kitchen. Eloise offered to lend a hand and followed her.

Alex grinned at Samantha, after the older women left the room. "See, I told you she wouldn't bite," he reminded Samantha, winking.

A moment later they were joined by their daughters, coming to show off their gifts. In less than a half hour, they sat down to dinner.

The girls chattered almost continuously through dinner, and afterward they played games while the adults talked over their coffee. It was almost nine-thirty when Samantha noticed Jessica yawning.

She nodded in the direction of the children. "I think we'd better get ready to leave. Unfortunately Jessica's getting too big for me to carry her upstairs to bed. It has been a long day," she observed.

"Jessica, it's time for us to leave. Help Melanie put the game away," she instructed her.

They said their good-byes, and Alex walked them to the car, giving her instructions to call and let him know that they had arrived home safely. It was odd that such a simple little consideration made her feel special. In fact, Alex had a way of making her feel special in so many ways.

The following week Samantha spent at home with Jessica. She tried to keep her occupied with little projects. Most of the time the child was content with this or with reading or watching television. An invitation from one of her other friends to a slumber party helped, but it was obvious that she missed her special friend. Samantha found that she missed the child's father almost as much as Jessica missed Melanie.

New Year's Eve arrived, dreary and snowing. It was a wet snow, nothing to cause a great deal of concern. Samantha thought it was a perfect day for building a roaring fire in the fireplace. She imagined it would be even better if the warmth were shared with a loving companion, which would probably generate more warmth and contrarily render the fire unnecessary. However, she mused, the romantic atmosphere created by the fire was one of the catalysts that would start the circle in the first place.

"Girl, you have got it bad," she mumbled to herself, when she realized her imagination was getting out of hand. "Men are the ones that are supposed to need the cold showers."

Hours later Samantha had put Jessica to bed and was sitting in a tub of bubbles, feeling a little sorry for herself. Her little trip to fantasyland earlier that day was partly to blame for her sagging spirits. Bringing in the new year alone had never bothered her before, but it didn't take much deliberation to understand why this year was different. It was just ten minutes before midnight when the telephone rang.

The water was so relaxing, she did not want to get out. In fact, it felt so good she began to doze off but was startled out of her lethargy when the telephone rang. Reluctantly she pulled herself out of the soothing water and, shrugging into her terry cloth robe, went to answer it.

"Hello, sweetheart." Alex's husky voice responded to her mumbled greeting. "How are you?"

Samantha felt the familiar acceleration of her pulse as his voice washed over her. "I—I'm fine," she stammered.

She slowly gathered her thoughts, wondering if she had misunderstood that he had planned to remain in Atlanta until after the holiday. "Where are you?" she asked.

Alex sighed. "Unfortunately I'm still in Atlanta. We returned from spending a few days at Disney World yesterday. I just wanted to hear your voice. This is no way to spend New Year's Eve. I miss you."

Samantha felt something inside her melt, and the weakness in her knees could not be blamed on exhaustion. Her emotions took over, and she spoke before her mind had a chance to weigh her words. "I miss you too."

"How was your week?" he asked. "Other than the fact that you missed me."

"Fine," she insisted, ignoring the last part of his comment.

"If you say so. Well, I know there are still a few minutes to go, but happy new year."

"Happy new year to you," she replied, her spirits lifting considerably. She could hear sounds of music and celebrating in the background.

Samantha cleared her throat. "It doesn't sound like you could be missing me very much. It sounds like you're at a party."

"Well, I guess I am, sort of," he said. "Barbara has some people over."

She almost asked why he was on the telephone with a party going on around him, but she was not sure she was ready for the answer. Instead she asked, "What did Melanie think of Disney World? As if I need to ask."

"You're right," he said, chuckling. "I think she might try to talk me into moving us down here if it weren't for one little problem."

"What's that?"

"She'd want Jessica to come with us."

"Well, it seems that feeling is reciprocated. Jessica has been a little down in the dumps too."

"I'm beginning to understand how they feel—about missing someone, that is. Why do you think I'm here on the phone, instead of out there with the crowd?"

Samantha felt her heartbeat quicken at his words. He had answered the question she hadn't had the nerve to ask. Her voice seemed to have deserted her, but he needed no response. She could hear the noise in the background growing, but his voice came through as clear as before.

"I guess that's the signal," he murmured. "Happy new year. I suppose I should let you go now—I think I hear Barbara calling me. She probably thinks I've slipped off to bed."

His comment broke the spell his previous words had cast. Samantha laughed at the idea of Alex sneaking away from his sister's party to go to bed.

"Do you do that to her often?"

"Well, not to bed, but I have been known to sneak out of her parties and find a quiet corner somewhere. I'll probably hear about it tomorrow. I'd better go now and let you get some sleep. You take care of yourself, and I'll see you in a few days."

Samantha went to bed a short time later, a smile still on her face.

Twelve

On Monday Eloise informed Samantha that she had accepted a speaking engagement at a conference the following week. The conference coordinator had contacted her at the last minute to replace one of the participants who had been forced to cancel due to an emergency. Samantha was in the process of making travel and hotel arrangements, when Amy poked her head in the door.

She entered quietly and stood waiting until Samantha hung up the telephone. Noting the smile on her friend's face, Samantha asked, "What are you up to, Amy? You look like the cat that ate the canary."

"Maybe I should be asking you that question, girlfriend. You have a visitor—Dr. MacKenzie."

"Alex is here?"

"In the flesh, if you'll pardon the expression." Amy cocked her head to the side and continued. "But speaking of flesh . . ."

"Okay, Amy, I get the message. I can see the wheels turning in your head, but it's rude to keep a guest waiting. Would you show him in, please."

Amy smiled and exited Samantha's office, leaving her door open. A moment later Alex entered.

"Hi, Alex, how was the trip?"

"Fine," he replied, closing the door and moving toward her. He came to a stop beside her, turned her chair to face him and, taking her hands, gently urged her to stand. Immediately his arms enclosed her.

"I missed you," he murmured, looking into her eyes.

Samantha opened her mouth to respond, but his eyes told her he was looking for more than words. Stretching up on her toes, she looped her arms around his neck. Pulling his head down to her level, she lightly touched his lips. When she pulled back, he smiled.

"Is that all I get for a welcome home?"

Samantha returned his smile and reached up once again, but this time her lips settled firmly on his. Alex's hands moved to her waist, lifting her just enough to set her on the edge of her desk. Samantha's tongue outlined his lips and sought entrance to the moist heat inside.

He moved closer, her full skirt allowing him to wedge his thighs between her legs, as he willingly allowed her the entrance she sought to his mouth and gave himself up to her tongue's exploration. When her tongue began to stroke the roof of his mouth, he could remain passive no longer, and his hand began moving up and down her rib cage, finally coming to rest on her breast.

Samantha moaned, tightening her arms around his neck. The sound fueled Alex's desire, but it also restored him to an awareness of their surroundings. He lifted his head and planted a few final, featherlight kisses at the corners of her mouth.

Samantha opened her eyes and murmured, "Welcome home."

Alex grinned. "I'll have to remember to challenge you more often. Only next time I'll be sure to do it when we have more privacy."

Samantha lowered her eyes to his chest as the heat crept up her neck. Unwinding her hands from around his neck, she slid from her sitting position and began to smooth her skirt. He was still so close that her hand brushed the front of his pants. If she had not already seen the desire blazing in his eyes, that accidental touch would have left no doubt about his reaction to her kiss.

Samantha felt as though her face was on fire, along with a few other parts of her body. Alex cleared his throat and moved back a few steps. Samantha looked away, trying to focus her attention anywhere but on him and his effect on her. The warmth in her cheeks began to subside.

"I almost forgot the reason I stopped by. Although," he continued, running his finger lightly down the side of her cheek, "I think I could be forgiven for forgetting any number of things after that demonstration."

Alex smiled and hugged her when the color spread over her face again. She was such a contradiction. One minute she was setting him on fire, and the next she was blushing from a few innocent words—well, maybe not so innocent. He held her for a moment, telling himself that it was to give her time to compose herself.

Samantha was the one to break the embrace. She stepped back and managed this time to look him in the eye.

"What was your reason for coming?" she asked.

"To ask you to have dinner with me on Saturday. I could have called, but I decided I'd rather have an excuse to see you. I don't think I could have waited until Saturday."

"Dinner on Saturday will be fine." She sounded prim, even to her own ears. She couldn't help it, she was still struggling to regain her composure.

Alex pretended not to notice the formal edge to her speech and was careful not to smile.

"Now that that's settled, shall I arrange for Sarah to baby-sit this time? You know the girls will be dying to have some time together."

"Yes, I know. As a matter of fact, Jessica asked me this morning if Melanie could visit this weekend. So in answer to your question, it will be fine to have Sarah baby-sit, as long as she doesn't have other plans. I really don't want to get into the habit of taking advantage of her good nature."

Alex held up his hand. "Sarah and I already have that understanding as far as any evening baby-sitting is concerned, but I promise to remind her that other arrangements can be made. Even if she has no other plans, but would simply rather spend the evening in her own apartment."

* * *

Later that week, as Samantha dressed for her date, she realized that a good portion of her preparation involved giving herself a lecture. Alex had promised that she was in control of what happened between them and when it happened. The real problem was that, given her recently awakened hormones, she did not feel in control. She also suspected that Alex was aware that he had the upper edge, in spite of his promise.

When Samantha opened the door to Alex, she suggested a change in plans. "You look exhausted, Alex. Sarah said you were at work when I dropped Jessica off this afternoon."

"I did go in today. There were some tests I wanted to finish. I'll be fine, though."

He did not tell her of the sleep he had lost in the past two weeks because he had missed her and had not been able to get her off his mind. He had told her the truth earlier that week, his need to see her had motivated his visit to her office.

"We don't have to go out, Alex. There are any number of restaurants that deliver. We can order in and just relax," she assured him, opening the closet and holding out her hand for his coat.

"You're sure you don't mind? After all, I did promise you an evening out."

"I don't mind. How do you feel about Chinese food?" she asked, hanging his coat.

"Chinese is fine," he said.

"Go in and make yourself comfortable. I'll find the menu."

They settled in the living room after dinner. Alex suggested making a fire, and Samantha recalled her fantasy less than a week earlier. Once the fire was blazing, he knelt in front of the fireplace for a moment, before joining her on the sofa. Samantha sensed that his thoughts were on something other than what had gone through her mind when he first suggested the fire. Even during dinner, he had seemed preoccupied.

Samantha waited patiently, as he took a sip of coffee. He surprised her when he commented, "You're a rather unusual woman, Samantha."

The puzzled expression in her eyes prompted his explanation. "Considering what I've already told you about myself, most women would have found a way by now to ask a few more personal questions."

"I guess I've been the victim of so many probing questions that I've learned to curb my curiosity. Besides, I believe it's rude to push someone into a corner with uncomfortable questions. I confess that Sarah told me some time ago that you're a widower. I decided you would volunteer any more information if and when you were ready. Anything more than that was really none of my business."

Alex gazed at her for a moment and nodded slowly. "As I said, you're an unusual woman. I appreciate your attitude, but at this point in our relationship, I think there is a little more information that you're entitled to have.

"I need to tell you a little more about my marriage, partly because it explains Melanie's problems. Aside from that I need to tell you because of our relationship. I'm aware that each of us brings some baggage into every relationship, and I believe that knowing what constitutes that baggage can help make the relationship work."

Samantha opened her mouth to speak, but he held up his hand. "Believe me, Samantha, I learned that lesson the hard way. Anyway, Marci and I were married right after I finished medical school. We moved to Chicago immediately afterward because I had been offered a residency there. She had hated Chicago from the beginning, but when she became pregnant I found that she hated that even more. Until then I had no idea she felt that way. It wasn't as if we hadn't discussed having a family before we were married.

"As if that weren't bad enough, late in her pregnancy there were some complications, and I found out that she had had two abortions before we met. I still wonder how I could have been so blind.

"She left when Melanie was just six months old. Sarah came to work for me, and I went on with my life. Melanie was four years old when she showed up again. By that time we were divorced, and any feelings I had had for her were dead. I allowed her to see Melanie, which she insisted was the reason she had come back, but after a while I started to notice money missing from the house mysteriously after her visits.

"She stayed in the city for about six months. That seemed to be her limit where Melanie was concerned. Unfortunately it was just long enough for Melanie to become attached to her.

"About a week before she left again, I discovered that Melanie's bank was missing. When I asked Melanie about it, she said she had given it to Mommy. I didn't even ask her why she gave it to Marci. Marci came by one evening to inform me that she was leaving for good, that she had decided she just wasn't cut out to be a mother.

"Melanie was asleep, and I confronted her with the money issue. Of course, she denied it. She even tried to blame it on Melanie, saying that she probably broke it herself and hid it from me. To say we argued is a gross understatement. It was the closest I ever came to hitting a woman."

Samantha saw the hurt and anger in his face as he stood and silently paced. She said nothing, just sat and watched him pace for a while, as though he was trying to walk off the feelings that had been revived.

Finally he took a deep breath and went on. "Evidently the noise woke Melanie. I looked up and there she stood. Marci didn't even make any effort to comfort her or even to stop to tell her good-bye. I went to Melanie, picked her up, and when I turned, Marci was gone.

"Two days later she and her new lover were killed when his private plane crashed over Colorado. Ironically she was carrying a card that listed me as next of kin. It wasn't long after that that Melanie started sleepwalking."

Samantha sat still, tears burning the backs of her eyes, unable to speak. She ached for him—she now realized that she was also deeply in love with him. She had seen it coming for months. In spite of her misgivings, she had fallen in love with Alexander MacKenzie.

She thought about Amy's romance novels where love always happened instantly, like a lightning bolt. It wasn't like that at all—her feelings for him had been growing for some time. She simply had not acknowledged it until now. Seeing his torment had made her realize the depth of her feelings.

She wanted to help him, comfort him, but she had no idea how to begin. Finally she murmured, "I'm so sorry, Alex."

Something in her voice made him turn and look at her. A moment later he was kneeling in front of her, and she was wrapped in his strong arms.

"Oh, baby, don't cry. I seem to have a habit of making you cry. I certainly didn't tell you this to upset you. Please, forgive me. I should have known better," he said softly, his hands tenderly stroking her back.

"I'm all right, Alex," she assured him, gently pulling away. She didn't quite manage a smile, insisting, "I should be the one comforting you."

"You are, sweetheart, just by being here and listening," he said. Gently wiping away the tears glistening on her eyelashes, he then kissed each eyelid.

His lips traveled down her cheek, leaving a trail of tender, tingling kisses before settling on her lips. Moments later he was seated on the sofa with her on his lap, his mouth never leaving hers. Her arms twined around his neck, and he pulled her closer. She shuddered in his arms, and his hand moved up from her waist to caress her rib cage, before cupping one lush round breast. Samantha moaned and clutched his shoulders, as his tongue slipped between her soft, full lips to play tag with hers.

His hands continued their exploration, one slipping under

her, to gently squeeze the tempting round cheeks that were settled on what was rapidly becoming a painful arousal. His other hand caressed the tempting curve of her hip and continued moving down to stroke her thigh. His roving hand then started on its return trip, moving her dress up with it, until his fingers came to rest on the inside of her thigh, inches from the center of the heat being generated in her body.

Just as his finger was reaching to explore that core of heat, a log in the fireplace fell, startling them both and bringing them out of the cloud of passion in which they had become immersed. Alex's hand retreated reluctantly from its quest and came to rest on her thigh.

He lifted his head a fraction of an inch and then planted a featherlight kiss on each corner of her mouth. Samantha felt as though her heart would burst from her chest. She laid her head against his chest and became aware that his appeared to be in the same danger.

"I'd better stop while I can," he whispered huskily, still holding her close.

A few moments later, sounding a little more like himself, he lifted her chin and scanned her face. What he saw there told him that she felt the same desire. "I think I'd better leave before I forget my promise."

Samantha nodded absently. The intensity of her own passion stunned her. He eased her gently from his lap, stood up, and walked over to the fireplace. He wasn't really concerned about the fire, in spite of the log that had fallen, but he needed a few minutes to regain his control.

Samantha was occupied with her own efforts to put her clothes in order and retrieve her shattered composure. Moments later, still slightly dazed, she was walking him to the door. He wisely bid her good night with a kiss on the cheek.

She did not know that Alex was mentally kicking himself as he drove back to his home. He had not expected to spend the evening in the privacy of her home. He had forgotten the primary code of his youth: 'Be Prepared.' Consequently he had been forced to call a halt to their lovemaking. Another cold shower was in store for him. The freezing temperature outside was not enough to cool the fire in his loins.

Lying in bed, Samantha relived the entire evening. Her awareness of her love for him had not prepared her for the intensity of the passion he had evoked. She knew it was only a matter of time before she cast aside her reservations about where their relationship was headed. She had suspected that her own desire equaled his. Considering how easily she had been aroused to a fever pitch that evening, it was no longer simply a suspicion.

She pondered the story he had told her about his ex-wife. Personally she could not understand any woman walking away from Alex. But then she might be slightly biased on that topic. Try as she might, though, she could not understand how Marci could just leave her child without a backward glance.

Thirteen

When Samantha went to pick up Jessica at the MacKenzie home late Sunday morning, she did not encounter Alex. Sarah informed her that he had left a few minutes earlier to run an errand. She was not sure if she was relieved or disappointed. She still felt some remnants of embarrassment, although she felt no regrets.

She had already admitted to herself it probably would not be long before they became even more intimate than they had the previous evening. She had not considered how soon this might happen, until he called that afternoon.

"I'm sorry I missed you this morning. I had planned to try to talk you into staying for dinner."

"I probably would have declined anyway. I really need this evening to prepare for next week."

"In that case how about dinner next week—say, Friday?"

"I'd love to, Alex, except I'm going to New York with Eloise on Wednesday for a conference. I probably won't return until late Thursday or early Friday."

"New York—that sounds interesting. What do you say to my joining you there for the weekend?"

"In New York?" she asked warily.

"That's right, in New York. I'm not sure if I'll be able to manage tickets to a play on such short notice, but I think we could find enough other activities to occupy us. If nothing else, we can always go dancing at one of the clubs. Most importantly it would give us an entire weekend together, just the two of us."

"I don't know, Alex. That will mean almost a whole week away from Jessica. It also means arranging for a sitter for the whole weekend, and that might not be easy."

"As far as the baby-sitting part is concerned," he said, "you know Sarah wouldn't mind keeping her."

"Yes, I know, but I won't take advantage of her generosity— not for the whole weekend."

"In that case who will be taking care of her for the week?"

"Amy is picking her up here Tuesday evening. Eloise and I will be catching an early morning train on Wednesday. I suppose I can ask Amy about the possibility of extending it for the weekend. If Cassandra is available, it may not be a problem."

"Good, then you'll consider it?"

There was a pause at Samantha's end of the line. She knew very well some of the other activities Alex had in mind.

"Samantha," he continued. "I know what you're thinking, and I won't deny that it crossed my mind. As a matter of fact, it crosses my mind at least once a day, but nothing is going to happen until you decide you're ready for it to happen. Trust me."

"I do trust you, Alex, and I have to admit the idea of a weekend in New York, for pleasure instead of business, sounds exciting."

As soon as the words left her mouth, it occurred to her that the pleasure and excitement she mentioned would not necessarily have anything to do with being in New York.

"All right, I'll check with Amy and Cassandra about the weekend. I'll let you know tomorrow."

The next day Samantha told Amy of her plans, and her friend assured her that there would be no problem extending her baby-sitting duties through the weekend. Before calling the hotel to extend her reservation, she talked to Eloise about her plans to remain in the city for the weekend and return by car with Alex.

"I think that's a wonderful idea," Eloise assured her. "I know you and Alex have been seeing each other for some time."

Eloise shook her head. "There I go again. I'm sorry. I guess I have a tendency to be nosy where you and Alex are concerned, and I should know better."

Samantha smiled. "That's all right, Eloise. I don't mind. If I think you're getting too personal, I'll just say, 'No comment,' " she assured her.

"As a matter of fact, we've had dinner a few times. At first, I had an idea that it was just a matter of being thrown together because of the girls."

When she hesitated, Eloise prompted, "And now . . . ?"

Samantha shrugged. "I'm not sure."

"Well, I certainly hope you realize by now that his interest has nothing to do with your daughters. You're a very attractive, intelligent woman, and Alex is neither blind nor stupid. In any event I'm glad you've overcome your original antagonism."

If you only knew, Samantha thought, but she made no reply to that observation.

"I think the weekend in New York is a wonderful idea. You and Alex deserve some time together, away from the children."

She called Alex later that day, to inform him of her decision. After she had hung up the telephone, she considered more fully what the coming weekend was likely to mean to their relationship. The more she thought about it, the more she felt that one outcome of the weekend was almost a foregone conclusion.

She recalled her conversation with Alex and his telling choice of words. He had said nothing intimate would happen "until" she was ready, not "unless." Actually his statement did not surprise her. She had not exactly remained passive to his increasingly intimate advances. She had already acknowledged her own desire, and her mind was almost made up. She was twenty-six years old . . . and she was in love.

There was still some apprehension on her part, but the anticipation was rapidly outdistancing any reservations she might have about taking the next step in their relationship. At one point in her musings, it occurred to her that Alex's statement might indicate that he had some reservations of his own—that it would be up to her to let him know how she felt.

If that turned out to be the case, a little subtle seduction might be in order. She could never picture herself making blatant overtures to let him know how she felt. So she would have to come up with some other way to get the message across.

He had mentioned dancing. She decided to treat herself to a new cocktail dress. She found the perfect one, black silk with a deep vee-cut neckline in front and a back cut almost to her waist. The full circle skirt fell softly over her hips and swirled enticingly around her legs to end just above her knees. Fortunately it was made with a built-in bra. Her figure had not been the type that could go braless since she turned fifteen.

During the train ride on Wednesday, Samantha had little time to think about the coming weekend with Alex. She and Eloise discussed the conference, which took her mind off the other reason for this trip and helped to settle her nerves. By the time they reached the hotel, she had pushed aside all thoughts except the conference.

When the conference ended, Samantha said her good-byes to Eloise. Her employer did not return to the hotel but went straight to the train station from the conference center. As the taxi carried her back to the hotel, Samantha's doubts about her decision began to resurface.

She had never before felt anything close to the desire Alex had awakened in her, and she questioned whether her feelings might be attributed to her lack of experience. She had dated sporadically over the years, but there had been only a few men in her life.

She had spent most of the last eight years getting her education, working, and taking care of Jessica. She had never felt the need for anything more, until she met Alex. It never occurred to her that anything was missing, until he became such an important part of her life.

She smiled to herself when she finally reached the hotel and realized that she had made up her own mind during that short ride. In spite of the initial antagonism, she had felt an attraction to Alex from the beginning, and it had steadily grown. She loved him. There was no more doubt about that.

As for her concern that she might have misread Alex's reason for joining her on this trip, she would stick to her plan. If the desire she had seen in Alex's eyes on several occasions had not dissipated, she was prepared to do whatever was necessary to achieve her own end.

Alex had told her that he would be arriving sometime Thursday afternoon. Somehow he had managed to get tickets to a show for Saturday evening. Other than that they had not made any specific plans, at least none that either of them had verbalized.

The final presentations at the conference had run longer than expected, and it was after six-thirty when she arrived at the hotel. She stopped at the desk to inquire as to whether Alex had arrived, and that was where he found her. Some sixth sense made her aware of his presence just before his arm came around her waist, and she felt his warm lips on her cheek.

"Hello, sweetheart. I've been waiting for you," he said softly, smiling down at her.

He was wearing navy slacks and a crew neck sweater in muted shades of burgundy, navy, and tan. Samantha tried to ignore her racing pulse, as she returned his smile.

"I had expected to get back here earlier, but it seems the most long-winded of the speakers were all scheduled for today. In addition to that, you always have people who have a million questions, even though the answers have sometimes already been given during the presentation. How long have you been here?"

"About a half hour. I've already checked in. When they rang

your room and there was no answer, I decided to wait for you here."

"You know, that was a rather reckless greeting," she chided. "With my back to you, how could you be certain you were accosting the right woman? There are plenty of other red-haired women in New York."

His gaze traveled down her body and back up, stopping when he captured and held her eyes. Samantha blushed and realized that, as usual, she had left herself wide open for his next comment.

"Honey, I'd recognize you from any angle, with or without the red hair."

He peered at her more closely. "You look like you've had a long day. Shall we just have dinner here at the hotel tonight?" he asked, steering her toward the elevator.

"If you want to go out, that will be fine," Samantha insisted.

They entered the elevator and Alex pushed the appropriate button, before turning to her.

"Samantha," he said quietly, "I don't want to go anywhere, in particular. I just want to be with you. In fact, we could order room service and you won't even have to get dressed." He grinned when she blushed at his suggestion.

"What I mean is, you won't have to change clothes at all, or you can change into something more comfortable."

He grinned again. The look in her eyes told him that they had both realized what 'slipping into something more comfortable' usually meant.

"I think I'd better give up on trying to explain."

Alex thought about his choices of words and realized that they, unconsciously, reflected what he really had on his mind.

Samantha smiled. "I get your message, Alex. But are you sure you don't mind staying in?"

"I'm sure. So, which will it be, the restaurant or room service?"

"I think room service. I like the idea of kicking off my shoes and relaxing."

As they walked down the corridor, Samantha asked, "What room are you in?"

"Next door to you."

Samantha stopped in her tracks. "How did you manage that?"

Alex shrugged. "I called early this morning, told them I had a reservation, that you would be checking in and I wanted a room adjoining yours. No problem."

Samantha shook her head and laughed. "Only you could manage something like that with 'no problem.' "

Alex could not confess to her that it had not, actually, been that easy. At first the clerk said that they could not assure him that his request would be honored. He had assumed that she and Eloise would have adjoining rooms and had mentioned to the clerk that he expected Eloise's room would be available.

When the clerk still hesitated, he decided to try a different approach. He said that she was his fiancee and he wanted to surprise her because it was the anniversary of their first date.

Afterwards, he had felt a little guilty about lying. He rationalized that it did not hurt anyone and, obviously, granting his request was possible, after all.

When they arrived at her room, he took her key, opened the door and held it while she entered. He closed the door and stood just inside while she set her briefcase on the table, immediately stepping out of her shoes.

"Shall I order dinner now or wait a while?" he asked, moving across the room.

"You probably might as well order it now. I should be finished changing in about half an hour and I'm sure it will take at least that long for them to deliver it." She picked up the menu, quickly scanned it and gave him her order.

Alex nodded. "I'll let you know when it arrives."

He leaned over, planted a quick kiss on her surprised mouth, and before turning to leave, added, "For now, I'll leave you to get comfortable."

Samantha stood still for a moment, her lips tingling from just that brief kiss. When the door closed behind him, she urged herself to action. She stripped off the navy blue business suit and white blouse and hung them in the closet. She stripped off her pantyhose and padded into the bathroom in her bare feet. After turning on the shower, she shed her remaining garments and stepped under the reviving spray.

Fourteen

Twenty-five minutes later, she was showered, lotioned, and dressed in a long emerald and gold print caftan. She pinned her hair up in a loose knot on top of her head, spritzed herself with cologne and walked over to the connecting door. She had just raised her hand to knock when it opened from the other side.

Alex stood there, a smile lighting his face when he saw her. "Perfect timing," he said. "The food just arrived."

His eyes scanned her body and his smile expanded. "I like your idea of getting comfortable."

Gesturing toward the wheeled cart behind him, he asked, "My place or yours?"

The heat rose in Samantha's cheeks. The looks he had been giving her since their encounter in the lobby had already told her there had been no lessening of his desire. His words reinforced that opinion.

She realized, too, that the fact that she had chosen to wear the caftan, as opposed to jeans and sweatshirt, probably gave him a clue as to what was on her mind.

"Since the cart's already here, we might as well eat in here," she suggested.

He stepped aside, allowing her to enter. He stood there for a moment, enjoying the sway of her hips through the soft fabric as she walked to the small table near the window. He followed with the cart and they settled down to their meal.

"How was the drive up?" Samantha asked.

"Not bad, until I hit the city, but I was expecting that. I had hoped to get away early enough to avoid the rush hour completely, but I couldn't quite manage it."

"Better you, than me. I don't think you could pay me enough to drive in New York City, rush hour or not."

"It's not much worse than Chicago. In fact, any big city at rush hour is probably hectic."

Alex asked about the conference and her train trip. He had turned the radio on earlier and soft music played in the background. The rest of the meal they were content to simply enjoy each other's company, commenting occasionally on the food and the hotel, in general.

They had finished dinner and were having coffee when Alex asked, "What would you like to do tomorrow? I did mention that I have tickets for a play on Saturday, didn't I?"

Samantha nodded. "Yes, you told me about the play. I know this will probably sound terrible, living as close to New York as I do, but I've never seen the Statue of Liberty. Do you think we could take the ferry to Staten Island?"

"It doesn't sound terrible. It's not as simple as it may seem to some people to pop up to New York for sightseeing. I do hope, though, that you're not going to tell me you haven't seen the Liberty Bell."

"No, I won't tell you that. I've seen the Liberty Bell and Independence Hall, and even Valley Forge." She laughed, softly. "But I have to confess that I probably wouldn't have bothered with any of it, if it weren't for Jessica."

Alex smiled and nodded. "If I hadn't grown up in the area, and had only lived here my adult years, I'd probably have to make the same confession. Melanie hasn't been to any of those places, yet. I plan to take her some time this summer.

"So, the Statue of Liberty it will be. If we have time, we can also do the Metropolitan Museum and dinner and dancing tomorrow evening. How does that sound?"

Samantha nodded. "That sounds like a plan," she said, as she started stacking the dishes on the cart.

Alex helped her and then wheeled the cart into the hall. Samantha was replacing the items that had been moved from the table while they were eating when he came back into the room.

She leaned across the chair to retrieve one of the brochures that had fallen to the floor. Alex took a deep breath in an effort to quell his body's response to the sight of the soft fabric of her caftan molding the tempting, round flesh of her buttocks. She put the brochure on the table and took a step back, colliding with Alex as he approached.

Placing his hands on her shoulders he asked, "Well, now that we have our plans for tomorrow, what about tonight?"

"Tonight? Isn't it rather late to plan anything for tonight?"

"Not really. I'm sure we could manage to go dancing somewhere."

"Is that what you'd like to do?"

His arms wrapped around her waist from behind, as he bent his head to nuzzle her neck. "Samantha," he whispered. "You know what I'd like to do, but I made a promise to a certain lady. I admit I've been hard pressed, no pun intended, to keep that promise, but I've never gone back on my word."

Samantha leaned back in his arms, arching her neck to allow him better access. His right hand traveled upward to cup one ripe breast, while the other slid down her abdomen, coming to rest at the triangle that shielded her womanhood. He could feel her heat through the silky fabric. His teeth nipped at her earlobe and, as he brushed his hand over her breast, he felt its tip harden immediately.

She moaned and he turned her in his arms. One by one, he removed the pins that had held her fiery mane in captivity far too long.

"Every time I see that twist, I'm tempted to do that," he murmured against her lips.

His lips fastened on hers, searing them with his heat, as his hands had already done to her body. He pulled her closer, his hands cupping and squeezing the enticing globes that had tempted him from across the room.

She opened her mouth to him and wrapped her arms around his neck, as their tongues played tag. Alex's arms tightened around her, as his whole body reacted in anticipation. They drank hungrily from each other, and still the thirst was not slaked. Finally, a hairbreadth away from losing control, Alex raised his head. Samantha clung to his shoulders.

"Samantha," he whispered huskily, "if you're not sure about this, you'd better stop me now because in about ten seconds it will be too late."

She looked up at him and whatever small doubts may have remained, immediately disappeared. She loved him and she wanted him. Whatever happened later, she wanted this night. Her answer was to twine her arms around his neck again, pulling his mouth down to hers.

When he broke the kiss, his hands had already raised her caftan to her thighs. Seconds later, he had pulled it over her head and dropped it to the floor.

She stood before him clothed only in two delicate pieces of emerald green lace and satin. Alex was unable to move, all he could do was stare at her full breasts, straining against the fabric, and the generous curves of her hips and thighs, begging to be caressed.

He lifted her in his arms and, in two strides, was beside the bed. With one hand, he managed to pull back the covers and lay her down gently near the middle of the king-size bed. Sitting on the side of the bed, he leaned over and pulled her into his arms. He kissed her once more, as his hands sought the clasp at her back and peeled off the lace shielding her breasts.

His lips settled on hers again, as his hand covered her breast, his open palm lightly skimming the soft mound. After a brief taste of the nectar, his lips left hers to trail a string of feathery kisses down her throat and across her shoulder. His tongue traced the curve of her ear as his hand continued the magic he was working on her breast. She moaned when his lips moved to her other breast, laving and teasing it into a taut peak.

His ministrations were driving Samantha crazy; coherent thought had fled long ago, all she could do was feel. She felt as though a fire was spreading through her veins. As she clutched at his shoulders, his lips traveled from her breasts down her abdomen, leaving a trail of heat in their wake.

The warmth of his breath penetrated the silky barrier shielding the triangle of red-gold curls as he leaned closer, skimming his hand down each leg. Seconds later the lace garment that had hidden those curls was skimmed off and dropped absently to the floor. He smiled when he realized that he had just received the answer to that long-ago question concerning the color of her hair.

He stood up and began removing his own clothes, his eyes boldly surveying her full breasts and lush curves. Samantha watched him, her own desire steadily increasing. She felt no embarrassment over his steady perusal, she was too captivated by the sight of his muscles flexing and stretching. He shrugged out of his sweater, revealing the broad shoulders and chest that had been hidden from her until now. She wanted to reach out and run her hands through the mat of dark hair that tapered downward, to disappear beneath the waistband of his slacks. A moment later, her eyes were drawn to the spot where that trail of hair ended, which was now exposed. Her breath caught in her throat as she gazed in fascination at his aroused manhood.

Alex saw the look in her eyes, desire mixed with something that looked, suspiciously, like apprehension. He lay down beside her, pulling her into his arms. His hands roamed over her body answering another of his earlier questions: her skin felt like warm silk.

"Don't worry, sweetheart. I'll take care of you, don't be afraid."

He kissed her then, gently at first, but he became more demanding as she began her own explorations. Her fingers played in the mass of curls covering his chest before her arms slid up to encircle his neck. She shuddered in his embrace when his mouth left hers to tease and tantalize the dark turgid peaks of her breasts, each in turn. Slowly, his hand slid across her hip and then even further, coming to rest on the silky pelt at the juncture of her thighs. His fingers insinuated themselves into that secret place and slowly stroked its sensitive core, until Samantha felt as though she were on fire and slowly melting.

His fingers continued their magic, stroking and probing, and she lost all sense of time and place. Nothing existed but him and the wonderful, almost unbearable pleasure he was creating.

She moaned deep in her throat and he whispered, "Ah, kitten, I knew I could make you purr."

When he turned away from her for a moment, she felt bereft. "Please, Alex."

Groaning, he quickly removed the foil packet from the night-stand drawer and a moment later returned to her, his lips fastening onto hers to drink greedily of all that she offered. He positioned himself between her soft thighs and she pulled him closer. Slowly he entered her and held his breath when her wet silky sheath welcomed him. Alex felt as if he had finally come home. They were both startled when he pushed forward and penetrated the thin barrier. Samantha gasped, and his body stilled.

"No, don't stop," she pleaded.

"Baby," he breathed hoarsely, "I couldn't if I wanted to."

He moved again and before long they had found the rhythm that moved them closer to that final rapture. His arms tightened around her, and she arched into him. Her legs twined themselves around his waist, drawing his throbbing shaft deeper into the wet cocoon of her womanhood.

His thrusts intensified, and Samantha felt something tighten inside of her. Just when she thought she could stand the tension no longer, his fingers again found that sensitive nub, and she cried out his name in her climax. She was still shuddering in the aftermath of ecstasy when his release came.

They lay in each other's arms for a few minutes, silent except for the sound of their labored breathing, exhausted but content and sated. Samantha's feeling of contentment was temporarily disrupted when he released her and sat up on the side of the bed, his back to her. She had almost drifted off to sleep when his words broke through her lethargy.

"Who is Jessica?" he asked quietly.

Samantha's eyes fluttered open, as she attempted to concentrate on his words. His face finally came into focus. He was leaning over her now with one arm on either side of her.

She was brought fully awake by the look in his eyes. She detected anger there, mixed with some other emotion she could not comprehend. The covers were tangled around her waist, her full breasts exposed to his gaze.

Flustered by his scrutiny as well as his question, she stammered, "What . . . what do you mean?"

"Let's not play games, Samantha," he persisted. "Whose child is Jessica? There is no way she could be your daughter. Until tonight you were a virgin. Did you think I wouldn't know?"

She could not tell him that she loved him and wanted him so much that those feelings had overridden any misgivings she'd had. She certainly could not admit that for a short time she had not even thought of Jessica. She sighed resignedly.

"I guess I convinced myself that the idea that a man could tell the difference was a just a lot of romantic nonsense."

Alex laughed, but it was not a pleasant sound. "I can't speak for other men, or other couples, but I told you some time ago that I notice everything about you. How could you think I would not be in tune to your every reaction when I'm making love to you?"

Samantha blushed and he continued. "Now back to my original question. Who is Jessica?"

"She's my sister, my stepsister actually," she admitted.

"Your stepsister? Where are your parents?"

"They're dead," she murmured.

Alex sat up, no longer imprisoning her with his arms. She

was thankful for the breathing space and quickly pulled the sheet up to cover herself. She hoped that he would be content with the sparse information she had given him. She should have known better—he was not the kind of man who would ever settle for less than the entire truth.

"I don't understand the need for the deception. Why are you posing as her mother? Does Jessica herself even know the truth?"

He shook his head. "No, she couldn't. It would be too much for a child to keep a secret like that. She'd have given it away by now."

He fixed his eyes on her, and she recognized that look of determination. "I think it's time you told me the whole story."

Samantha took a deep breath, her mind working frantically in an effort to think of a way to tell enough of the story to satisfy him without disclosing all of it. Alex watched her closely and could almost hear the wheels turning in her head. He reached out, grasping her chin gently but firmly, and turned her face up to his scrutiny.

"All of it, Samantha," he said fixedly.

Alex dropped his hand from her chin, but he continued to face her. "All things considered, I think I deserve that much."

Reluctantly she resigned herself to yielding to his request, although it had not actually been a request. She sat up, propped up the pillows and leaned back against the headboard.

"My mother died when I was twelve, and when I was seventeen my father remarried. Martha was widowed herself, with a two-month-old baby, Jessica.

"She'd been through a terrible ordeal. She had just learned she was pregnant when her husband, Barry, was diagnosed with a brain tumor. He died before Jessica was born. She and my father met at a grief counseling session. My father had started going soon after losing my mother. Afterward, he continued to attend the sessions, in hopes that he could help others cope with the grief he had experienced.

"Anyway, before long, they fell in love. They had been married for less than six months when Martha was diagnosed with a terminal illness. Dad was devastated when she died two weeks after their first anniversary.

"I graduated from high school that same year. There was a baby-sitter, Mrs. Cummings, who watched Jessica during the day—Martha had been unable to do it for quite some time. In the evenings Jessica's care fell mostly to me. Dad tried, but he never really got over Martha's death. A little over a year later he had a heart attack. In the few weeks that he was hospitalized, he had two more attacks. He clung to life for a while, but they couldn't save him.

"By that time Jessica was calling me 'Mommy.' I tried correcting her at first, and then I let it go. I was the only mother she had ever really known."

She paused and Alex commented, "You could have explained when she was old enough to understand."

"I would have, but . . ." She stopped.

"But what, Samantha? What happened?"

"I had started college before Dad had the heart attack. Afterward I went back to school, and Mrs. Cummings continued to baby-sit Jessica during the day. She suggested several times that maybe it was too much for me to handle, and I should consider giving her up for adoption.

"I became even more concerned when Mrs. Cummings began making statements to the effect that I really had no right to keep her, since I didn't have legal custody. She said I was too young to be raising a child—and since the child wasn't mine anyway, I should let the Child Welfare Agency find a foster home for her.

"I couldn't let that happen. I had taken care of her since she was a baby, and I had promised my father that I would continue to do so. I became afraid that someone would tell the agency, and they would take her away from me.

"When she saw how much it upset me, she apologized and never mentioned it again. It didn't matter what she said at that point—the seed had already been planted.

"And then, to top it off, Mrs. Thomas showed up at the house one day."

"Who is Mrs. Thomas?" Alex asked.

"The aunt of Barry. Jessica's biological father."

"What did Mrs. Thomas want?"

"Jessica. At first she said she just wanted to be able to see her, but before long she was hinting that I should give Jessica up for her to raise. I was afraid, but I think I was more angry than anything else.

"I remembered Martha saying that her husband's aunt had visited him only once when he was ill and had never contacted her after the funeral. His parents had both died before they were married, and his aunt was the only close relative he had—close in blood only.

"After the anger cooled down, I became really afraid that she might actually try to gain custody of Jessica."

"Is that why you moved away?" he asked.

"It was the only thing I could think of," she admitted.

Alex watched her closely, imagining the weight she had carried and then having it compounded by fear.

"But how could you manage financially? Child care can be expensive and with the cost of college, too . . ."

"My father had been an insurance broker, so he knew how important it was. He not only had life insurance, the mortgage was paid off too. Until he died, I didn't know he had put the house in my name soon after Martha died.

"I was very grateful for that when I decided to move. After Mrs. Thomas's second visit, I started making plans to get away. I went to a real estate agent to put the house up for sale, but I told them I didn't want them to put a sign on the property. I was afraid if Mrs. Thomas saw it, she really would take action to get Jessica.

"With the money from the insurance, I had enough to carry us for a while. I was very careful about spending, and I took out loans to finish school. I decided that I could always pay the loans off early, if I found a job soon enough after graduating.

"We moved here. I worked part-time and finished school, and then I was lucky enough to get the job with Eloise. I decided it was best to let everyone believe Jessica is my child and avoid the problems I had run from."

Samantha took a deep breath. "Well, you wanted the whole story. There it is."

Alex shook his head in disbelief. She had uprooted them, turned her whole life upside down and taken on an awesome responsibility when she was barely out of her teens—and all by choice. However, parts of her story were unclear.

"Samantha, I understand why you did what you felt was necessary years ago, but what about Jessica's records? Didn't you need a birth certificate to register her for school?"

She hesitated, her hand nervously pleating the covers. He took her hand in his and gently prodded, "You were going to tell me all of it, remember."

She nodded and went on. "When Dad married Martha, he adopted Jessica so the last name was the same. A new birth certificate was issued after the adoption."

"But her mother's name would have been on the certificate too," he insisted.

"Well, yes," she agreed. "That's where I had another stroke of luck. I just made some changes in the parents' ages, added two letters in front of Martha's name and changed the *r* to an *n*. Then I deliberately smudged the whole thing and the school authorities never noticed. I guess their main interest is verifying the child's age."

"You changed the birth certificate? That's an official document, Samantha."

"I know that," she replied shortly. "I didn't have much choice. I didn't find out until later that I could get a state-issued birth certificate that had only the child's name, not the parents' names at all."

"All right, kitten, all right," he said soothingly. "But you can't continue with this deception. I have a friend who's an attorney. I want you to talk to him. You have to take some action to obtain legal custody."

"No!" she said quickly. "I can't take that chance. No one else knows the truth. If I go to court, they might decide against me with the excuse that I took custody of her when I had no right to it or just because I'm single. They might even use the changed birth certificate against me. She'll end up as a ward of the court in some horrible foster home. I won't risk it, Alex."

He saw the tears in her eyes and he gathered her now-trembling body into his warm embrace. He wished he could shelter her from any more trouble or upheaval. Having heard the whole story and knowing what she had already been through to keep Jessica, he knew there was little chance of persuading her to change her mind about taking her case to court.

"I think you're wrong Samantha. If you have it settled once and for all, you won't have to be afraid anymore. Knowing what you've been through, I can understand your reluctance, but will you at least give it some thought?"

She nodded against his chest but could not bring herself to verbalize her agreement. He showed no inclination to release her from the circle of his arms, and she was in no hurry to leave the shelter of that enclosure.

Her warm breath teased the hairs on his chest and his fingers slowly stroked up and down her spine. She raised her face to his, and the covers fell to her waist. Their eyes locked, and the flame of desire that had so recently been extinguished, ignited with a speed and intensity that rivaled any case of spontaneous combustion.

Their lips met in a frenzy of tasting and searching, their tongues stroking and swirling around each other's in an erotic dance of love. He lowered her gently to the pillows, and his lips left hers to cover her body with warm kisses, while his hands rediscovered the silky texture of her skin.

His lips claimed hers once again, and her fingers splayed across his chest before twining themselves in the mat of hair. She became bolder in her fever of passion, and her hands moved lower to caress the dark curls surrounding the fully aroused shaft of his manhood. He groaned and she felt a keen sense of power when he shuddered, burying his face in her breasts.

He covered her body with his, entering her swiftly and deeply. His thrusts came hard and fast, and she matched his ardor stroke for stroke. Moments later they lay still, their passion spent, the conflagration of desire extinguished once again. They drifted off to sleep locked in each other's arms.

Fifteen

The next morning Samantha awakened to the sound of running water. When the haze of sleep lifted, she realized that what she heard was the shower. It took a few more minutes for her mind to register that it was Alex's shower she was hearing, Alex's bed in which she had been comfortably sleeping, and Alex's body which had fully awakened her passions the previous night.

She moved to sit up and realized just how fully her passions had been awakened. She ached in some rather unusual places and was made aware of muscles she had not previously known existed. Along with that, though, there was an amazing sense of completion and fulfillment.

She was not surprised that her muscles were now staging a minor protest. They had awakened and made love twice during the night, and each time she had marveled at the intensity of her own responses.

Forcing herself to stand and move, she retrieved her caftan and undergarments and went to her own room. Walking made her even more aware of her aches and pains. A shower was not likely to be very helpful—she needed a good soak in a hot bath.

She was lounging in a tubful of bubbles with her eyes closed when Alex walked in. Freshly shaved and clad only in a towel around his waist, he was a more tempting sight than Samantha had ever seen. She suddenly felt a need to add more cold water to the bathtub when moments earlier it had felt quite comfortable and soothing.

"I was beginning to think you had deserted me," Alex said, smiling.

He walked over and sat on the side of the tub. His hand began trailing a path through the bubbles, and Samantha felt as though the temperature of the water had risen ten degrees.

Samantha's voice was just barely above a whisper when she replied, "Since you were using the shower, I decided to come in here."

"That wasn't necessary. You were perfectly welcome to join me," he said, reaching over to tilt up her chin so that she had no choice but to look at him.

He planted a brief kiss on her lips before asking, "What would you like for breakfast?"

"Breakfast?" she echoed.

He nodded. "I thought I'd order now. It should arrive by the time you've finished soaking."

"Oh," she murmured. "It doesn't matter. Coffee and juice and anything else will be fine."

He released her chin and stood up. "I'll let you know when it arrives. Don't stay in there too long, you might turn into a prune. Your skin is too beautiful to allow that to happen."

After the bathroom door closed behind him, Samantha closed her eyes and took a deep breath. "Girl, what have you gotten yourself into? You thought you had it bad before—that was nothing. The man had you melting before he touched you."

Twenty minutes later Alex knocked on her door. "Breakfast is here," he announced.

Samantha had just slipped into her robe. She went to the door and opened it.

"I'm not dressed yet."

Alex grinned. "I think it would be perfectly acceptable for us to share breakfast in our robes, all things considered."

He stepped aside, and Samantha entered the room. She sat down at the same table they had shared the previous night and looked at the array of food spread out there.

"What did you do, order everything on the menu?"

Alex shrugged and smiled. "Not quite, but when I dialed room service, I suddenly realized that I seemed to have worked up quite an appetite overnight. I can't imagine why."

Samantha blushed and he explained further. "I thought there might be a possibility that you were experiencing the same problem."

"You really are incorrigible, you know," she responded, pouring their coffee.

Alex laughed and helped himself to several samples of the food on the table. They ate in companionable silence for a while, until they both reached for the cream and their hands touched.

Their eyes met, and Samantha felt the heat from his gaze travel from her face down to her toes, but most of it seemed to settle in the lower region of her torso. She couldn't tear her eyes from his—the coffee, cream, and food were forgotten. Alex's body responded immediately, and the fire in his eyes intensified.

"If you keep looking at me like that, you may not see the Statue of Liberty or anything else today except this room."

Before taking time to think about her response, Samantha replied, "You can't be serious. Not after last night."

"Is that a challenge? You seem to have forgotten that I have something to prove. After all, I seem to recall some reference to my being almost 'over the hill.' "

"In other words, you're only trying to prove a point."

Before she could say another word, he had risen from his seat and was standing beside her. Seconds later he was seated on the side of the bed, with her on his lap.

"You are now sitting on the only proof you need to verify

what you do to me. And I have a feeling that you'll still have this effect even when I'm way beyond the hill."

His eyes held hers as he commented, "Do you know your eyes change color with your emotions? Normally they're the color of dark amber: When you're angry, they become a little darker, like fine whiskey. Last night . . . ah, yes, last night . . . they were a little lighter than usual with flecks like golden honey. Right now they've returned to their normal color, but I think they could easily be changed. It gives new meaning to the phrase, 'Go for the gold.' "

His hand slipped inside her robe as his mouth descended to claim hers. His mouth tasted and teased and nipped at her lips, while he kneaded and molded the silky globe in his hand. She moaned, and her tongue began its own exploration. His hand left her breast, loosening the tie on her robe and slipping it from her body. He eased her naked body onto the bed and continued his caresses.

Her arms encircled his neck, clinging tightly, when his hand caressed her knee and then moved slowly upward, until it reached the fiery curls guarding the entrance to the core of her desire. Samantha gasped when his finger probed and then entered the sheath that had more than once enveloped his throbbing manhood.

"Oh, baby," he murmured in her ear, "you're so hot and wet and ready."

"Yes, Alex, yes."

"Soon, sweetheart, very soon."

She whimpered when he slid his finger out, but moaned her pleasure when two fingers were inserted. Samantha lost control when his thumb began to caress the sensitive nub. Her hips moved in the rhythm of his fingers, thrusting and retreating. He bent his head down to replace his thumb with the most intimate of kisses and Samantha's body arched, as she cried out in release.

A moment later Alex had removed his robe and lay beside her, pulling her into his arms. Samantha's hand strayed down to caress his still-aroused shaft. Alex could hold out no longer. He settled himself between her soft thighs, and his first thrust sent Samantha over the edge once more. In the aftermath of her contractions, he soon found his own release. Desire sated, they drifted to sleep in each other's arms.

Alex was the first to stir, opening his eyes to gaze contentedly at the woman lying in his arms. No woman had ever affected him the way she did, not even Marci during the best part of their relationship. But then, when he looked back on it, he realized that even the best part of his relationship with Marci had been sorely lacking in terms of friendship and companionship.

He had believed himself to be in love at the time, but he now knew that what he had felt then was nothing compared to what he felt for Samantha. Samantha filled more than his physical needs and desires, he loved just being with her—he loved her.

Alex caught his breath, his arms tightening involuntarily around the precious woman lying in his embrace. He understood, now, the meaning of "cherish." But how did she really feel about him? He had made the mistake of declaring his love too quickly, just once, and he had paid dearly for it. He would not make that mistake again.

Samantha stirred and he loosened his arms. Leaning up on one elbow, he murmured, "It's decision time. We can get up now and go see the sights, or we can stay here for the rest of the day."

A smile spread across Samantha's face. She reached up, twining her arms around his neck. Her lips brushed his gently, her breasts grazing the mat of hair on his chest.

"That's tempting, but I wouldn't want you accusing me of sapping your already meager strength," she replied, just before pushing him onto his back and scooting toward the opposite side of the bed.

She wasn't quick enough. She shrieked in surprise when Alex grabbed her leg, dragging her back into his arms. Trapped in his close embrace, Samantha had no room to struggle, even if the idea of struggling had crossed her mind.

"Meager strength, huh?" he said, smiling. "I'll show you how meager my strength is."

He lowered his head and captured her mouth in an all too brief kiss. Samantha frowned when his lips left hers. Alex laughed and playfully squeezed her buttocks. He sighed.

"You do tempt me, lady, but you might have a hard time explaining to Jessica that you never found time to see the Statue of Liberty."

It was Samantha's turn to sigh. "You have a point. Even if I managed to come up with an excuse, she'd probably ask so many questions that I'd never get away with it."

Alex laughed as he loosened his hold and rolled away from her to sit on the side of the bed. He stood up and stretched, giving Samantha an enticing view of flexing muscles and taut buttocks. She had never been much of a football fan, but the term "tight end" came immediately to mind.

"Stop torturing yourself, Samantha," she mumbled under her breath.

"What was that?" Alex asked, picking up the robes that had been discarded earlier.

"Nothing," she insisted. She hadn't realized that she'd spoken aloud.

Totally at ease with his nakedness, he placed her robe on the bed, draped his own clothes over his arm, and started toward the bathroom door. In spite of her earlier admonition to herself, Samantha could not tear her eyes from his imposing masculine form. She blushed when he turned toward her, the gleam in his eyes telling her that he was aware of her fascination.

"I'd invite you to share the shower with me, but we both know that would definitely be the end to any sightseeing plans. If we avoid getting sidetracked again, we should be ready to leave in an hour."

* * *

After their trip to the top of the Statue of Liberty, they stopped for lunch before catching the ferry back to the city. Alex suggested a trip to Rockefeller Center, and they spent an hour watching the skaters. Although she wore wool slacks and a sweater under her full-length coat, he noticed her cheeks and nose turning pink. He put his arm around her shoulders, pulling her close to his side.

"Why don't we get some coffee or hot chocolate," he suggested. "You look like you could use some warming up." He grinned and Samantha knew immediately what was going through his mind.

"Don't say it, Alex. Hot chocolate sounds fine. Your other remedy for the cold might be a bit embarrassing in this crowd."

Alex laughed. "How do you know I was even considering another remedy?"

"Because you seem to have a one-track mind," she declared.

"Only where you're concerned, sweetheart," he insisted, urging her away from the rink. "Only where you're concerned."

It was after five when they returned to the hotel. Alex opened the door to her room, flipped on the hall light, and stepped aside for her to enter. Samantha walked past him, expecting him to follow, but he was still standing in the open door when she looked back.

"You might as well just use the connecting door," she suggested, shedding her coat. She retraced the few steps she had taken to hang her coat in the closet.

Alex shook his head. "I don't think so. I'm afraid if I step any further into this room, we'll end up resorting to room service again, and that wouldn't be anytime soon."

Samantha cursed her fair skin for the hundredth time since meeting him when she felt the blush spread upward from her neck. She looked at him and caught her breath at the naked desire that glowed in his eyes.

"I'll be back at seven." He then turned and exited the room.

As he showered and shaved, Alex admitted that Samantha was rapidly becoming an addiction to him. He had known, as soon as he entered her room, that he was in danger. When she had brushed past him he had not dared to take one step closer. He had been so preoccupied with watching her that even his normally ingrained manners had deserted him. It had not occurred to him to help her off with her coat until she was in the process of hanging it.

The major factor that had aided him in maintaining his self-control was the realization that they would be returning to these rooms in a few short hours. Unfortunately the more he thought about it, the less he anticipated that those hours would be short.

He would just have to take advantage of the two days and nights that they had left to spend together. On the other hand, no matter how much time they had together, he knew it would never be enough.

Promptly at seven there was a knock on Samantha's door. She opened the door and looked up into Alex's eyes. What she saw there took her breath away. When he had left her less than two hours earlier, she had been tempted to call him back—to take him up on his suggestion to order from room service. Not that she had been interested in food—she was more interested in his statement that it would be a while before they actually got around to calling room service.

Her nerve endings began tingling just recalling the previous night of passion. She could almost believe that he was, indeed, a man with a mission—to prove that he was a long way from being over the hill. If it had ever crossed her mind to seriously entertain such an idea, he had definitely fulfilled his mission.

They stood silently gazing into each other's eyes, as if suspended in time. There was no need for words as each made a silent appraisal of the other, envisioning what they knew lay beneath the clothes.

Alex was the first to break the silence. "To say you look absolutely beautiful is a gross understatement."

He had noticed that she'd pinned up her hair again. He smiled.

In due time he would remedy that. For now he would not comment on it. After all, he was possessive enough to like the idea that the vision of those fiery curls tumbling around her shoulders was reserved for him alone.

Samantha turned her back to him, and Alex drew in a long breath. The bare expanse of silky skin was almost his undoing. She took her coat from the closet and handed it to him.

"I'll be ready as soon as I get my purse."

Alex smiled and looking down remarked, "I think you might want to get more than your purse."

Samantha followed his eyes and realized she was still in her stocking feet. She blushed, well aware of the reason for her forgetfulness. Opening the closet again, she slipped her feet into the black peau-de-soie pumps. The tingling in her nerve endings grew to the intensity of an electric current when his hands brushed her neck as he helped her on with her coat. She knew it was going to be a long evening.

By the time they sat down to dinner, she had regained her composure, only to find herself in danger of losing it again a short time later on the dance floor. His fingers caressed the bare skin of her back, playing up and down her spine as they moved in time to the slow rhythm of several romantic tunes, one after the other.

When the tempo of the music picked up, Alex raised an eyebrow in question. Samantha shook her head. She was not in the mood for gyrating around the floor. They returned to their table and chatted desultorily over coffee. If questioned, they would have both been hard pressed to repeat their conversation.

When they heard the beginning bars of "I Believe In You and Me," their eyes met and locked. Without a word, Alex held out his hand. She placed her hand in his, and moments later they were in each other's arms on the dance floor but barely moving. The music ended, and Alex loosened his hold enough to look down at her face. What he saw there put a greater strain on his control than he had ever known.

"I think we'd better be leaving," he murmured.

Samantha was beyond speaking; all she could do was nod. The cab ride to the hotel was made in silence, their hands clasped on the seat between them, as though any closer contact or words would ignite the time bomb of suppressed desire.

When they reached her hotel room, her hand trembled as he took her key. She stepped into the room, and he was right behind her, taking her into his arms. It was all that was needed to set off the explosion of passion that threatened to consume them.

His lips teased the corners of her mouth, his tongue outlining its curves and indentations, before settling firmly on hers. She opened to him eagerly and he drank hungrily, tasting again the sweet nectar inside.

His tongue probed and explored, rediscovering every sweet, moist crevice of her mouth. His hands molded and shaped every curve, before reaching up to remove the pins from her hair. He buried one hand in the thick curls, while the other found the zipper to her dress.

Samantha whimpered, and her hands sought the buttons that would give her access to the warm skin and curly pelt beneath his shirt. Unable to make her fingers work fast enough, she began tugging at it from his waist. She finally succeeded in getting her hands under the fabric, but it was not enough.

"Please, Alex, I want to touch you."

She had managed to loosen only two buttons, but it was enough for him to pull the shirt off over his head. Samantha sighed in pleasure, as her fingers splayed across his chest and then began roaming at will over the hard muscles and then playing in the mat of hair. Alex knew his control was almost spent and retrieved the foil packet from his slacks, just before she found the hook at his waistband.

Moments later their clothes lay in heaps at their feet and when they came together again, mouth to mouth and skin to skin, she shuddered with uncontrollable need. Alex scooped her up in his arms and in two strides was beside the bed, which had been turned down by the maid.

He laid her down, gave her one long kiss before taking a moment to tear open the foil package. The frenzy of passion had not diminished with that brief delay. He settled himself between her thighs, fighting for control. His hand found her moist heat, and she arched to meet the gentle probing of his fingers.

"Oh, baby, you're so wet and hot."

"Alex, please. I need you, now."

Alex groaned when his pulsating shaft entered her wet, welcoming sheath. She felt so good. He wanted to prolong the moment, but when she twined her legs around his hips, he was lost. His thrusts came fast and hard, and she met each one. He felt the contractions, signaling her climax, and together they were transported to ecstasy.

Sixteen

Samantha came slowly to her senses the next morning. She stretched languorously, unaware of the sensuality of her motions. The first indication that she was being watched closely came with Alex's warning.

"Another movement like that, lady, and I may not let you out of that bed today, or at least not until sometime late this afternoon."

Startled by his voice, she sat straight up in bed, the sheet dropping to her waist. She looked in the direction of his voice and saw him sitting in a chair he had pulled to the side of the bed. His eyes were fixed on her bare breasts, and she felt the color flushing her cheeks.

Seconds later he was seated on the side of the bed, clasping her hands in his and effectively preventing her from hiding her nudity. His eyes drank their fill, and she blushed at the thoroughness of his examination.

"It's hard to believe this blushing kitten is the same tigress that shared my bed last night."

Samantha's face was now on fire, and he smiled at her unexpected shyness. She had matched his passion for two days and nights, and still she blushed at his open perusal of her considerable charms. Leaning over, he captured her lips in a long, lingering kiss. Only his hands, still holding hers, and their lips, touched, but Samantha's entire body was tingling when he finally ended the kiss.

He released her hands, pulled up the sheet over those tempting mounds of flesh, and sighed. "I'd better leave you to get dressed. It wouldn't take much for me to forget the plans we made for today. I'll meet you downstairs in the lobby in"—he glanced at his watch—"one hour?"

She nodded and, after one last brief kiss, he left. She ordered a pot of coffee from room service. While she waited for it to arrive, she ran her bath and laid out her clothes for the day. She noticed that Alex had hung her dress from the previous night. Her other garments had been carefully folded, and she wondered how long he had been watching her before she had awakened.

An hour and fifteen minutes later, she stepped from the elevator, looking around for Alex. She spied him sitting patiently reading the newspaper. She had taken only a few steps when he set aside the paper, as though he had sensed her presence. He smiled as he stood and walked toward her.

"You're late," he observed, but his admonition held no anger.

She returned his smile, defending herself. "We women require more time and effort to make ourselves presentable."

He was standing inches away now, and he leaned over to whisper in her ear. "That excuse won't cut it, you know. I've seen you 'au naturelle' and with no effort at all on your part, I've never seen a more 'presentable' sight in my life."

Samantha felt the color creeping up her neck, but she could not pull her eyes away from his. Alex had mercy on her and simply took her hand, and they started toward the door.

They spent the day roaming through the Metropolitan Museum and window shopping on Fifth Avenue. It was after six when they returned to the hotel. Alex deposited her at her door, serving notice that he would be back for her at seven. They had stopped for a quick meal while they were out since there would be no time for a leisurely dinner before the play.

She took a quick shower and was dressed in record time. She had just spritzed herself with perfume when Alex knocked on her door. She opened it and smiled.

She loved this man more than she would ever have dreamed possible. She felt as though she had been caught up in one of Amy's romance novels. She would never again make fun of them. It was hard to tear her eyes from him, but somehow she managed.

Turning toward the closet, she informed him, "As you can see, I'm ready on time."

Alex nodded and, looking down at her feet, observed, "So I see. You even remembered your shoes this time."

She laughed as he helped her on with her coat. Her laughter changed to something else when he whispered in her ear.

"The total picture is lovely, as usual."

"Thank you," she replied softly. "You're looking rather splendid yourself."

"I think we'd better be going," he suggested, taking her arm, "or these tickets may be wasted."

She picked up her purse and they were on their way. Once they left her room, and the temptation of the bed they had shared, the tension eased.

The play was a poignant story of the trials of a struggling African-American family, set in the early seventies. Halfway through the story, Samantha tried unobtrusively to wipe the moisture from her eyes.

She was surprised when a snowy-white handkerchief appeared before her. She took it and, as she dabbed at her eyes with one hand, Alex reached over and clasped the other. They remained that way until the end of the play.

They stopped for a late supper after the play. Alex was feeling guilty about the effect the play had had on her. He had wanted her to enjoy the evening, but it had not occurred to him that it would sadden her.

"I guess I should have given more thought to choosing a play," he said halfway through their meal.

"Didn't you enjoy it?" she asked.

"I thought it was very good, but you might have better appreciated something more lighthearted," he explained.

"Alex, I enjoyed the play very much, tears and all," she said, reaching across the table to place her hand on top of his.

He placed his other hand on top of hers, squeezing gently. She smiled, as if to prove her words to him. He returned her smile.

"You're quite a woman, Samantha Desmond."

They finished their meal over a quiet discussion of the play, its characters and implications. He could not have pinpointed exactly what made up his mind, but by the time dinner was ended, he reached his decision.

It was after midnight when they returned to the hotel. They reached her room and Alex took her key, opened the door, and followed her in. She turned to him unaware of the look of expectancy in her eyes. Alex groaned inwardly. There was nothing he wanted more than to take her in his arms and relive the rapture and ecstasy that had filled their previous nights. But first, they had to talk.

"Samantha," he began hoarsely. "There's something we have to discuss. I've been thinking about what you told me about Jessica, and I have a suggestion that might help. Marry me."

She opened her mouth to speak, but he touched his finger lightly to her lips. "Let me finish. Marrying me will remove any possible concerns about your being a single parent, although in this day and age, I can't imagine it being a big stumbling block. Neither can I imagine your age being a problem now. You're not a teenager anymore.

"As far as Mrs. Thomas is concerned, if she should surface again, as a settled, married couple we could show that we are more than capable of providing a good home for Jessica.

"It would also give Jessica a father and Melanie a mother. I know how much you care about Melanie, and I hope you realize that I feel the same about Jessica."

Samantha was stunned, but she was also hurt. Not once had he mentioned anything about his feelings for her. She forced her reply past the lump in her throat.

"I can't, Alex. I can't marry without love."

It was Alex's turn to be shocked. He had been sure that she loved him. She had not voiced the words, but he had attributed that to her shyness, even though she had shown no shyness in her responses to him. He could feel the anger rising.

"That's great. You can't marry without love, but you can . . ." The stricken look on her face made him stop.

"Go ahead and finish it, Alex. But I can sleep with you, go to bed with you, have sex with you. It doesn't matter which phrase you had in mind, I get the meaning."

"Samantha . . ." he began soothingly.

"No, Alex, please don't say anything else. I suppose I should have seen this coming," she said, her own anger rapidly escalating.

"You really have nerve, you know. You're so busy giving me advice about how to run my life, but your decisions about your own life are rather questionable. You implied that I've been burying my head in the sand, but you're guilty of the same. You reacted to your own problems by running away."

Alex looked stricken but did not reply. Samantha knew she had gone too far. She was immediately sorry she had uttered those last words, but her lips could not form the words to apologize. She was hurt, and she had instinctively sought to inflict that same pain on him.

"Just go, Alex. Leave me alone. Please."

He stood still for a moment, just looking at her. After what seemed an eternity to Samantha, he turned to leave.

"If that's the way you want it. I'll see you in the morning. We should plan to be on the road no later than one o'clock."

There was no response from her, and reluctantly he made his

departure. When the door clicked shut behind him, Samantha sank into the chair behind her. She did not even realize that she was crying until the drops fell on her hands that lay clenched in her lap. It was enough to rouse her, and she forced herself to get up.

As she prepared for bed, she fought to come to grips with the turmoil inside her. She was forced to admit that he was right. She had given herself to him willingly and completely because she loved him. It had made no difference that there had been no declaration of his own feelings.

How could he condemn her for using the fact that he did not love her as a reason for refusing to marry him? Maybe she should have agreed. Maybe her love would have been enough for both of them.

She shook her head. No, she had been right to turn down his proposal. She could not have lived with him day in and day out, knowing that he did not feel the same about her. Knowing that there was a possibility that he would eventually meet and fall in love with another woman. That would be hard enough to handle under any circumstances. It would be impossible if she were married to him.

She thought about the hurtful words she had uttered. She was angry with herself for losing control so completely that she was oblivious to his feelings. She was no better than he. She was blaming him for using her passion against her, but what she had done was worse. He had opened up to her, confided his grief and frustration, and she had twisted it and used it as a weapon. How could she have been so cruel?

Next door Alex was struggling with his own disappointment. After Marci he had never expected to find a woman he could trust, a woman he could love. He had thought she loved him. She had held nothing back when they made love. How could she give herself to him so unreservedly, and why to him?

He was also upset with himself. How could he have been so

foolish again? He had almost confessed his own feelings, but he had not been able to say the words. He had proposed for all the reasons he had given her, but had not been able to tell her the real reason he wanted her for his wife. When she rejected him, his ego had been hurt. He had struck back, reproaching her for something that had been more beautiful and wonderful than anything he had ever experienced with any other woman.

He was in love with her and would always love her. What he had felt for Marci was nothing compared to this, and now he had probably lost her for good. She had not hesitated to let him know that she did not love him or to remind him that the changes he'd made in his own life had been prompted by the urge to run from his problems.

Her words had hurt, but he realized that she was only retaliating for his own careless implications. It had taken no more than the short walk to his room for him to forgive her for her angry words. If he had not uttered those stupid words himself, she would not have felt the need to strike back, and he might have had the opportunity to win her love. He'd blown his chances of that. He sighed. It was going to be a long night . . . and a long trip home.

Samantha awoke the next morning with the germ of an idea. She had lain awake most of the night and was not looking forward to facing Alex, let alone being confined in the limited space of his car for two hours. She threw back the covers and started emptying the drawers. If she hurried, she could pack and catch the train back before he realized she was gone.

She could leave a message for him at the desk. She owed him that much. She had no idea what she would say, what possible explanation she could give. After their conversation the previous night, there was probably no need for an explanation. In fact, he might be relieved himself not to have to share the return ride with her.

She did not deceive herself that she could avoid him forever.

Cutting off all contact would mean punishing Jessica and Melanie. Maybe a few days' breather would at least give her time to bring her emotions under control.

"Sure, Samantha," she murmured to herself. "You're as deeply in love as a person could be. How do you plan to control that?"

She wiped away the tears that had sprung up. "Well, they say time heals all wounds. I guess I'll find out firsthand whether or not that's true."

An hour later she was packed and dressed. She looked around the room one last time, to make sure she had not left anything behind. She assumed the knock on her door signaled the arrival of the bellman. She picked up her purse and coat, but it was not a bellman she confronted when she opened the door.

"Good morning, I see you're ready," Alex greeted her, as he entered the room to collect her bags.

"We should have time for breakfast before we check out."

So much for her earlier plans, she thought. Aloud she informed him, "I just called for a bellman. I'm not really hungry."

As if to reinforce her words, there was another knock on the door. Samantha gave her bags over to the bellman, who offered to have them stowed at the desk until she was ready to check out. Alex had insisted on having breakfast, leaving her little choice but to join him.

She tried to relax during their meal but had little success. She took two bites of her English muffin and managed to swallow them only with the help of the coffee.

Alex made no mention of the previous night's discussion, and she was grateful for that much. She retrieved her luggage, which he promptly took from her.

Although he showed no outward signs of anger, the tension did not diminish during the trip back to Pennsylvania. As she settled herself in the car, Samantha considered their present situation. On one hand, she wished they could talk, clear the air. On the other hand, she concluded that there probably was not anything more to be discussed. She was in love with him, he was not in love with her. What more was there to say?

Any decision as to whether or not there was to be further discussion was soon taken away from her. They had barely settled themselves in the car when Alex turned on the radio, not loud, but at a volume that effectively discouraged conversation.

When they reached the highway turn-off for Yardley, Samantha noticed that they were heading in the opposite direction from her house. She looked over at Alex questioningly.

"I might as well take you to pick up Jessica."

"That's not necessary . . ." she began. A look from him silenced her. "But thank you," she finished lamely.

After Alex dropped them off, she quickly unpacked, eager to get back into her familiar routine. However, her desire to get back to normalcy did not extend to cooking dinner. She just wasn't up to it. She bundled Jessica into the car and took her out for dinner.

She would be glad to get back to work. She had no doubt that whatever she had thought was happening between her and Alex was now ended. The only drawback in getting back to work was Amy.

When Alex had decided to take her to pick up Jessica, she had not been thrilled with spending the extra time in his company. As it turned out, it gave her the perfect excuse not to linger. Amy had asked about her trip, and she was afraid, if she went into detail, she would not be able to keep the tears at bay.

She wished she could be angry with Alex, but she could only feel hurt. How could she be angry? He had no more control over his feelings than she had over hers. She couldn't even claim that he had led her on or seduced her. She had wanted him as much as he wanted her, and he had wanted her—that had been real. He had been honest too. He never said he loved her, only that he wanted her.

After she had tucked Jessica in bed, she treated herself to a long leisurely bubble bath. She told herself that getting Alex out of her mind was just a matter of time. Eventually she would be able to think of him without feeling the pain of losing him.

Seventeen

The next day Samantha was too busy to worry about her personal problems. She had guessed correctly that Amy would want to know the details of her trip, but they had no opportunity to talk until early that afternoon.

Samantha had had no appetite, but her friend entered her office a few minutes after one o'clock, holding up the paper bag that had just been delivered.

"I know you said you weren't hungry, but I ordered a sandwich for you anyway. You can't work on an empty stomach."

"Amy, I'm really not hungry," Samantha insisted, just as her stomach put up a protest.

Amy cleared her throat. "You were saying?"

Samantha closed her eyes and sighed.

"Obviously you are hungry," Amy observed. "So your lack of appetite must be due to some other cause."

She watched her friend closely. "All kidding aside, I can tell there's something going on, girlfriend. The question is, do you want to talk about it? Or would you prefer to tell me to mind my own business and leave you alone?"

Samantha sighed again. "When have I ever told you to mind your own business? The problem is, I can't see that talking about it will help or change anything."

Amy put her hand on her hip. "Haven't you learned, in all

the years you've been working here, that you never suggest to a psychologist that talking won't help?"

Samantha smiled in spite of herself. "I beg your pardon."

"That's better," her friend said, pulling a chair up to the opposite side of the desk. She pulled out two sandwiches and gave one to Samantha.

Samantha accepted it and asked, "Since you decided I was hungry, what did you decide I should eat?"

"Chicken salad with lettuce and tomato."

Before taking the first bite of her sandwich, Amy urged, "Before we get into the problem area, how was your trip in general? Did you manage to do any sightseeing?"

Samantha told her about the play and the sights she had seen. She even told her about the evening of dancing. Of course, she kept to herself the details of the night that followed.

"I'm missing something. It sounds like it was a great trip. What happened that has you so down in the dumps?"

"Nothing really happened. Well, that's not quite true," she said, looking down at her sandwich.

Amy cleared her throat. "I guess this is the part where I bite my tongue to keep from prying into your personal affairs."

Samantha looked up sharply.

Amy shrugged. "Sorry, poor choice of words. Although the look on your face, and the fact that you're almost the color of that tomato on your sandwich, answers my question—and then some."

"That isn't really the problem, believe it or not," Samantha insisted. "The problem is, I now know what it's like to be in love with someone who isn't in love with you."

She stared at Amy when her friend showed no reaction to this revelation. Amy continued to chew her food, returning her look.

Finally she responded. "Am I supposed to be surprised that you finally admit you're in love with Alex MacKenzie? I've seen that coming for quite some time. I'm not a psychologist for nothing."

Amy put down her sandwich and rested her arms on the edge of the desk. "What I want to know is, why are you so sure he's not in love with you?"

"For one thing, the most obvious reason, he's never said the words. In fact, he implied just the opposite."

It was Amy's turn to become absorbed in the contents of her sandwich. Looking away from her friend, she softly inquired, "Have you said the words, Samantha?"

"Not exactly."

"Not exactly, but he should know how you feel, right?"

"All right, Amy, I get the message. There's more to it than that though. We had a big argument. We both said some terrible things to each other. I'm not sure we can get beyond that."

"You can always get beyond hurtful words if you want to."

Samantha sighed. "At this point I'm not sure he wants to."

Amy reached over and patted her friend's hand. "I think you both probably just need some time to cool off. I've seen the way Alex looks at you, and I don't think he's going to let a few words come between you."

"I wish I had your optimism."

"Give it time. I am a little older than you, remember?"

She picked up her sandwich but paused before she continued eating. "There is one more thing you should consider. Men, in general, have been known to have a problem with the big C—commitment. Alex in particular has more reason to be wary. I don't know the circumstances surrounding his divorce, and I don't need or want to know. I do know that anyone who's been divorced is usually a little leery of getting involved again. Be patient. From what I've seen, the prize will be worth the wait."

Samantha felt a little better for having had her chat with Amy. Maybe her friend was right, maybe their words hadn't done irreparable damage. If she could find the courage and the right opportunity to apologize, maybe they could reestablish their friendship at least. She shook her head. Who was she kidding?

She would never really be satisfied with just friendship. On the other hand, it was better than nothing—unless he fell in love with someone else.

The next morning she met with Eloise. Her employer reminded her that she would be leaving in a few days, to take a two-week cruise. As usual, once the business was out of the way, the conversation turned to personal matters.

"Did you enjoy your extra days in New York?" Eloise asked.

"Very much. I finally saw the Statue of Liberty, although I dare say I could have chosen better weather to make that visit."

"As I told you before you left, I'm glad you and Alex had an opportunity to spend some time together, without the children. You know, Samantha, you and I have had many discussions over the years. I've always been mindful of being careful not to pry into your personal life and to respect your privacy.

"I have to be honest with you, though, as far as your relationship with Alex is concerned. From what I've seen, it's done him a world of good. He's been through some rough times, and I like the changes I've seen in him in just a few short months. I have to credit you with that. I can't imagine any other explanation."

"I've always appreciated being able to discuss things with you, Eloise, for the very reason that you don't try to pry any more out of me than I'm willing to divulge. However, as far as Alex is concerned, you might want to prepare yourself for some other changes in him. I don't think we'll be seeing much of each other anymore."

"I'm sorry to hear that. I think you two were good for each other."

Samantha looked away. She had thought so too. Eloise watched the expression in her young friend's face alter and decided it was best to change the subject.

"I'm sure I don't need to ask if Jessica enjoyed her weekend. Those girls of Amy's keep her occupied every minute."

Samantha laughed. "Sometimes I get the impression that she thinks she's their contemporary. Yesterday she informed me that she wants to wear her hair out, like Cassandra's.

"I agreed to compromise, she can get rid of the braids for special occasions. Her hair is so long and thick, she needs the braids to keep it under control. I can't say she was thrilled with the compromise, but I'm sure she would be less thrilled with having the tangles combed out of it every day."

Eloise smiled, nodding her head in agreement. "I'm sure she would. I can still remember those days. Even though it's easier with today's relaxers, I think my memories of having those tangles combed out greatly influenced my decision to cut it all off—well, almost all. It's so much easier to handle this way."

"You're fortunate because it's also becoming. Not every woman could handle a style like yours."

"Thank you," Eloise said, rising from her chair. "Now before we get into another session of our mutual admiration society, I'd better be on my way. I have some last-minute errands to run before I leave on Thursday."

"Have a good time. You deserve the break."

On Thursday Sarah called at Melanie's request to invite Jessica for an overnight visit on Saturday. Samantha acquiesced, and they settled on a time for her to bring Jessica.

Samantha had known that sooner or later she would have to see Alex again. She also knew that given the friendship between the girls, it would probably be sooner rather than later. She spent the next day muttering to herself, trying to prepare herself for their meeting.

In the back of her mind was her resolve to offer an apology for her damaging words. In addition to steeling herself for their meeting, she was trying to muster the courage and the right words to make amends.

There was no need for her to be concerned. Alex was not at home when she arrived. The girls greeted each other as though they had been apart for months. There had been no overnight visits since before the holidays. As far as the girls were concerned, seeing each other in school every day did not count.

Samantha started to ask more questions when Sarah informed her that Alex was out, but she bit her tongue and resisted the urge. After all, she told herself, she should be glad of the reprieve. Besides, his comings and goings were none of her business.

When Alex was not at home the following day, she could not help being disappointed. It occurred to her that he might be deliberately avoiding her. He would have known when she would be coming, and it would have been simple to invent an excuse to be somewhere else.

Samantha was right about Alex's planned absence. He, too, wanted to apologize for his indirect insult, but he was not yet ready. Aside from that, her words had hit home and given him food for thought. He had some serious thinking to do about the direction of his own life, and his career.

He was still determined to win her love somehow, but he realized that he had to face the unresolved issues concerning his career first. He was no longer content to simply ignore those issues.

He had avoided her for the past week, but not seeing her had only reinforced his realization of how much she meant to him. He had been testing himself by keeping his distance, and he had failed. He hoped his deprivation had not been in vain.

If nothing else, maybe the time apart had made her forget the pain of his foolish words. He was relying on her reaction to his hurtful words being an indication that she cared about him. If she had no feelings for him, he would have had no power to hurt her. He had to win her forgiveness and her love.

By the end of the following week, Samantha had almost given up on any possibility of rescuing her relationship with Alex.

On Saturday she took the girls to the movies, but it was Fred who brought Melanie to the house. When Samantha returned her to her home that evening, Alex was once again absent.

She had heard nothing from him and, as much as it hurt, she admitted that it was time to start putting him and the entire relationship behind her. Of course, that was much easier said than done.

She dreamed of him at night, sometimes waking in the wee hours of the morning, expecting him to be lying beside her. The first time it happened really stunned her. It was not as though they had been sleeping together for years. Those few nights in New York had been enough to make her subconsciously hunger for more.

She even had trouble concentrating on her work, something she had never before experienced. Her work had always been challenging and interesting enough to hold her complete attention, but not now. Thoughts of him intruded into every aspect of her life.

Monday Samantha received a call from Alice, informing her that she would be out for at least a week. Her son, Mark, had a bad case of bronchitis.

"I'm sorry to leave you shorthanded. I thought it was just a bad cold until I took him to the doctor today."

"Don't worry about it, Alice. Take care of Mark, I hope he feels better soon."

When she hung up the phone, Samantha considered calling a temporary agency, but that seemed like a waste for just a week. Surely she could manage to handle the reception area and filing for a week. The only problem would be the short time that she had to leave the office to pick up Jessica, but Amy or Karen would be there.

She checked the patient schedule and figured that while they were seeing their three o'clock patients, she would have time to pick up Jessica and return before the four o'clock patients were due. At least with Eloise away on vacation, there would be fewer patients.

Having made her plans for managing in Alice's absence, she was convinced that she could handle a week of double duty. That was before she received a call from Amy on Tuesday. Her friend had gone skiing the previous weekend and had taken a day off Monday.

"Samantha, it's Amy. I'm afraid I have some bad news. I won't be in today. As a matter of fact, I won't be in for at least two weeks. I fell this weekend and broke my leg. Can you believe it? I've been skiing for years and never even had as much as a sprained ankle—now this. I really did a number on it."

"Oh, Amy, I'm so sorry. Are you in much pain?"

"It's not too bad. I have pills for when it's unbearable. The worst part right now is the fact that the doctor wants me to stay off it completely for a while. I'll probably be stir-crazy in a week. I really feel terrible about leaving you to cope with juggling the appointment schedule, especially with Eloise away on vacation. The groups can probably be canceled for this week. Eloise is due back next week, isn't she?"

"That's right. I expect her in the office on Tuesday."

"Maybe you can get Karen to come in the extra days for the rest of this week. Hopefully I'll be in next week."

"Don't worry about it, Amy. It couldn't be helped. I'll manage," she assured her, sounding more confident than she felt.

With Eloise on a cruise in the middle of the ocean, there wasn't the option of having her cancel part of her vacation and return early. She had no way to even contact her, unless it was an extreme emergency, and this could hardly be considered that.

Even when Eloise returned, it would not be the same as having an extra person. Eloise had her own patients already scheduled. In fact, Dr. Middleton was seeing two of her patients and was on call in case of emergencies. He would not be able to handle any more of the regular appointments.

She reminded herself that she was being paid to manage the

office, and that was what she would do. She called Karen, who agreed to work two extra days until Amy returned. She then began contacting patients to either cancel or reschedule their appointments.

By the time Jessica was in bed that evening, Samantha was ready to call it a night herself. Trying to cope with telling people who were already emotionally disturbed that their appointments would have to be canceled or rescheduled had taken its toll on her nerves. She had had to have Karen call a few of them that had become extremely agitated over the change.

Eighteen

The remainder of the week did not improve. She had been unable to contact three of the patients for the groups that had been canceled and had left messages on their machines. On Thursday they came into the office anyway, insisting that they had received no message.

When Samantha tried to explain the situation, it only increased their irritation. Karen had had to intervene to calm them down. Finally the disgruntled patients left, and the office had settled back into a somewhat normal routine once again.

In addition to the aggravation of trying to run the office with the unexpected absence of two employees, she had been having trouble sleeping. She had been unable to erase Alex from her mind or her dreams since their return from New York. Not hearing from him or seeing him should have made it easier, but she missed him terribly and her guilt was eating at her.

By the end of the week she was exhausted. She was glad to see Friday arrive. Hopefully the worst was over. Eloise and Alice were both due back in the office on Tuesday, but Amy had called to say that she would still be out the following week.

She felt a little guilty about resorting to pizza for dinner, but she had no energy left to cook. Unfortunately she had promised to take Jessica to the movies the next day. In addition, Jessica had asked to include Melanie, and Samantha had acquiesced.

After all, taking both children was no more trouble than taking Jessica alone.

When she had called to invite Melanie, Mrs. MacKenzie had answered the telephone. Hearing his mother's voice on the other end had resurrected her guilt. It had taken her a moment to gather her thoughts and issue the invitation.

Saturday morning she awoke feeling no better than she had the previous evening. She felt the beginnings of a cold, but she couldn't bring herself to disappoint Jessica—she had been in such a sour mood and had spent so little time with her all week.

She arrived at the MacKenzie home after lunch, hoping to catch a glimpse of Alex, but once again he was absent from home. It had been nearly three weeks since she had seen or heard from him. Before they left, Mrs. MacKenzie had insisted that they plan to stay for dinner when they returned.

Samantha accepted, not wanting to admit to herself that the likelihood of seeing Alex weighed heavily in her response. Although she probably would not have an opportunity to speak with him privately, she would be happy just to see him.

It was hard to hide her disappointment when she was informed that he was out for the evening. She was convinced now that he was avoiding her. It had to be more than a coincidence that he was absent every time she came to his home. In addition to that, she felt a twinge of jealousy, wondering if he was out dining and dancing with some other woman.

The girls chattered through dinner, drawing the adults into their conversation. They got into a discussion of valentines. They had to make an important decision as to whether they would pick and choose the recipients for their favors or simply send cards to all of their classmates.

Samantha was hard pressed to maintain her composure. She had been so busy the previous few weeks that she had not realized the traditional lovers' holiday was the following week.

After dinner the children went up to Melanie's room to play, leaving Samantha alone with Alex's mother. Suggesting they have their coffee in the living room, Mrs. MacKenzie rose from the table and began clearing away the dishes. Samantha finished loading the dishwasher while the older woman prepared a tray.

Once they were settled on the sofa, Mary poured coffee into two cups and handed one to her guest. Samantha felt a little uneasy about their little tête-à-tête. She was wary of saying too much, since she had no idea what Alex had told his mother about her or their relationship. She breathed a sigh of relief when the older woman spoke.

"I must tell you, dear, that I admire what you've managed to accomplish. You've done a remarkable job of raising your daughter alone. You should be very proud."

Samantha looked down at her hands, a little embarrassed by the compliment. She tried to appear nonchalant.

"I've had quite a lot of help from Eloise. First the job, and then allowing me to bring Jessica to the office with me. I'm not sure I could have managed without her help and patience, to say nothing of her advice on occasion."

Mrs. MacKenzie shook her head. "Eloise is a kindhearted woman and, although she's an excellent doctor, she's somewhat lacking when it comes to the business side of her practice. She's intelligent and humble enough, however, to recognize her own shortcomings. I'm sure she knew that what she gained in hiring you to manage the business end far outweighed any concessions she made for your convenience.

"We've kept in touch over the years, and she's always spoken highly of you and your abilities. She'd had a few qualms about opening the second office, but she was determined to fill the need she had seen in that area. She's always had a tendency to spread herself thin, but you eliminated a lot of her worries. You could almost say you made it possible for her to have her cake and eat it too."

She looked at Samantha intently. "I think perhaps you're a very kindhearted woman too."

"Thank you," Samantha murmured, looking down at her hands. She was a little uneasy at the older woman's scrutiny.

She did not know how much Alex had told his mother about her.

Mrs. MacKenzie's next words brought her out of her musings.

"Samantha," she said hesitantly, "I don't want you to think I'm a meddling old woman, but there's something I have to tell you. You've been very good for Alex. He's had some rough times in the past few years and, until you came along, he was starting to seem a lot older than his years."

Her feeling of guilt returned. She was now certain that whatever Alex had told his mother, he had mentioned nothing about their disagreement. She would hardly think of Samantha as being kindhearted if she knew of the angry words she had thrown at him.

She could not find any words to respond to Mrs. MacKenzie's confidences. All she could think was that now that their relationship appeared to be ending, everyone insisted on telling her how wonderful the two of them were together. She was glad when the girls came running into the room.

"Will you play a game with us, Grandma?" Melanie pleaded, holding up the Scrabble box.

"You, too, Mommy," Jessica chimed in.

Samantha agreed readily, focusing her hostess's attention away from her speculations concerning Alex and herself. They played a few games until she decided it was time to take their leave.

By the time she and Jessica arrived home that night, Samantha had a splitting headache. As she climbed the stairs, she was aware of aching muscles, in addition to the throbbing in her head. She could not tell if it was because she was, indeed, coming down with a cold, or a result of the tension during her conversation with Mrs. MacKenzie.

She downed some aspirins as soon as she arrived home and sat down with her head back and eyes closed, while Jessica prepared for bed. After she had tucked her in, she drew a hot bubble bath for herself. Maybe it would ease the tension in her muscles and help her relax. She needed a good night's sleep.

Samantha was almost ready to cry when she received a call from Eloise the next day. Her employer had returned from her much deserved vacation on Saturday morning and had promptly come down with the flu.

"I'm sorry to put you in a bind, Samantha. You'll have to cancel some of my appointments again this week."

Samantha hesitated a moment before replying. "I hate to add to your problems when you're not feeling well, but I've already done some juggling with the schedule. Amy's been out for two weeks.

"She broke her leg skiing and won't be able to return until next week. Karen has been seeing some of the patients for her. Shall I call Dr. Middleton and ask him if can continue to cover for you next week?"

"I've already spoken with Sam. He'll continue to see the two patients he's been seeing for the past two weeks. After you contact the others, let me know if there appears to be a problem."

By Tuesday Samantha's cold was full blown, and then some. Her body ached and she had a slight fever. She had called Eloise's patients the previous day to cancel their appointments. One of them had beat Samantha to it—she called early in the morning because she, too, had the flu. Three other patients of Amy's or Karen's had also canceled for the same reason.

Samantha tried not to feel glad of the cancellations; she was sorry they were sick, but she could not help being thankful that there were four less patients she had to call. Having less patients to schedule, Samantha decided to try to rearrange the schedule.

She discussed it with Karen and contacted the only two patients left with appointments on Friday, rescheduling them and leaving Friday free. Samantha was hopeful that an extra day off would help her shake the cold that was worsening with each day. Her coughing had increased in frequency and intensity, and she felt even worse than she had the previous week. She knew she had a fever but had refrained from actually taking her temperature. She was afraid that knowing the figures would increase her anxiety.

When Samantha returned from picking up Jessica on Thursday, she realized that the temperature in the office had dropped in her absence. Karen was leaving just as she arrived, and Samantha asked her if she had changed the thermostat. Although she had not touched it, she agreed that the temperature had cooled considerably in the past hour.

Samantha checked the thermostat and realized the heater was not working. She called the repairman, who informed her that he would be unable to come until the next day. She called Eloise and told her about the furnace, assuring her that she would take care of it. So much for staying home and nursing her cold.

The next morning she dragged herself out of bed. She took some cold tablets and cough medicine, but they did nothing for the tightening in her chest and not much for the other symptoms. She was more concerned than she had been before, but still she refused to take her temperature. It would do her no good to know how high it was since she had no choice but to go into the office. She had been keeping her distance from Jessica, and luckily the child had shown no signs of illness.

After seeing Jessica off, her bag packed with her books, papers, lunch, and her valentines, Samantha wanted nothing more than to crawl back in bed. Unfortunately the repairman would be coming to fix the furnace. He had been unable to give her a specific time, so she would be stuck there until he arrived.

At noon she was still waiting for the repairman and shivering. She had been careful to dress warmly—a heavy sweater, wool slacks, and her coat—but it made no difference.

She tried pacing, but before long she was exhausted and out of breath. She had to content herself with turning on the space heater Alice always kept behind the desk.

When the repairman had not arrived at two o'clock, she realized that it was unlikely he would finish in time for her to pick up Jessica. Even if he arrived and she left him there alone until she returned, she did not want to bring the child back to a freezing cold office. She called Sarah.

"I have a very large favor to ask. I'm stuck here at the office, waiting for the furnace repairman. Would it be possible for Fred to pick up Jessica at school and take her to your house? I'll come and get her when I leave here."

"No problem, child. We'll take care of it," the older woman assured her. "Are you all right? You don't sound well."

"I'm okay, it's just a cold. I'll call the school and let them know. There shouldn't be a problem since Fred is in the records as having permission to sign her out. I'll be there as soon as I can."

"Don't worry. We'll take good care of Jessica until you get here."

"Thanks, Sarah." She hung up the telephone and called the school.

The repairman arrived just after three o'clock. She had just shown him the way to the furnace when she had another visitor. She opened the door to a man from the florist's, who arrived carrying a vase of beautiful yellow roses.

"I have a delivery for Samantha Desmond," he said.

"I'm Samantha Desmond," she replied, when she had recovered from her shock.

He handed her the vase and turned to leave. He looked back and smiled, as he opened the door. "Happy Valentine's Day."

Samantha closed the door after him, carried the flowers over to the desk and set them down, pulling off the card that was taped to the vase. Her eyes misted over when she read the words: *I've missed you.*

Two hours later the repairman was still working. Samantha was becoming increasingly uncomfortable. She was just recovering from a coughing spell when she heard the bell over the door and looked up to see Alex striding across the room.

"What the devil do you think you're doing?" he asked angrily. "It must be thirty degrees in here."

"What are you doing here?" she asked hoarsely.

"Sarah told me you had called to have Fred pick up Jessica. She said you sounded terrible and was worried about you. I decided to come and see about you. Why is it so cold in here? And why are you sitting here in this cold?" he questioned.

"The furnace is broken. Didn't Sarah tell you? I explained to her when I called that I was waiting for the repairman. He's back there now," she explained and began coughing again.

Alex looked at her more closely, taking in her flushed face and the slightly glazed look in her eyes. "You have no business sitting here in the cold all day. What are you trying to do to yourself?"

"It's only a cold, and I have the space heater," she mumbled, attempting to keep her teeth from chattering.

"A space heater that warms a space of about two square feet. Come on, you can't stay here," he ordered, pulling her up out of her chair.

"I can't just leave with the repairman here," she protested.

Taking her by the shoulders, he impelled her gently toward the door. "You can wait in my heated car. I'll take care of the repairman."

"My purse . . ." she began.

"I'll get your purse," he told her, urging her out the door.

He retrieved her purse and followed her. After settling her in the car, he started the motor. Leaving one window slightly open, he turned up the heat full blast.

"After it warms up in here, you can turn it down," he instructed her. He fixed her with a determined stare. "Don't leave this car. I'll be back."

He returned to the building to find the repairman emerging from the back of the office. "Well, the heat should be coming through any minute."

He held the clipboard out to Alex. "I need a signature."

After seeing the repairman out, Alex turned off the space

heater and unplugged it. He took a look around and, satisfied that everything was as it should be, he turned out the lights and locked up.

When he joined Samantha in the car, he took another look at her and was even more convinced that her problem was more than a mere cold. He was torn between wanting to shake her for letting her illness get to this stage, and wanting to comfort her and ease the misery he could see in her face. She looked exhausted, and he detected her labored breathing from where he sat. In spite of that, he also saw what appeared to be a spark of anger in her eyes. He sighed and put the key in the ignition, but she stopped him before he started the motor.

"My flowers. We can't leave them here." She fumbled for the handle of the door, but he stopped her.

"Samantha," he said patiently, "give me the key. I'll get the flowers. You stay put."

"I'll wait in my car," she insisted, handing him the office key.

He accepted the key and stated, "I'll drive you."

Without giving her a chance to respond to that statement, he stepped out of the car. A few minutes later he returned, handed her the vase of flowers and the card. He slipped in beside her and started the engine.

"I can drive myself home, Alex. I would appreciate it if you could bring Jessica home though."

"Stay where you are, Samantha. I don't think you're in any condition to be driving."

"What about my car?" she asked. She was beginning to feel that she was fighting a losing battle.

"I'll see that your car gets back to the house."

Samantha fingered the card he had handed her and remembered her manners. "Thank you for the flowers," she murmured.

He looked at her, the expression in his eyes recalling that weekend in New York. "I meant what I said on the card. If you weren't so ill, I'd show you exactly how much I've missed you."

Samantha managed a weak smile. "I've missed you too."

Alex took a deep breath, the desire springing to the surface with her softly spoken words. It didn't seem possible, but his feelings for her had increased. He looked at her again and his desire fled. All he wanted to do at that moment was comfort her, take care of her. He tore his eyes from hers and put the car in gear.

By now Samantha's head was throbbing in addition to her other aches and pains. One minute she was burning up and the next she was shivering. She was too miserable to argue, she couldn't even think straight. She leaned back and closed her eyes as he pulled away from the curb.

Nineteen

When they reached her house, she was shivering again and Alex had to help her out of the car. After rummaging through her purse, she finally found her keys. Alex promptly relieved her of them and opened the door, ushering her into the living room. She sat down wearily, and he sat down beside her.

"Samantha, do you think you can make it up the stairs to get some clothes together for yourself and Jessica?"

"Clothes?" she asked, looking puzzled.

"Clothes for you and Jessica for the next few days at least. I'm taking you home with me where someone can look after you. Between Sarah, my mother, and myself we'll be able to see that you're taken care of until you feel better."

"You can't do that," she said without much conviction. "You have to work, and I can't impose on Sarah and your mother. We'll be fine."

Her words held even less conviction when she was seized by a racking cough. When she had quieted, she looked up to find him staring at her with such a look of tenderness that she was unable to tear her eyes away from his.

"I'll be fine, really. I have cough medicine upstairs, and once I settle down I'll be better."

Alex knelt down in front of her and took her hands in his. He was shocked by the heat emanating from her body, and his concern increased.

"As I was saying, I'm taking you home with me. I'm not giving you a choice. My mother and Sarah would be very angry with me if they found out that I had left you to manage on your own, in your condition. You're too ill to take care of yourself, so how are you going to manage to take care of Jessica too?" he questioned solemnly. "I'll bet you haven't even seen a doctor, have you?"

"Until today I didn't see any point in paying a doctor to tell me to go home and rest and drink plenty of fluids. I had decided today though that I would call the doctor if I didn't feel better by Monday."

Alex shook his head in frustration. "Come on. I'll help you upstairs, so you can show me where your clothes are. I'll get a few things for Jessica too. I can send Fred back later with either Sarah or Mother and Jessica herself to make sure she has everything she needs."

When they reached the top of the stairs, she began coughing again, and Alex noticed that she was almost out of breath. He helped her into her bedroom and went to Jessica's room to collect the clothes she would need. He returned with a bundle of clothes to find Samantha slumped on the side of the bed. She told him where to find the luggage, and he quickly packed the child's belongings.

"Now it's your turn. Where do you keep your pajamas?"

"I don't wear pajamas," she informed him.

She blushed when he looked at her with one eyebrow raised and said, "Not ever? And here I thought that was only for my benefit."

He kissed her gently on the forehead. "Sorry, sweetheart. I shouldn't tease you when you're feeling so lousy."

Samantha tried to smile, but she couldn't quite manage it. "My nightgowns are in the bottom drawer."

Alex gathered her gowns, robe, slippers, and a few other articles of clothing and carefully packed them. He went into the adjoining bathroom and collected a few toilet articles, although he was certain she would be too ill for the next few days to care about her appearance.

"I think that should be enough for a few days. You wait here while I put these in the car. I'll come back and help you to the car. I don't think you should try to navigate those stairs alone."

Samantha closed her eyes and tried lying down on the bed, but that only made it harder to breathe. Alex returned within a few minutes and found her slumped against the headboard. He helped her to stand, took another look at her and lifted her into his arms, carrying her down the stairs.

He settled her in the car, strapped her in and a few minutes later, they were on their way to the MacKenzie home. If she had been able to think straight, she probably would have continued to put up an argument. As it was, she realized that she did not have much choice. Her misery was growing minute by minute. The tightness in her chest had increased, and she felt totally drained.

They reached his home, and he helped her out of the car. When he lifted her into his arms, she protested.

"I can walk, Alex," she wheezed.

Alex never broke his stride. "I know," he replied.

He carried her up the stairs to the front door. Unable to manage the key, but not willing to release her, he rang the bell. Fred opened the door to them. Alex set her on her feet, bracing her when she looked as though she would keel right over.

Sarah came into the hall as Fred was hanging their coats. Following behind, while he led Samantha to the living room, she informed him that Jessica and Melanie were upstairs in his daughter's room. Mrs. MacKenzie was slightly alarmed when she saw them enter with Samantha leaning heavily on his arm.

"Good heavens, child, what's the matter?"

Alex answered for her. "I found her sitting in the office with no heat, coughing her head off. I decided that she and Jessica should stay here until she's feeling better."

Samantha glared at him, but could not muster the energy to

argue or explain. He settled her on the sofa and left to retrieve the bags, motioning to Sarah to follow him.

"I apologize for springing this on you, but I think you can understand why I did it. Would you prepare the room next to mine for her?"

"You hurt my feelings, Alex. You know you don't have to apologize for doing something like this. One look at that child, and I can see that she needs someone to take care of her for a while."

He put his arm around her shoulder, hugged her, and kissed her cheek. "Thanks, Sarah. I don't think I say it often enough, but I don't know what I'd do without you."

Sarah was touched by his confession and his actions. His decision to bring Samantha home with him had not surprised her.

"You're a good man, Alex," she said, patting his cheek. "If I'd had a son, I couldn't be any prouder of him than I am of you. And no son could have been any better to me than you've been."

She cleared her throat. "Now I'd better go see to that room. Samantha looks like she needs to be resting in bed, the sooner, the better."

Left alone with Alex's mother, Samantha tried to be sociable, but all she wanted to do was curl up somewhere and sleep for about a week. Mrs. MacKenzie could see that it was a struggle for her to keep her eyes open. She had seen Alex motion to Sarah and guessed that she had gone to prepare a room for their guest. She excused herself, telling Samantha that she would go and check on the girls.

As soon as she left the room, Samantha closed her eyes and rested her head on the arm of the sofa. That was how Alex found her when he returned from taking the luggage upstairs. As he approached, he saw that she had dozed off. He intended to simply carry her upstairs without waking her, but she stirred when his arm came around her shoulder.

"Let's get you to bed where you'll be more comfortable," he

suggested. Giving her no chance to protest, he lifted her in his arms and made his way upstairs.

A half hour later, with the help of Mrs. Henderson, she was tucked up in bed. She had lain there only a few minutes before she was seized by another coughing attack. Alex came in while she was in the midst of it and poured her a glass of water from the carafe Mrs. Henderson had left on the nightstand. Her coughing subsided and, with one arm around her shoulders, he held the glass for her as she sipped the cool liquid. He was alarmed by the heat emanating from her body and more than a little concerned.

She finished drinking and slumped against his shoulder, her eyes closed. Alex could barely hear her when she whispered, "I couldn't breathe lying down."

He plumped the pillows behind her and gently eased her back against them. "Is that better?" he asked tenderly.

She nodded, her eyes still closed. "Jessica . . ."

"Jessica is fine," he assured her. "You don't have to worry about her right now. You just relax."

He could see that she was dozing off again as she murmured, "I have to take care of her. I promised. I have to . . ."

"Samantha, I know you're exhausted, but you can't sleep just yet. I want to examine you."

"You?"

"I am a doctor, remember?"

"Not a real doctor," she mumbled.

She was unaware of the stricken look that came over his face when she uttered those words. In her opinion the fact that he had given up the active practice of medicine evidently meant that he was no longer a real doctor. His expression relaxed with her next statement.

"You're for babies," she said, her mind on a completely different wavelength.

"I think I can manage to treat an adult. There's not that much difference, as far as the basics are concerned."

He left her for a few minutes and returned with his bag. After

popping the thermometer in her mouth, he pulled out his stetho-
scope, placing it around his neck. His examination confirmed
his suspicions, but he was still alarmed when he removed the
thermometer from her mouth and read it.

"What is it?" she asked.

"Very high," he said vaguely.

"It appears that you have pneumonia, Samantha, and my instructions involve more than rest and fluids, although those will
be part of the treatment."

He would have considered hospitalizing her, but he knew that
no insurance company would consider her ill enough for that. It
seemed there were very few circumstances that insurance com-
panies considered worthy of hospital admission. Unfortunately
that determination was becoming less and less the doctor's decision. He would just have to keep her in his home and see that
she received the proper treatment until she recovered.

"Rest now," he said. "I'll be back soon with some medicine
that should help you feel better."

When he returned, she was asleep. He was tempted to give
her the injection of penicillin before she awakened, but that
would have been taking unfair advantage. He spoke her name
softly, and she stirred.

"Samantha, I have to give you an injection," he explained.

He turned her gently on her side. Before she could awaken
completely, he had completed the task, but not without arousing
her anger.

Jerking away from him, she rolled onto her back. She was
too weak to do anything more than glare at him. It was quite
enough to get her message across.

"I'm sorry, Samantha. It was important to get that first dose
into you as soon as possible, and that's the quickest way."

Alex poured a glass of water from the carafe Sarah had left
on the nightstand and sat down on the side of the bed. His arm
around her shoulders, he helped her sit up. Her hand trembled

as she grasped the glass, and he held it for her, urging her to drink.

She managed to swallow almost half of it before she pushed it away. He fluffed up her pillows and helped her get settled once again.

"Try to stay awake for just a little longer. I'll get Sarah to bring you some soup and sponge you off. It should help bring down that fever and make you feel more comfortable."

He smiled and couldn't resist adding, "I'd do it myself, but I think I've taken advantage of you enough for one day."

He started toward the door, but her voice made him turn around.

"Jessica . . ." she murmured.

"She's fine," he assured her. "She and Melanie are enjoying this unexpected time together. You know we'll take good care of her."

He sat back down on the side of the bed. He smoothed her hair back and kissed her forehead. "Now will you stop worrying and rest?"

She nodded slowly, and he left her reluctantly. He found Sarah in the kitchen, already preparing a tray for Samantha.

"I see you've anticipated me again," he said, hugging her. "There's one thing I'd like for you to do before she eats though."

He explained about the sponge bath. "I know you didn't count on being a nurse, but I think you and Mom would hit the ceiling if I offered to perform that particular duty."

Sarah rolled her eyes at him but stopped what she was doing. Taking her apron from around her waist, she crossed the room and hung it on a hook in the pantry.

"I'll take care of Samantha. Dinner is ready. You, Mary, Fred, and the girls sit down and eat."

"I'll call the others in a few minutes, and you can come down and join them after you've sponged Samantha," Alex said. "I'll take her tray up and see that she eats something."

* * *

Twenty minutes later he entered Samantha's room. She had almost dozed off when she heard the door close. Alex set the tray down on the dresser and walked over to the bed.

"It's dinnertime. And don't even think about giving me an argument. I know you probably don't have much of an appetite, but I want you to try to eat something."

He helped her sit up and placed the tray across her lap. He then tucked a napkin into the neck of her gown and began feeding her. Samantha wanted to tell him she could do it herself, but she wasn't sure that was the truth.

A half hour later, he removed the tray. Samantha pulled the napkin from her neck and handed it to him. He took it and she lay back against the pillows, her eyes closed.

Samantha was still asleep when he and Jessica tiptoed into the room later that evening. She roused herself just long enough to say goodnight, but dozed off again before the child had left the room.

After tucking the children in bed, Alex returned to her room. He pulled the covers up under her chin and kissed her cheek.

"Good night, sweetheart," he murmured, turning off the bedside lamp.

Samantha slept fitfully that night, as Alex had expected. Her bedroom was separated from his by the bathroom. He would have preferred to have her closer, so that he could hear her if she awakened during the night. Since that could not be arranged, he had resurrected Melanie's baby monitor and placed it beside her bed.

He awakened several times during the night to give her a dose of medicine. Concerned by the fever, he sponged her face and arms each time he went to her, although she was too exhausted and dazed to be fully aware of his care.

Samantha slept most of the day on Saturday, except when she was awakened by a coughing spell or Alex roused her for her medication. Alex knew the violent coughing was not un-usual, but that did nothing to alleviate his concern.

Aside from the coughing, he was concerned about her fever. He had decided to allow a few days for some sign of improvement, before considering an attempt to hospitalize her.

Sunday afternoon her fever broke. Alex took her a lunch tray and found her just awaking, drenched in perspiration. He set the tray on the table and went to examine her. Although her temperature had not returned to normal, he was pleased to see that it had lowered a few degrees.

He called down to Sarah and, while she helped Samantha to bathe and change, he put fresh sheets on the bed. Afterward he helped her back into bed while Sarah took the tray and left to reheat the soup.

"I'm sorry to be so much trouble," Samantha apologized, her eyes misting over.

Alex gently wiped away the tear that had escaped. "There's no need for apologies, Samantha. I told you in the beginning, neither Sarah nor Mom would have forgiven me if I had left you to manage on your own. None of us mind doing whatever we can to make you more comfortable."

"I know. I just feel so helpless. I've never been really sick before."

"Then you've been very fortunate. Considering the present situation, your feelings are understandable. You've been accustomed to managing on your own for a long time. You don't have to do that now."

At that moment Alex's mother entered with the tray. Alex took it from her and placed it on Samantha's lap. Mary watched her son for a few minutes, smiling contentedly as he arranged the napkin and began spooning the soup into his patient's mouth.

* * *

When Alex returned to work on Monday, Sarah and his mother took over Samantha's care. He had considered calling a service to arrange for a part-time nurse, but when he voiced this idea, they both became indignant. They insisted that they could handle the simple tasks involved, and there was no need to hire a professional.

The next few days passed in a haze for Samantha. She slept most of the time. During the evenings, Alex continued to take care of her. Her fever had diminished, but she was still having trouble breathing and was very weak. Jessica had been allowed in to visit with her for a few minutes each day to relieve their concerns about each other.

Twenty

The following weekend Alex began to feel more comfortable about Samantha's condition. Her temperature had almost returned to normal and the flushed look was gone from her face. She was still weak, and he could see that it frustrated her.

Saturday night he was awakened by a thud and a muffled cry. Jumping out of bed, he rushed through the connecting bathroom and jerked open the door. She was standing, barefoot, just on the other side. The lamp that had been on the dresser near the door lay shattered on the floor near her feet.

"Don't move," he ordered.

He lifted her in his arms and carefully picked his way across the room. He set her on the side of the bed and knelt in front of her, taking her feet in his hands.

"I'm sorry. I'll replace it. That is, if it's not an antique or anything." That possibility had just occurred to her. She closed her eyes and thought, *Please don't let it be an antique.*

Alex looked up from where he was kneeling. "Samantha, the lamp isn't important. It's not an antique or anything special. Even if it were, I'm more concerned with whether or not you were cut. Did any of the slivers of glass hit you?" he asked, examining her feet and legs.

"I don't think so."

He stood up and went to pick up the pieces of the lamp. After disposing of the larger pieces, he went to get the electric broom.

"Alex, you can't run that. You'll wake everyone."

"It's not very loud. Besides, I can't take the chance that there are still some slivers left in the carpet."

He finished cleaning up the glass and returned the broom. She was sitting up in bed when he entered her room. He came to sit on the side of the bed.

"Now why didn't you call me to help you? I know you feel much better than you did a week ago, but you're still too weak to manage some things on your own."

She sighed. "I didn't want to disturb anyone. I thought I could do it on my own. I was on my way back when I started to feel dizzy. I reached out for something to hold on to and knocked the lamp over."

"Next time, yell for help."

Samantha smiled. "Yell for help?"

"You know what I mean. The monitor is still on, so I'll hear you."

He reached over and cupped her chin in one hand. "It's good to see you smile again. I've missed that."

He pushed her gently back onto the pillows and pulled the covers up. "Go back to sleep now. I'll see you in the morning."

From then on Samantha made steady progress. On Wednesday Mrs. MacKenzie came to sit with her for a while.

"I imagine you must be getting cabin fever by now," she told Samantha. "I thought perhaps a little company might help.

"I've been spending quite a bit of time with the girls since you've been ill. They've become quite a team. Of course, by the time I leave here, I'll probably never want to see another game of Monopoly."

"I know that feeling. No matter how many other games you play, they always come back to Monopoly."

"Samantha," Mary MacKenzie continued, "Alex mentioned that you were feeling guilty about being here. I just want to add my assurances that having you here has not been an imposition in any way."

She reached over and patted Samantha's hand. "I'm just sorry we haven't been able to spend any time together. I'll be returning to Atlanta in a few days, but I'm sure we'll be seeing each other again."

The two woman chatted for a while longer. Samantha was glad that she asked no awkward questions, nor did she make any further embarrassing observations concerning Samantha's relationship with her son.

When the girls came home from school, they came looking for her. With only a few days left to spend with her granddaughter, Mary excused herself and allowed them to cajole her away from Samantha.

Although Samantha would never have admitted it, she was glad to have their conversation interrupted. She had enjoyed chatting with the older woman, but she was beginning to feel drowsy. She had become used to her afternoon nap, and she could think of no diplomatic way to ask Mrs. Mackenzie to leave. Within minutes of Mary's departure, she was sound asleep.

It was almost lunchtime on Saturday when Alex came in and informed her he was leaving in a few hours to take his mother to the airport. Samantha was seated in a chair across from the bed, the same chair in which Alex had spent quite a few hours himself, since she had become ill.

"I thought I'd take the girls along for the ride," he told her.

"I was also thinking you might like to join us for lunch before we leave."

"Join you? Downstairs? You mean you're finally going to let me see something besides these four walls for a change?"

Alex was amused but also a little touched by her evident pleasure at the idea of being allowed downstairs. He knew she had been less than happy with the restrictions that had been placed on her, but he was now beginning to understand how bored she must have been. He had brought her books and magazines, but for a woman as busy as she, in normal circumstances, they had probably been of little help.

He knelt down in front of her and took her hands in his. "Only if you promise not to overexert yourself."

Samantha stared into those black fathomless pools and nodded. He kissed each palm in turn and the tingle that traveled up her arms told her that she must be well on the road to recovery. For the past two weeks, she had been so ill she had hardly been aware of him, but the awareness and the butterflies were now returning with a vengeance. Both feelings increased considerably when he lifted her in his arms, insisting on carrying her downstairs.

For Alex, too, desire had taken a backseat during her illness. His concern for her health had driven all other thoughts from his mind, but the old feelings were beginning to reassert themselves.

Both children were excited to have Samantha join them for lunch. They were even more excited when Alex informed them of his decision to take them with him to the airport. They chattered happily throughout the meal. Sitting there, listening to them, Samantha realized how much she had missed them.

After lunch, Samantha said her good-byes to Mary, while Alex loaded the luggage in the car. They left after he had seen to it that she was settled in a comfortable chair in the living room. She had just picked up a magazine from the side table when he came back in.

"Did you forget something?" she asked, as he came toward her.

"Yes," he said. Before she could ask any more questions, he pulled her gently from the chair and took her in his arms.

"Something I've missed desperately in the last few weeks," he murmured.

His mouth settled firmly on hers in a long kiss. He wasted no time before his tongue rediscovered the sweet honey, waiting to be tasted and reclaimed. The heat permeating Samantha's body had nothing to do with her illness. Neither did the weakness that overcame her, prompting her to raise her arms and entwine them around his neck. His hands cupped the round cheeks of her derriere, lifting her, pulling her against him and making her aware of his own heat, and his need.

All too soon he raised his head and lowered her slowly, until her feet touched the floor. Samantha clung to his shoulders, unwilling to trust herself to stand alone. Alex urged her back into the chair and leaned over with one arm braced on each side of her.

"Unfortunately I have three people waiting for me in the car, so I'd better be leaving. Remember, being allowed downstairs does not mean you're completely recovered, although after that kiss I'm not so sure about that," he said softly.

After one last brief kiss, he murmured, "I'll be back in a few hours." A moment later he was gone.

Samantha remained downstairs through dinner, although when Alex returned from the airport, he found her asleep on the sofa. He sent the girls upstairs to play, covered her with a blanket, and left her to nap.

After the girls were in bed, he helped her up to her room and insisted on one last examination. Samantha was alarmed at his suggestion after he listened to her lungs.

"I have to take you to the hospital on Monday, Samantha."

"No, Alex, I won't go to the hospital. Why are you doing this now? I'm better, I can feel that I'm better. I can't go to a hospital, I won't." She had started crying and babbling before he could finish explaining.

He took her by the shoulders and gently shook her. "Samantha, stop and listen to me."

She sniffed and stopped crying. Looking up at him, she opened her mouth, but he put his finger on her lips to stop her.

"Will you let me finish now?" he asked softly. She nodded.

"I need to take you to the hospital for an X-ray. Your lungs sound good, but I'll feel better if you have an X-ray to confirm it. Okay?"

"I'm sorry I carried on like that. It's just that when you mentioned the hospital, I . . ." She shook her head. "Never mind. If you think it's necessary, I'll go and get the X-ray."

"Will you tell me why you were so upset at the mention of the hospital?" he murmured.

She hesitated. Alex waited patiently.

"With what you've already told me, I can guess that it must have something to do with your father," he said at last.

Samantha nodded. "Not just my father. Both of my parents, and Martha, died in the hospital. My father was already in the hospital when he had his last heart attack, and they still couldn't save him."

Alex took her in his arms. "Sweetheart, I know it's hard to accept, but I'm sure they did everything they could."

"I know that, Alex. I'm probably being unreasonable, but I can't help it. Hospitals make me uncomfortable. In fact, they scare me a little."

"Well, that's understandable under the circumstances. For right now we only have to concern ourselves with the short time it will take to have the X-ray done."

After her X-ray Alex informed Samantha that she was almost well enough to resume her normal life. He strongly suggested that she not return to work until the following week.

"That will give you a few days to gradually get back into your routine. Promise me you won't overdo it though. You'll probably tire easily, and we don't want you to have a relapse."

Monday evening Samantha informed Jessica that they would be returning home on Wednesday. She could see from the look on the child's face that she was torn between wanting to settle back into her own room and not wanting to leave her friend. Melanie was not pleased with the news either. If the girls could have read their parents' minds, they would have known that the adults were not exactly overjoyed at the thought of the impending separation.

After she returned home and had settled in, Samantha called Amy and Eloise to thank them for the flowers they had sent. She also informed Eloise that she would return to work on Monday. When she started to apologize for leaving her employer shorthanded, Eloise forestalled her.

"Samantha, considering what you went through trying to keep the office running during the weeks before your illness, I'd be a poor excuse for a human being if I became upset about your taking time to recuperate," Eloise commented.

"I believe we've managed to keep everything current. Alice has been handling the billing, and I hired a temp to help with her other duties and manage the scheduling. My major concern was to maintain a reasonable level of efficiency to keep you from being inundated on your return.

"One thing I want to make clear, Samantha," she stressed, "if the accounts aren't quite up to date, Alice can continue to help you and the temp can stay on for as long as necessary. I don't want you exhausting yourself working overtime."

"I appreciate your concern, Eloise, but I'm sure a few extra hours a week wouldn't cause a relapse," Samantha insisted.

"No overtime, Samantha. At least not for a few weeks. I'm sure Alex would agree."

Samantha couldn't help smiling at Eloise's veiled threat. "I get the message, Eloise."

"Good. You take care of yourself and I'll see you on Monday."

The remainder of the week seemed to drag for Samantha. Back in her own home, but not back at work, she had trouble keeping busy. While Jessica was in school, there was little to do. She had even resorted to rearranging kitchen cabinets and bedroom closets and drawers, not that any of them needed it. Alex had been right though—even those tasks tired her out by the end of the day.

No matter how tired she was, when he called each evening, something inside her perked up. Neither of them had spoken of the argument. It no longer seemed important.

Twenty-one

Samantha was usually the first one to arrive at the office, since there was always at least an hour before the first patient. Monday morning, when she walked through the door, she was greeted by Eloise, Alice, Karen, and Amy. They were gathered at the reception desk beneath a large banner that exclaimed, WELCOME BACK, SAMANTHA. Samantha's eyes misted over. She tried to wipe them unobtrusively, which was impossible since everyone was watching her. Amy hurried over to her.

"It's good to see you, girlfriend. This place hasn't been the same without you," Amy said, hugging her.

"Thanks, Amy. It's good to be back."

By the time the workday had ended, Samantha understood why Eloise had stressed the fact that she did not want her to work overtime. She would have been hard pressed to manage more than her regular eight hours. In spite of that it felt good to be back at work.

She was glad to see that Eloise was right about the accounts. She expected that, with Alice's help, she would have them totally up to date within a week.

She had just tucked Jessica in for the night when Alex called. "I thought I'd better check to make sure my patient survived her first day back at work. How do you feel?"

"A little tired, but other than that I'm fine."

"A little isn't unusual. Getting back into your normal routine will probably take a while. Just take your time and don't try to rush it."

"I will, Dr. MacKenzie," she promised. "Actually I don't think my body will allow me to overdo it. I just put Jessica in bed, and I'm ready to call it a day myself."

The thought of Samantha in bed conjured up images for Alex that, all things considered, were best left alone. He took a deep breath, but he was unable to control the extra huskiness in his voice.

"Well, I'd better let you go and get your rest. Good night, Samantha."

Slowly Samantha regained her strength. Her first real test came the weekend after her first week back at work. She went grocery shopping Friday evening, and Saturday morning she was up early, cleaning and doing laundry. She was afraid that if she allowed her normal chores to slide it would be much harder to get back on track.

Saturday afternoon she was given a break. Cassandra had called that morning, offering to take Jessica out to a movie. She arrived as Samantha was putting in the last load of laundry. Even without the prospect of the movie, Jessica was excited and the two greeted each other with hugs and kisses. Within minutes they were on their way, and Samantha went back to her chores.

She changed the linens on the beds and realized that she probably should have performed that particular task earlier that morning. The bed looked too inviting. She lay down, intending to rest for just a few minutes, and was soon sound asleep.

A few hours later, Samantha was awakened by the telephone. Still half asleep she fumbled for the receiver and dropped it.

Retrieving it from the floor, she picked it up and placed it at her ear in time to hear Alex's voice.

"Samantha, it's Alex. Are you all right?"

"Alex," she replied, not quite stifling a yawn. "I'm fine. I'm sorry—I dropped the phone. I just woke up."

She sat up. "What time is it?" she asked, trying to focus on the clock.

"It's almost five. How long have you been asleep?"

"A few hours. Cassandra came and took Jessica to the movies. I hadn't really intended to take a nap."

"Obviously you needed the rest. You haven't been overdoing it, have you?"

"No, I only did a few household chores," she insisted. "So did you call just to check up on your patient again?" she asked, finally fully awake.

"As a matter of fact, I considered inviting you to go out for dinner, but I knew as soon as you answered the phone that you're not up to it yet. Maybe we can try it next week."

"You're right about my not being up to it. I'd probably keel over facedown in my salad."

Alex chuckled. "What about next Saturday?"

"Next Saturday sounds fine. I'd love to have dinner with you. I think I'll be much better company by then."

"Good. I'll call you later this week. Take care of yourself."

"I will," she promised.

"Samantha, one more thing. If you need anything, call me."

His last words were more a statement than a question.

The following week as she dressed for her date, Samantha could not help thinking about her earlier promise to herself to offer Alex an apology. It now seemed so long ago that she had uttered those hasty words. Maybe it was better not to bring it up at all, to just let bygones be bygones. But then how could you do that without first clearing the air and getting the feelings out in the open?

She sighed. "You know you can't let it go," she muttered to herself. "If you don't speak up, it's going to gnaw at you."

They were both aware of the undercurrent of desire as they chatted over dinner. The romantic atmosphere, soft music, and candlelight were superfluous. Each time their eyes met, the passion simmering just below the surface threatened to boil over.

Alex had decided that a quiet dinner was best. Although she insisted she was back to normal, dancing might prove to be more than she could handle. Samantha was glad for this, not for his reasons. She had enough trouble maintaining her composure, without having to cope with the feeling of his arms around her.

She knew he wanted her, just as she wanted him, but what else did he feel? The care and concern he had shown her during her illness should have given her some answers, but she was still unsure.

Caring for her when she was ill might mean nothing—after all, he was a doctor. He had mentioned that he was taking her to his home because he could see that she was unable to care for herself. Maybe it was just an inherent kindness that had prompted him.

When Alex brought Samantha home, she invited him in. The restaurant had not seemed the proper place for the apology she was once again determined to express. With Cassandra and Jessica upstairs, she knew there was no chance that they would be likely to do much more than talk.

She waited until they were settled on the sofa, with the coffee in front of them on the table. After taking a sip of her coffee, she turned to him. At first, the words stuck in her throat. There was a strange look in his eyes.

"Alex . . ."

"Samantha . . ."

They both spoke at the same time. Alex smiled.

"You first," he insisted.

"Alex," she started and cleared her throat. "There's something that's been bothering me for some time—in fact, since we returned from New York."

She looked down at her hands, unable to look him in the eye. "I owe you an apology for the things I said to you. You had confided in me something that was very painful to you, and I threw it back in your face. I'm sorry. I had no right to say what I said to you."

"Samantha, I accept your apology, but you weren't the only one at fault. I've been thinking about my own choice of words. I've been guilty of saying the wrong thing to you more than once. Believe me, I never meant to demean what happened between us, it was beautiful. I think I pushed you into saying what you said, and I owe you an apology for that. Will you forgive me?"

"Oh, Alex, of course I forgive you."

He leaned over, enfolding her in his arms. Neither of them spoke for a few minutes. Soon his lips found hers, and all of the pent-up desire was in danger of exploding. Lost in the rediscovery of the tastes and textures, their tongues and hands slowly exploring, it was hard to bring the passion under control.

Alex's hand slid up under her sweater, to cup her breast, and Samantha moaned. Alex swallowed her moan, his fingers teasing the nipples, before forcing himself to remove his hand from further temptation.

He raised his head reluctantly, breaking the kiss. She opened her eyes, with their golden flecks shining up at him. He took a deep breath and forced his wayward body under control.

"Now that the coffee's cold, I think it might be best if we called it a night," he suggested. "I think this could very easily get out of hand."

Samantha nodded. She walked him to the door. After one last brief kiss, he made his exit.

* * *

The following weekend, she invited Alex to dinner. She knew she was playing with fire—Jessica was spending the night with Melanie. There would be no chaperone this time. Being honest with herself, Samantha admitted that she wanted no chaperone. Now that the breach between them had been healed, her desire seemed to be increasing.

Who do you think you're kidding, Samantha? she thought. *You couldn't love him or want him any more than you have for months.*

Saturday evening Samantha put the finishing touches on her makeup, pulled on her sweater, and slipped into her shoes. She started to twist her hair up and changed her mind. Alex had said more than once that he liked it loose and flowing. She couldn't bring herself to leave it completely untamed, but she decided to compromise by clipping it loosely in back with a barrette.

Taking one last look in the mirror, she went downstairs to check on the pot roast. She had arranged it on the platter with the vegetables, covered it with foil, and returned it to the oven to keep it warm, when she heard the doorbell.

She opened the door to Alex. He was dressed casually in slacks and a white Aran knit sweater. He stood there for a moment, just looking at her. It had also occurred to Alex that they would have no chaperone.

After dinner Alex built a fire. Although it was the end of March, there was a definite chill in the air. Besides, few things were more romantic than the glow from a fire in the fireplace. He had seen the desire in her eyes. With a little encouragement, he would soon learn whether her thoughts were on the same wavelength as his own.

He settled himself on one of the oversized floor pillows, holding his hand out for her to join him. She set the tray of coffee on the raised hearth and sat on the matching pillow beside him. Samantha poured the coffee and they chatted for a while, neither of them really interested in anything that was being said. The tension built until Samantha felt compelled to say something to ease it. However, the words she chose did just the opposite.

"Would you like some dessert?" she asked.

"What did you have in mind?" he asked, smiling.

Samantha did not see the gleam in his eye. "I have a lemon meringue pie."

"Hmmm, actually I'd rather have peaches and cream," he replied, taking her into his arms.

The flames of passion ignited the instant his lips touched hers. Before long, both their sweaters were lying on the floor. Alex disposed of her bra and lifted her onto his lap. He kissed her hungrily, her response fueling his passion.

His hands caressed and explored, easing her out of the remainder of her clothes. In minutes she was lying naked on the pillows, his hands and lips working the magic only he could create.

"It's not fair," she gasped, as his fingers probed her hidden femininity.

His mouth left her breast just long enough for him to ask, "What's not fair, sweetheart?"

She tried to answer, but she was having trouble forming a coherent thought. "What's not fair, Samantha?" he prompted.

"Your clothes," she whispered.

"All in good time, baby. All in good time."

His mouth returned to her breast, suckling and teasing while his hand continued stroking and probing. When he felt her body tightening against his fingers, he began planting kisses down her body. She moaned when his tongue circled her navel, and when his thumb touched the sensitive nub that had become the center of her universe, she came apart. She cried out in sweet release, before collapsing in his arms. He kissed her briefly and then stood, removed the foil package from his pocket, and shed his remaining clothes.

Easing himself between her thighs, he entered her slowly and sighed with pleasure at the warm, wet welcome. Samantha was sated and would not have believed there was any more pleasure in store for her, except the satisfaction of knowing that he, too, had achieved the same sweet release he had given her.

Her eyes closed, she began moving in rhythm with him. Her eyes came open in surprise when she felt the tension of pleasure building inside her again.

"Alex," she gasped.

"That's right, baby, come with me. This time we'll reach it together."

Moments later they did, indeed, reach the pinnacle of rapture together. Desire slaked, Alex rolled onto his back, taking her with him. She lay on top of him, their bodies still joined.

As their passion cooled, so did their bodies. The fire began to die, and Samantha shivered slightly in his arms. Alex reluctantly eased her back onto the pillows and stood up. Lifting her in his arms, he started toward the stairs.

By the time he reached her bedroom, pulled back the covers, and laid her down, she was almost asleep. He lay down beside her and pulled her into his arms. He knew he could not stay with her through the night, but could not bring himself to leave—not yet. In moments he was asleep.

A few hours later Alex awakened. He looked at the clock beside the bed and the woman in his arms and sighed. He had to leave, to go home. He was not comfortable with the thought of Melanie and Jessica awakening to find that he had not returned home.

He eased Samantha from his arms and left the bed, making his way down the stairs. He checked the fireplace, making certain there were no live embers, and closed the flue. After retrieving their clothing, he went back up the stairs.

Seeing that she was still asleep when he returned, he took a quick shower and got dressed. Samantha stirred and opened her eyes when he sat on the side of the bed.

"What are you doing?" she asked groggily.

"I have to leave, sweetheart. As much as I'd like to stay right here with you, we both know that I need to be at home when our inquisitive daughters wake up."

She sighed. "I suppose you're right," she agreed.

He leaned over and kissed her briefly. "You go back to sleep. I'll see you later, when I bring Jessica." He stood up and started toward the door.

Samantha called after him, and he turned around. "I just wanted to tell you, I like your idea of dessert better than what I had planned," she said, smiling.

Alex groaned. "I'd better leave while I still have some semblance of control. I'll see you later."

Samantha snuggled back under the covers after he left. She had wanted to tell him of her feelings, that she loved him. Her courage had deserted her. She wasn't ready to open herself to the possibility that those feelings were one-sided. She lay awake for a short time, but eventually exhaustion claimed her and she slept.

Twenty-two

On Friday Jessica received an invitation to Melanie's birthday party. Although the child's birthday was on Thursday, the party was scheduled for a week from Saturday, the day before Easter.

Samantha had spoken with Alex on the phone but had not seen him since the previous weekend. He and Melanie were in church on Palm Sunday, and Samantha felt a little guilty when her eyes strayed in his direction several times during the service.

Afterward they chatted in the parking lot. Every time she looked at him, images of the previous weekend floated through her head. The girls carried on their own conversation, which, of course, centered around the party scheduled for the following week.

The parking lot was almost empty when she murmured, "We'd better be going. I promised Jessica we'd go shopping today for a gift. I have a feeling the process may take a while. After all, one has to find something very special for a best friend."

Alex smiled. "The mall closes early, so you can always use that fact to impress upon her that she has a limited time to make a decision."

"Let's hope that works and I don't end up having to make a second trip to the mall."

She turned her attention to the girls, calling to Jessica, "We'd better be going, if we're to make that trip to the mall."

Alex saw them to their car, and they said their good-byes.

He watched them drive off and seemed rooted to the spot, until his daughter called to him. Minutes later they pulled out of the lot and headed for home.

Later that week Samantha called Sarah. It had occurred to her that she might welcome her help for the party preparations. From her experience she had learned that the women were usually the ones who took charge of the decorations and the food. Alex was a good father, but how much did he really know about little girls' parties?

"I called to see if you could use some help with the party, Sarah," she explained.

"You don't have to do that, Samantha. Alex will help with the decorations before he goes to work. I can manage the food."

"Sarah, I know I don't have to do it, but I don't mind helping. What about the games?"

"Melanie mentioned an Easter egg hunt. You could help with that."

"Fine. I'll be there early to hide the eggs and help with anything else you might need. I'll see you Saturday."

Fortunately Saturday dawned clear and a little warm for early spring. They would be able to have the egg hunt outside, after all. In addition to real eggs, there were plastic ones filled with trinkets. Although there were other games, too, in Samantha's experience, nine-year-old girls were often so busy chattering that games were unnecessary.

Samantha had dressed in jeans and an oversized sweatshirt. She had considered wearing something a little nicer, but decided that it would be safer to wear something that could not be ruined by grass stains, ice cream, or punch.

They were greeted at the door by Fred, and a few minutes later she was again outside, hiding colored eggs. Sarah had promised to keep the girls busy indoors, assigning them the task of setting the table. There were other games to occupy the guests if they arrived before Samantha finished hiding the eggs.

She knew Alex was at work, but she was sure he would be home in time for his daughter's birthday party. As Sarah had said, he had arranged a banner and balloons earlier that morning.

She was on her hands and knees, concealing the last of the eggs under the forsythia bushes, when Alex found her. He stood watching her for a moment, enjoying the view of her rounded derriere. An image of her minus the jeans floated through his mind, and his loins tightened in response.

Don't even go there, Alex, he thought. *This is hardly the time or place.*

"I always thought the Easter bunny had long, floppy ears and a fluffy tail," he said, smiling.

Startled, she turned around and looked up into those jet-black eyes. Her pulse was racing, and she had difficulty finding her voice. She realized that he would probably have that effect on her for the rest of her life.

She was aware of his thorough perusal and blushed at the knowledge that he now knew exactly what lay beneath her jeans and sweatshirt. From the look in his eyes, he not only knew, he was actually envisioning it at that very moment.

She finally managed to ask, "How long have you been there? I didn't hear you coming."

He held his hand out to help her up. "I've been here a few minutes, enjoying the view," he replied meaningfully.

She hesitantly put her hand in his. Once she was on her feet, she busied herself dusting her clothes off to avoid looking at him.

Alex leaned over and retrieved her basket, avoiding the temptation to help dust her off. "I see you've completed your task," he observed. "How many did you hide?"

"Three dozen," she told him. "I just hope I can remember where I put them, in case the children don't find all of them. I'd hate to have Fred run over a rotten egg with the lawn mower two weeks from now, or even worse ruin the mower running over one of the plastic ones."

He smiled and Samantha would have sworn that the sun had suddenly become brighter. "Well, at least they're not inside," he commented. "I'd hate to come downstairs one morning to the smell of rotten eggs filling the house."

It was her turn to smile, and his reaction to it matched her own feelings. He leaned over and kissed her cheek, and her body responded immediately.

"I'm glad you came, Samantha. Thanks for volunteering to help. I'm not sure I could handle ten giggling nine-year-old girls."

Samantha cocked her head to one side. "So now the truth comes out. I'm appreciated only as a buffer."

She heaved an exaggerated sigh. "I don't mind though. I know they get a little carried away sometimes."

Alex put his arm around her waist. He leaned over and nibbled her ear, sending shivers down her spine.

"One day, lady, you'll pick the wrong place to issue a challenge. You know that here and now I can't demonstrate some of the other reasons you're appreciated, specifically the X-rated ones," he whispered.

Samantha cleared her throat. "Since I am here to help with a party, I'd better get back to the house. The guests have probably started arriving, and right now Sarah's the only one inside to cope with them. I'm sure she can use my help with the food too."

They entered the kitchen to find the girls folding napkins. They had set the table that had been temporarily set up on the enclosed porch, but Sarah decided they needed some extra napkins.

"Daddy, can you blow up some more balloons, please."

"More balloons? I thought I had taken care of all of them."

"Aunt Sarah found another whole bag of them in the drawer."

Alex rolled his eyes at Sarah. "That was very helpful. Thanks a lot."

She laughed as she handed him the bag. "You should learn to hide things better, or at least let other people in on your intentions," she whispered.

Less than an hour later, the egg hunt was in full swing. Samantha and Alex stood side by side watching the children scrambling across the lawn. The temptation of standing so close to her became too much for Alex, and he reached down and clasped her hand in his. Samantha was amazed that such a small gesture could set her hand to trembling. She looked up at him, but his eyes stayed on the children. She was unaware that his simple gesture was part of his larger plan. He was still working to rebuild the bridge between them.

Obviously the passion was still there. The apologies had restored the friendship, but he wanted more. He wanted her total and unreserved love, but he was still in the dark as to how to win that particular prize.

Sometimes when she looked at him, he could swear she was in love with him. Then he remembered that he had been convinced of that before, in New York, and had been painfully proven wrong.

A few hours later they sat drinking coffee. The children had gone, and the house had been restored to a semblance of order. Melanie had pleaded for Jessica to stay after the party was over, and the two of them were now happily ensconced in Melanie's bedroom, playing with her new computer game. The adults had been happy to have a chance to sit down and relax.

The Hendersons had retired to their apartment, and Samantha was left alone with Alex. She had just decided it was time to call it a day when he asked, "Will you have dinner with me next Saturday?"

Samantha remembered how their previous dinner date had ended and hesitated. She also remembered telling him months ago that she would not have a casual affair with him. Well, as far as her feelings were concerned, their relationship was much more than that. But what was it for him?

When she hesitated, Alex considered that she might be thinking that he would take for granted that their date would end with them in bed. He had to make it clear that passion was not all he wanted from her.

"Samantha, we'll have dinner at a restaurant. We'll talk, enjoy each other's company, maybe go dancing. The fact that I want your body hasn't been a secret for a long time, but that's never been all that I want. Besides, you seem to forget, you usually have two very effective chaperones."

Samantha smiled. "Yes, that's true. Dinner and dancing sounds very nice, Alex."

She and Jessica said their good-byes a short time later. Alex walked them to the car and gave her instructions to call when she reached home.

The next day, Easter Sunday, she called Mrs. Cummings. She had kept in touch with Jessica's former baby-sitter over the years, although she had never really explained her reasons for moving. Mrs. Cummings had been there for her when she needed her and had taken very good care of Jessica. In spite of their differences, she had been unable to bring herself to break off completely. Samantha felt that she deserved to know that her former charge was well and happy.

Samantha had spoken with her during the Christmas holidays and told her about Jessica's new friend. This time her call elicited some disturbing information. She learned that Mrs. Cummings had been released from the hospital just a few days earlier. Her daughter explained that she'd had a fall and broken her leg, but was doing fine.

She chatted with her former neighbor for a few minutes, bringing her up to date. After she hung up, Samantha began to feel guilty. She really should have taken Jessica to see Mrs. Cummings before now, but she had always been afraid that it was just too dangerous. She had to admit that Alex had a valid point in that, if she had legal custody, she would not have to be afraid. Maybe eventually she would have enough courage to take that step, but not yet.

On Monday she mailed a get-well card to Mrs. Cummings and, to further assuage her guilt, ordered flowers to be sent. She had enclosed a personal note in the card and at the last minute dropped a snapshot of Jessica into the envelope.

Her dinner date with Alex on Saturday was as tame as he had promised, if being held in his arms on the dance floor could be called tame. She knew the temptation might prove to be too much for her, so she had kept Jessica at home and hired Cassandra.

She invited him in for coffee, and he accepted her invitation but refused the coffee. Her insurance against temptation proved to be a smart decision. Until she was more certain of his feelings, she had to learn to control her libido.

When he took her in his arms and kissed her, she forgot all about her decision to keep her own counsel. Alex lifted his head and she stared into his eyes.

"I love you," she whispered.

Alex thought his heart had stopped.

Before he could respond, she added, "It's all right, Alex. You don't have to feel compelled to return the words. I just wanted you to know how I feel."

Alex shook his head. "I don't have to feel compelled to return the words? I love you, Samantha. I've been in love with you for months, maybe even since the first time I met you. Certainly since that day you stormed into my study, berating me for being a terrible father."

She pulled away from him. "I never said that," she denied.

"Not in so many words, but the implication was there. I admit at the time your accusations were understandable. I recall you looked like some avenging angel, standing there with those eyes practically shooting sparks. You were absolutely beautiful, and I think I fell in love with you right then and there, although I didn't admit it to myself until much later."

"You really love me?" she asked.

"Sweetheart, if those two chaperones weren't upstairs, I'd show you how much."

He kissed her with all the love he had been wary of revealing. Before long they both realized they were in danger of forgetting about the two girls asleep upstairs. Alex broke the kiss but continued to hold her.

The knowledge that she loved him sent his heart soaring, but it also put a greater strain on controlling his desire. He was tempted to take the next step, here and now. He wanted to marry her, but his own life was not yet completely in order.

Samantha contented herself with being held in his arms, although she wanted much more. She could not help recalling his earlier proposal. She would not hesitate to agree to such a suggestion now, but she admitted that it might be too soon to consider that step.

They had just overcome one hurdle and had openly declared their love, but there were two issues that were still unsettled. There had been no further discussion concerning his refusal to resume his medical practice. On her part she had not yet made a decision about taking the first step toward obtaining legal custody of Jessica.

They remained locked in each other's arms for some time, lost in their own separate thoughts. Neither was willing to break the spell by broaching the subjects that had so recently caused such unpleasantness. When Samantha's hand strayed from his waist to settle on his thigh, Alex's body tensed.

"As much as I hate for this evening to come to an end, I think it might be wise to call it a night."

Moments later she walked him to the door. After seeing him out, she put the living room in order, turned out the lights, and went to bed with a smile on her face.

Twenty-three

For almost a week Samantha was on cloud nine. She and Alex had spoken on the phone almost every day. If the first few months of their relationship had been lacking verbal expressions of love, they had made up for it.

But for all that, Samantha had some misgivings about their relationship. Although she had accepted the need to work out their individual problems, she had concluded that they should do it together. The fact that Alex had not repeated his proposal was the major cause of her apprehension. He had proposed even before he said he loved her. So why did he hesitate now?

Alex's reasons for holding back had nothing to do with a change of heart. He was more determined than ever to make her his wife, to build a life together, to grow old with her by his side. He had no doubts that she was the one for him.

His doubts were centered on whether he was prepared to be the man she deserved. In order to do that, he had to resolve once and for all the issues concerning his retirement from the active practice of medicine.

He had recently taken the first step in that direction by contacting one of the medical clinics in the city to volunteer his services for two weekends a month. He would be part of a mobile unit that provided free medical care to residents of homeless shelters.

They would be dealing in general with regular examinations and immunizations, and it would enable him to get back into active practice gradually. It had been less than a year since he had left his practice—not long enough to feel that he was out of touch with that side of his profession.

On Friday Samantha's feeling of elation came abruptly to an end. After unlocking her front door and seeing Jessica inside, she heard footsteps approaching. A middle-aged woman was coming up the walk.

"Miss Desmond? My name is Ms. O'Brien. I'm from the Office of Children and Youth, the County Child Welfare Agency. I need to speak with you concerning your daughter."

Samantha felt as though her heart had dropped to her stomach. "No," she whispered.

Jessica came back to see why she had not come in behind her, and Samantha sent her back inside. "What do you want?" she asked.

"I'm here in answer to a complaint. We have received information that the child you have in your custody is not actually your child. Is that true?"

"Why?" Samantha asked curtly.

"Well, Miss Desmond, if the child is an orphan, she should be a ward of the court. Unless, of course, you have legal custody," the social worker informed her.

"What are you trying to do? Why are you doing this? Who sent you here?"

"I'm only trying to do my job, as I explained. I'm afraid I can't tell you who filed the complaint. Do you have custody papers, Miss Desmond?"

"Please, leave us alone. Just go away," Samantha pleaded. "Leave us alone."

"I can't do that. I have no choice but to file papers to have the child made a ward of the court."

Samantha was becoming extremely agitated and frightened. She could not believe this was happening, not after all these years.

"Why?" she asked again. "She's happy and healthy. What good will it do to uproot her?"

"Miss Desmond, I haven't said that the child would be uprooted—that's not my decision to make. However, it is the responsibility of my agency, and the courts, to determine that the child is healthy and happy."

She watched the other woman and became angry at her business-like attitude. She was completely unfeeling. With this observation all of her own feelings of courtesy disappeared.

"Get off my property, Ms. O'Brien. Leave us alone."

With those last words she opened the door and escaped to the shelter of her house. After she had closed the door in the other woman's face, she leaned against it for support, shaking uncontrollably.

Jessica. They were going to take Jessica. They would make her a ward of the court—the social worker had said that. And then they would put her in some awful foster home. She said someone filed a complaint, but who? No one knew—no one but Alex. He wouldn't do this to her—he couldn't.

She remembered what he had said about getting Jessica's custody settled once and for all—that she would feel better if she did that. He wouldn't do this just to prove his point, would he? He knew it would force her into taking action, but surely he wouldn't put Jessica's happiness in jeopardy. He wouldn't deliberately put them through this anguish.

Maybe this was why he had refrained from reissuing his marriage proposal. He would not want to marry her with that hanging over their heads, and she had already made it clear that she had no intention of bringing the situation to the attention of the courts.

She kept coming back to the main piece of evidence against

him. He was the only one who knew the truth about Jessica. Even Eloise didn't know—only Alex. How could she have trusted him? She had let herself be taken in by him again. All his seeming care and concern, his confession of love, and he had turned around and done this. She had forgiven him for his hurtful words to her, she had thrown out a few of those herself. This was much worse, and she would never forgive him for putting Jessica's happiness in danger.

She managed to get through the evening, but before Jessica was in bed, she felt the beginnings of a monumental headache. She had to get her emotions under control. She had never been so hurt and terrified in her life.

What would she do if they took Jessica away from her? What would happen to the child? How could she possibly explain why she was being torn away from the only home she had ever known? How could anyone explain it? Why would anyone do such a thing?

She forced these thoughts from her mind. She could not allow herself to consider that possibility. There was a chance that they would decide that there was no reason to take her from her home. They would have to see that she was healthy and happy.

But could she afford to do nothing and take that chance? The answer was obvious. There was too much at stake to leave it to chance. The first thing she had to do was talk to a lawyer, but she would have to survive the weekend before she could do that.

The longer she thought about it, the more the hurt feelings dissipated to be replaced by anger. How dare he take it on himself to do this? She could just hear him trying to explain that he did it for her own good. She wouldn't put it past him to try to convince her that she would eventually thank him, when she succeeded in gaining custody of Jessica. But what if she did not succeed? Time and again she had to force those thoughts from her mind.

* * *

That weekend she tried several times, unsuccessfully, to contact Eloise in hopes that she could recommend a lawyer. Alex had called several times during the weekend, but she had left the answering machine on to screen her calls.

Eloise had no patients scheduled on Monday. Before Samantha had a moment free to call her again, her employer walked into the office.

"Eloise, I'm glad to see you, I was going to call you. If you have a moment," she said, clasping and unclasping her hands, "I need your advice."

The strain of the weekend was evident on her face. "Of course, dear. Why don't we go into my office?" Eloise suggested.

Samantha poured coffee for both of them. She took one sip and said, "I'll get right to the point. I need a lawyer, and I thought you might be able to recommend someone."

"A lawyer? Well, I can recommend the firm I use. Do you want to tell me about it?"

Samantha took a deep breath and told her about her weekend visitor. After that, she had to tell her the whole story. When she had finished, Eloise asked, "But how did they know about Jessica after all these years."

"Alex told them," Samantha informed her.

"Alex? I don't understand. Why would he do that? How did he know?" her employer inquired.

"I told him," she admitted. "I didn't have much choice. He knew she wasn't mine."

As soon as she uttered the last sentence, Samantha realized she had told Eloise more than she intended. She blushed, but the other woman simply nodded her head in understanding.

"That answers one question, but I still can't believe that Alex would do that. Are you sure? Did the social worker tell you who made the call?"

Samantha shook her head. "No, she said she couldn't give me that information. It doesn't matter though. I didn't want to believe it, either, Eloise, but it had to be him. No one else knew the truth. That's why I moved here years ago."

"Well, I'll call my attorney now and you can speak with him."

A few minutes later, Samantha had scheduled an appointment for later that week. Before she left Eloise's office, her employer tried to reassure her that there was no reason for her not to be awarded custody.

"I appreciate the vote of confidence, Eloise, but let's be realistic. I'm sure one strike against me will be the fact that Jessica is not actually a blood relative. On top of that the fact that I uprooted her and moved away so abruptly will probably be taken into account. Originally, I was concerned that my age would be a factor, but that shouldn't be an issue now. I am still single though, and I have no idea whether that will have any bearing on the situation."

Her eyes misted. She had tried to maintain her composure and put on a brave front, but it was beginning to crumble. "I just don't know. And I don't know what I'll do if they take her away from me, Eloise. It scares me to think what it would do to her."

Eloise patted her hand and offered words that she hoped would be of some comfort. "Try not to worry, Samantha. My mother used to say that even though we may not believe it at the time it's happening, somehow things usually work out for the best. Not only that, I find it very hard to believe that the court would have any valid reason for taking Jessica away from you.

"If there's anything else I can do to help, let me know. If you like, I'll be happy to keep Jessica when you have your appointment with the attorney."

Samantha nodded, and Eloise rose from her chair. She came around the desk and hugged her. She felt compelled to make another stab at keeping her from making another mistake.

"Samantha, I really think you're wrong about Alex. I just

can't believe he would go behind your back with something this serious. It's not like him at all."

Samantha made no reply. She was not surprised that Eloise would defend Alex. After all, she had known him for years and she was his mother's friend. Her loyalties would naturally lie with him. She had not convinced Samantha though.

Wednesday afternoon Samantha had her appointment with the attorney. When she left the attorney's office, she was not sure if she felt better or worse. He had given her no indication of what he thought her chances would be of winning.

Although she had explained her reasons for all of her actions, he had not been pleased with the fact that she had tampered with the birth certificate. He asked for character references and scheduled to meet again after he had filed the petition.

She had accepted Eloise's offer to pick up Jessica at school, and had asked her to keep her until the evening. She had not told her employer the reason for her additional request, simply explaining that she had to attend to some other business after her appointment. Eloise had agreed with no hesitation.

Samantha felt some guilt about not confiding her plans, knowing that Eloise would have tried to dissuade her if she knew the real reason for her wanting Jessica out of the way for a few hours. She had tried to ignore the anger that ate at her every time she thought about the part that Alex had played in her present dilemma.

She left the lawyer's office and went directly to see Alex. She was determined to have it out with him. She had not called first. She did not want to give him any warning, to give him time to come up with excuses for his actions.

She had tried to prepare herself for this confrontation, but she almost lost her composure when Alex himself answered the door. He smiled, but there was no joy on her face and his smile quickly faded.

"Samantha, what's the matter? I've been trying to get in touch with you for days. I've left several messages."

He'd barely gotten his words out before she told him. "I want to talk to you privately."

He ushered her into his study and offered her a seat, which she refused. He had seen the anger in her eyes, but he had no idea what had put her in such a mood. Before he could question her further, she lashed out at him.

"I just came from an appointment with a lawyer. I have to go to court for custody of Jessica. I guess you're satisfied now."

"Samantha, I'm glad you've taken this action, but I don't understand why you're so angry about it."

"You missed the point, Alex. I said I have to go to court. I didn't take this action by choice—as if you didn't know. You can stop pretending innocence."

"Me? I merely suggested—"

"Come off it, Alex. A social worker from the Child Welfare Agency showed up on my doorstep Friday. She said they received a complaint informing them that Jessica is not my daughter, and they plan to take me to court to get custody, to have her made a ward of the court. They'll take her away from me and put her in a foster home."

He took a step toward her, but she backed away. "I'm sorry, Samantha. But I—"

She cut him off. "You're sorry. You've wreaked havoc with my life and Jessica's happiness, and now you say you're sorry. How could you do this to me, to Jessica?"

The tears were flowing now, but she hardly noticed them, and the anger had not abated. Once again he attempted to defend himself.

"Samantha, I think you're overreacting. I can't believe they'll actually take Jessica away from you. As for your accusation, I didn't call anyone. I don't know who made that complaint, but I had nothing to do with it."

"Liar!" she accused. "No one else knew. Don't try to deny it. It's easy for you to tell me that I'm overreacting. It's not you that's being threatened. If they take Jessica away from me, it will be your fault. Why did you do this? How could you do this? I'll lose her, and I'll never forgive you for that. Never."

Without giving him an opportunity to say anything else, she turned and ran sobbing from the room and from the house. She was gone before he could stop her. He could hardly believe what she had told him. How could she believe that he would do that to her?

How would he ever convince her that she was wrong? He would lose her. Whether she won the custody case or not, he would lose her. Aside from that, he did not want to contemplate what it would do to her if she lost.

After she left, Samantha drove only three blocks before she was forced to pull over to bring her emotions under control. She had to stop the tears—she could not let Jessica see her like this.

It was forty-five minutes later when she finally pulled up in Eloise's driveway. Eloise could see that she was upset, but could not ask questions in front of Jessica. Samantha stayed only long enough to thank her employer.

She arrived home and put the child to bed, before retreating to her own room and slumping down in the chair by the window. She rose slowly when the telephone rang.

"Hello," she murmured.

"Samantha, thank God," Alex replied. "I had visions of you ending up in a ditch somewhere or worse, considering the state you were in when you left here. I had to make sure you had reached home safely. I've been calling every ten minutes for the past hour."

"I'm fine," she assured him, her tone lifeless. "Thank you for your concern. Good-bye, Alex." Before he could reply, she replaced the receiver and immediately removed it so it would not ring again.

The next two weeks Samantha barely slept or ate. The date for the custody hearing had been set, and she could think of nothing else. The lawyer had decided that she had a good chance of winning and had tried to reassure her, but she could imagine only the worst possible outcome.

Eloise and Amy were scheduled to appear as character witnesses, and her employer had also promised to stay with her during the entire hearing, to lend moral support. Unknown to Samantha, she had been the subject of a conversation between Eloise and Alex.

Alex had called his godmother and arranged to visit her the Sunday before the hearing. It had not taken much perception on Eloise's part to guess that Samantha was the reason for his request.

"I came to ask a favor of you, Eloise. Samantha came to see me about a week ago. She told me she has a custody hearing coming up. How is she?"

Eloise sighed. "She's holding up, Alex. She's anxious and very scared. I find it hard to believe that any court would take that child away from her, but you never really know. I don't like to think of the effect it would have on her, if she lost Jessica. I would guess that her entire adult life has revolved around that child."

"I suppose you know she blames me for all of this."

"Yes," she admitted, "although I wasn't aware she had actually confronted you with those accusations."

"Oh, she confronted me all right," he said wryly. "She was so upset when she left that I was afraid she would end up wrapped around a telephone pole."

Eloise shook her head. "I'm sorry Alex. She's just not thinking clearly. I told her that you would never do anything so underhanded."

"But she didn't buy it. She's wrong though, Eloise. I had urged her to file for custody, but I would never take it on myself to make that decision for her. I certainly would never do anything that might harm her or Jessica," he insisted. "But that's not why I came here. Do you know her attorney?"

"As a matter of fact, she asked me to recommend someone so, yes, I know him. Why?"

"If he hasn't already told her what his fee will be, I'd like to make an agreement with him to charge her some nominal fee and bill me for the balance. I know she wouldn't accept my assistance willingly, but I'd like to help."

"That's very kind of you, Alex. Actually when I referred her, I asked him to do just that, except he'll bill me, of course."

"In that case I would appreciate it if you forwarded that bill to me." She opened her mouth to speak, but he urged, "Please. It's not a matter of being kind. I'm sure it comes as no surprise to you, but I'm in love with her. The way it looks now, I'll probably lose her—whatever the outcome of the hearing. I need to do this for her . . . and for myself."

Eloise had agreed, and they had chatted a while longer. She watched him closely as he talked. She could see his mind was still on Samantha. She wondered how Samantha could believe a man so deeply in love could deliberately cause her pain. She had to be aware of how much this man cared for her.

Twenty-four

The day of the hearing dawned warm and sunny, belying the gloom that pervaded Samantha's world. She sent Jessica off to school with some difficulty, not knowing for how many more days she would have that right. She had explained to the child that Amy would pick her up from school, although she had been careful to keep from her the possibility that her whole world might change drastically in the next few weeks.

When she entered the courtroom with her attorney and saw the social worker sitting there so calm, her hackles rose. She seemed totally unaware and uncaring about the devastation she was trying to bring to their lives.

At first, the hearing proceeded much as Samantha's lawyer had led her to expect. Ms. O'Brien presented the agency's petition for custody, repeating the reasons that she had previously given for her actions.

"The child is an orphan and should have been placed in the care of our agency so that we could make determination concerning a suitable home for her. Miss Desmond is not a blood relative of the child and had no right to assume custody. We are requesting to have her made a ward of the court at this time, to give the agency that opportunity."

Samantha did not hear the rest of her presentation. Her mind kept screaming: *She has a suitable home.*

The judge looked over some papers and addressed Ms.

O'Brien. "I understand another relative has expressed an interest in the child. Is that correct?"

"Yes, Your Honor. The child's paternal great-aunt, Mrs. Thomas, has been trying for some years to locate the child and file such a petition."

Her attention was drawn back to the proceedings by this statement. *Mrs. Thomas!* Mrs. Thomas was behind all this? But how?

Her attorney then presented her petition, noting that Samantha had been raising the child for a number of years. He ended his plea by informing the judge of the character witnesses and presenting several letters from Jessica's teachers and school principal.

As the judge accepted the letters, the social worker stated, "Your Honor, we are not questioning the possibility that Miss Desmond may be a moral and upstanding citizen. The point is that our agency has the duty to determine the proper home for the child, and Miss Desmond usurped that duty when she ran away with the child.

"We are prepared to examine the environment in which she has been living as well as other possibilities and decide which alternative would best suit the needs of the child."

Samantha reached the end of her patience with Ms. O'Brien's stilted unfeeling attitude. She lost her temper, stood up, and blurted out, "The child's name is Jessica. She's not some nameless, faceless entity to be used as a pawn for you to prove your agency's authority. You can't shuffle her around at will and feel complacent because you've seen to her physical needs.

"She has emotional needs too. That woman who is trying to get custody of Jessica has seen her exactly twice in her entire life. She wanted nothing to do with her own nephew and now she wants his child?"

The judge had to call her name twice before she heard her. She finally ended her tirade when her attorney grasped her arm, urging her back into her seat.

"Miss Desmond, you will have to control yourself," the judge admonished her, when she finally had her attention.

"I . . . I'm sorry, Your Honor," she replied meekly as she resumed her seat.

The judge nodded and began her own questions. "Miss Desmond, I understand you have been caring for Jessica for a number of years. You were quite young when you assumed this responsibility. How were you able to manage financially?"

Samantha explained about the insurance and the house. She was puzzled at the next question. "Did it ever occur to you to apply for financial aid? Jessica must have qualified for Social Security benefits from one of her parents."

Samantha shrugged. "I never really thought about it. We were able to manage with what my father left and later, when I started working, it became easier."

Ms. O'Brien's statement about her running away with Jessica led to the judge questioning the reasons for Samantha's relocation to Bucks County. Those questions led to the revelation of the altered hospital birth certificate. The judge frowned when she received this information, and Samantha's heart sank.

Samantha felt compelled to explain further. "Your Honor, I did not simply take it on myself to assume custody of Jessica. It was the request of both her mother and my father before they died.

"Although she had no way of knowing that my father would not be there to care for Jessica, Martha recognized that a little girl has needs that only a woman can fulfill. Having lost my own mother when I was twelve, I had to agree with her. As wonderful as my father was, there were times I wished for a woman to talk to. When my father was dying, I promised I would take care of Jessica, and that's what I've done for almost seven years."

Samantha's narrative was the first time Eloise had come close to hearing the whole story. She now understood more completely the reasons for her panic. How could she have been expected to think clearly and logically under this stress?

The judge questioned both parties a while longer and then

brought the hearing to a close. Her words left Samantha with mixed feelings.

"I'm going to continue this hearing in two weeks. In that time I'm going to arrange to have a psychological profile done on Jessica. I'll send you a letter with a date and time, Miss Desmond. It will be your responsibility to see that this appointment is kept. If you have not as yet told Jessica what is happening, you need not fear that anything will be said about the reason for the interview."

Samantha nodded, relieved that no questions would be asked that might raise the child's suspicions concerning her future.

"Thank you. Jessica knows nothing about this."

As they left the court, Samantha tried to tell herself that the continuance was a good sign. At least it showed that she had a chance of winning. Surely she would not have kept her on tenterhooks for two weeks if she was not considering the possibility of awarding her custody.

Now that she could be assured of having Jessica for the next two weeks, she could go ahead with the plans for her birthday party. Jessica's birthday was in eight days' time, and Samantha had hesitated to begin any preparations or issue any invitations.

As a first order of business toward that end, she stopped at a store after leaving the court. She purchased invitations, decorations, and all of the paper supplies she would need. She picked up the child at the office, where she had spent the afternoon with Amy, and headed home.

If there was some extra measure of love and joy in the hug and kiss with which Samantha greeted her, Jessica did not notice it. They spent the evening preparing the list of guests and writing invitations.

The next week passed swiftly with the arrangements for the party and the appointment with the psychologist. Samantha had refused to allow herself to dwell on the possible outcome of that interview. She was determined not to let her anxiety ruin the festivities.

Saturday Jessica awakened Samantha even earlier than usual, bubbling over with anticipation. She had been excited about the party since the day she gave out the invitations.

"Hurry up, Mom. We have to get ready for the party," the little girl urged.

Samantha groaned. "Can I at least have a cup of coffee first? Your guests won't be coming until one o'clock. We have plenty of time."

"But we have to blow up the balloons and put up the decorations and—"

Samantha interrupted the girl's chatter. "Don't worry, sweetheart. Everything will be ready on time, I promise. But first, I think it's a good idea to have some breakfast. We'll need a lot of energy for the party. Now you go get dressed. I'll fix breakfast, okay?"

"Okay," Jessica reluctantly agreed.

A few hours later the decorations were up and the food was ready and waiting. Eloise arrived just as Samantha was setting the table. It was a beautiful, warm spring day, perfect for holding the party outdoors. She had set up the picnic table on the deck, and there were balloons and streamers proclaiming the festive occasion.

"Everything looks great, Samantha," Eloise observed. "I thought you might need a little help, but you seem to have everything well under control."

"I should, since Jessica awakened me practically at the crack of dawn." She led her into the kitchen. "Would you like some coffee?"

Eloise nodded and Samantha poured two cups, joining her at the table. "I'd better take advantage of the lull and relax for a few minutes."

Her employer regarded her silently for a moment as they

sipped their coffee. "Is Melanie coming to the party?" she inquired.

"As far as I know," Samantha replied, her attention focused on her cup. "I haven't received any indication to the contrary."

She looked up at Eloise. "You didn't think I would leave Melanie out of this, did you? My disagreement is with her father. I would never take my anger out on the child."

Eloise shook her head. "I didn't think you would, dear. I never meant to imply that."

"Anyway," Samantha continued, "there really isn't any more argument. I told him what I thought of him, and now it's over."

Eloise opened her mouth to make another plea on Alex's behalf but changed her mind. From the stubborn set of her young friend's jaw, she knew it would be useless. She sighed. There was only so much a meddling old woman could do.

It was yet another reason to pray for the custody petition to be decided in Samantha's favor. At least that would give them a chance to work out their differences. Otherwise Samantha would never forgive him, and the three of them would suffer: Samantha, Jessica, and Alex.

Samantha had tried to sound brave in insisting that it was all over between Alex and herself. She was honest enough with herself to admit that, although the relationship was over, her love for him was still very much alive.

She had not seen him nor heard from him since her tirade, and she was not certain how she would react if she had to confront him again. She was hoping she would not have to find out, that Fred would be the one to bring Melanie to the party.

She was not to be so lucky. Several other children had arrived when Alex showed up with Melanie. Samantha was pouring punch, waiting for the rest of the guests to arrive, before starting the games.

She almost dropped the pitcher at the sound of his voice. "Hello, Samantha."

She whirled around to see him standing in the doorway, his ebony eyes watching her intently. He was wearing those same form-fitting jeans she had seen before or a pair just like them. His red knit shirt was opened at the neck, revealing enough of his chest to cause her pulse to accelerate.

She recalled all too well the sensations generated by running her hands through that mat of curly hair. She remembered, too, resting her head on that muscular chest with those strong arms holding her tightly. With some effort she shook herself free of those disturbing memories.

"Hello, Alex. Where's Melanie?"

Alex had not moved. He had watched the play of emotions on her face. It was obvious that she was as much affected by his presence as he was by seeing her again. He was relieved that her immediate reaction to him was not anger.

"Eloise took her outside with the other children. I came to see if I could repay you for your assistance with Melanie's party. Do you need any help?"

"No, thanks. I have everything under control."

He had noticed the circles under her eyes and the look of exhaustion. Children's parties were hectic but could hardly be responsible for the anxiety evident on her face.

"Samantha . . ." he began, but she did not allow him to finish.

"Alex, please don't say anything else. In fact, I think it would be best if you left. I'll call you when the party's over, or I can bring Melanie home."

She did not see him clench his jaw in an effort to control his anger. "I'll pick her up," he said curtly. "I wouldn't want to put you to any trouble. Good-bye, Samantha." Seconds later he was gone.

Samantha fought back the tears, mumbling to herself, "I refuse to feel guilty. After what he did, I don't owe him anything, not even courtesy." However, she could not stop the feelings of regret that rose in her.

She had no time to dwell on the exchange that had taken place in the kitchen. Minutes after his departure, she had a yard full of children, and soon the party was in full swing. She was kept too busy to worry about anything else.

When Alex came to pick up Melanie, they barely exchanged greetings. Eloise watched it all. She was saddened by the turn in their relationship and said a silent prayer that they would eventually work through their differences.

Twenty-five

Samantha was saying her own prayers when she entered the courtroom the following week. Her stomach was tied in knots, and she had not fallen asleep until the early hours of the morning.

The hearing began with the judge recapping the main points of each petition. She then moved on to the matter of the character references.

"I've read the letters you presented on your client's behalf, Counselor. I would like to hear from Dr. Simon at this time."

Eloise's testimony was brief. She described meeting and eventually hiring Samantha. When questioned about her observations concerning Jessica's care, she explained how the arrangement of bringing the child to the office after school had transpired.

Eloise stressed the fact that Jessica had always been content, for the short period of time involved, to occupy herself with her books and toys. She added that the child was always well behaved, and her presence had never interfered with the operation of the office.

When asked about Samantha's various trips to medical conferences, she told the judge of her original reluctance to leave the child. She stressed that Samantha's agreement had not come until after a few years and only when she was certain that Jessica was familiar and comfortable with being left in Amy's care.

"Are you aware of any other times the child was left in the care of a baby-sitter for any extended period of time, perhaps to take vacations on her own?" the judge asked.

"For an extended period of time, no. Only an occasional evening here and there—and as far as I know, that's been only in the last few years. In fact, I believe her actions have always been carefully thought out, her uppermost concern being the effect they would have on Jessica. Whenever she took vacations, she took her daughter, Jessica, with her."

When Eloise had stepped down, the judge directed her next question to the social worker. "Do you have anything further you would like to add? Have you discovered any reason to question Ms. Desmond's conduct or care of the child?"

"Only the fact that Miss Desmond tampered with an official document. I feel that deserves some consideration. It would seem to me that this may be an indication of an irresponsible attitude.

"Although Dr. Simon leads us to believe that she has subjugated her own needs to the child's, Jessica's, we cannot really be certain of that. After all, Miss Desmond is young and single, and it's highly possible that in time she will begin to feel stifled by a responsibility from which she has evidently had no relief since she was a teenager.

"Furthermore Ms. Desmond ran away with a child for whom she had no legal custody. In fact, as I stated previously, she has no blood relationship to the child, Jessica. As you know, from the papers we submitted, we have a request from the paternal great-aunt. The aunt of the child's biological father, not the adopted father. She is ready and willing to provide a stable two-parent home for the child."

"Yes, Ms. O'Brien, I have read the information you submitted. I admit I don't quite understand her reasons for waiting this long to make the request."

Listening to this last information about another request for custody of Jessica, Samantha recalled that there had been some mention of it at the previous hearing. She had been so upset at the time that she had failed to fully absorb that piece of information.

She looked around the room, expecting to see Mrs. Thomas. She wasn't there, but she didn't need to be there. Ms. O'Brien was doing her dirty work for her.

"Your Honor, until recently Mrs. Thomas was unaware of the child's whereabouts."

Samantha couldn't hold back her angry response to the implied accusation. "She knew the whereabouts of Jessica for over two years, prior to our move. She also knew the whereabouts of Jessica's parents during their entire marriage, including the nearly two months her father lay in a coma and she never once visited him."

"Miss Desmond," the judge said patiently, "I understand your anger and frustration—but once again you must control yourself in my courtroom."

"Yes, Your Honor," she responded quietly.

"Your Honor," Ms. O'Brien continued, "I would like to remind the court of the reason for our agency's existence."

"Thank you, Ms. O'Brien, and let me assure you that this court needs no reminder of the function of your agency. However, that is also the function of this court." She turned to Samantha.

"Miss Desmond, I have read the report from the psychologist. He indicates that Jessica appears to be a normal, well-adjusted, happy child."

Samantha's hopes rose with these words but plummeted again as the judge continued. "I, too, was displeased when I learned of the alterations made to Jessica's birth certificate. However, I must consider your age at the time you took that action and the stress of having lost both parents. The circumstances under which you had this responsibility placed on you would naturally affect your judgment. I can understand your reasons for resorting to such measures.

"Considering the caseloads already being carried by overworked caseworkers, I see no reason to add to it. I'm sure Ms.

O'Brien would investigate Mrs. Thomas prior to placing the child in her care. However, I see no need to place that additional burden on your agency.

"The fact that Jessica has been in Miss Desmond's care for the vast majority of her young life has a large bearing on my decision. I have no reason to doubt Dr. Simon's assessment of Miss Desmond's concern for Jessica, and I have never subscribed to the attitude that it requires two parents to provide a loving, nurturing, stable environment.

"To tear Jessica away from the only parent that has been a constant in her life, with no real basis for such an action, would not only be unjustified, it would be cruel. Therefore I am awarding Miss Desmond total and permanent custody of Jessica."

Samantha finally let go the breath she had been holding as tears misted her eyes. "Thank you," she whispered.

The hearing was adjourned, but Samantha was hardly aware of the congratulations from her attorney and Eloise. She came out of her daze when she heard her name spoken. She stiffened as Ms. O'Brien approached.

"Miss Desmond, I want to congratulate you. I also want to assure you that there was nothing personal in this action. I was only doing my job."

Samantha just stared at her. She could not quite bring herself to believe what she was saying, but she decided she could afford to give her the benefit of the doubt. She nodded and started to walk away.

The social worker continued. "I didn't know the background of Mrs. Thomas's relationship with Jessica's parents, but I am bound by regulations. If a child is orphaned, and a relative indicates their willingness to accept the responsibility of raising the child, I'm required to investigate the situation. I'm also required to determine whether the child's welfare is at risk. I don't think she filed the complaint with any malicious intent, and I hope you will see fit to allow her to see Jessica."

"I'm not convinced that you're right about her intent, but she's welcome to visit Jessica whenever she pleases, as long as she calls first. Neither do I believe that she really wanted the responsibility of raising Jessica," Samantha insisted.

"Unfortunately," she continued, "my limited contact with her leads me to believe that she hoped that gaining custody of Jessica would also give her control of the trust fund her mother set up for her after Barry's, her biological father's, death."

"I'm sorry you feel that way, but I am glad to know that Jessica has a good home. After all, that's what my job is all about."

Samantha was urged away by Eloise and her attorney. Once she and Eloise were settled in the car, she replayed in her mind some of the caseworker's testimony. The most important fact was that Mrs. Thomas was behind the complaint. That news in turn presented another problem: the accusations she had made against Alex.

Eloise watched the play of emotions on her young friend's face as she drove. Having heard Ms. O'Brien's statements concerning Mrs, Thomas, she guessed that there could be only one reason for her look of remorse. They arrived at the office, but Samantha made no move to get out of the car.

"He didn't do it, Eloise," she whispered. "Alex didn't call them. It was Mrs. Thomas." She shook her head.

Eloise was at a loss for words. She did not want to remind her that she had tried to convince her of that, so she simply nodded.

"How can I ever face him? I accused him . . . I said such awful things to him."

"Samantha, dear, I think Alex is a big enough man to accept your apology. I'm sure he'll understand that you were under an enormous strain."

She shook her head but could make no reply to Eloise's optimism. She got out of the car, and the two women entered the office to be greeted by Jessica. Samantha hugged the child to her, thinking, *At least the most important thing went right today*. She glanced at Amy over the child's head and answered her questioning look with a smile and a nod.

"I feel like celebrating," she murmured.

"What are we celebrating, Mom? Is it someone's birthday?"

"No, sweetheart, something much more important. Someday I'll tell you all about it. Right now why don't you gather your belongings—we're going home."

Even with the hearing a thing of the past, Samantha couldn't dismiss the questions running through her mind. From the general information she had gleaned, she knew only that Mrs. Thomas had contacted the Child Welfare Agency. But how had she known where they were living? And why had she waited until now?

For days she mulled over these questions. Then she stumbled across the bill for flowers she had sent Mrs. Cummings. She had never told her former neighbor where she lived. Their only contact had been by phone, until she sent the flowers and the card—a card on which she had automatically written her return address. She had to know the answer.

Picking up the phone, she dialed her number. She chatted for a few minutes, Mrs. Cummings thanking her for the flowers and exclaiming over Jessica's snapshot. Samantha was uncertain as to how to broach the subject of Mrs. Thomas. In the end it was the other woman who volunteered the information.

"Did Mrs. Thomas contact you? She'd been here several times asking about you and Jessica, but I didn't have your address until I received your card."

Samantha saw no need to upset the older woman. Obviously it had not occurred to her that Samantha had deliberately refrained from telling her their whereabouts all these years.

She simply replied, "Yes, she contacted me. She didn't really want anything important."

They talked a while longer, Samantha bringing her up to date on Jessica and assuring her that they were both doing well. She hung up after promising to bring the child to see her one day soon. There was no longer any need to keep her away from their former neighborhood.

Once she had spoken with Mrs. Cummings and had her curiosity satisfied, Samantha tried to unwind from the tension of the previous weeks. Her worst fears had been overcome, but she was now trying to cope with the realization that she had wrongly accused Alex. She knew she had to face him, to apologize, and she was not looking forward to it. There was no way she could rationalize what she had done.

If she could raise even the least hope of restoring their relationship, it would be easier—but she was convinced that she had destroyed any chance of that. Even without that hope, she could not ignore the wrong she had done to him. She had to apologize. He deserved that much. She thought about calling him, but she could not be that cowardly. She had delivered her diatribe in person—he deserved no less with her apology.

It was almost two weeks after the custody hearing when she decided the time had come, that she could not put it off any longer. Jessica had been invited to a slumber party the coming weekend to celebrate one of her friend's birthday.

It was the perfect opportunity since she was uncertain what state her emotions would be in after her confrontation. She would not have to be concerned about upsetting Jessica if she was a basket case when she returned.

Friday evening she drove Jessica to her party and went directly to see Alex. Unknown to her, he had learned the outcome of the custody hearing from Eloise, although his godmother had told him nothing about the information concerning Mrs. Thomas.

Samantha had summoned every ounce of her courage to bring her as far as his doorstep, and it almost deserted her when she saw the look on his face. Having heard nothing from her, he assumed she still held him responsible for her suffering. He also still harbored some anger for the way she had brushed him off the day of Jessica's party.

"Hello, Alex," she greeted him warily. It had not occurred to her until that moment that he might not even hear her out—that he might simply ask her to leave, as she had done to him.

"Samantha. What brings you here?" he asked tersely.

"I'd like to speak with you. May I come in?"

"Well, this is a switch—you're asking my permission. Usually when you show up on my doorstep unannounced, it's to demand an interview."

Samantha blushed, acknowledging the truth in his words, and was again faced with the possibility that he would throw her out on her ear. He saw the color flood her cheeks, and he knew his comment had hit the mark. His curiosity was piqued, but he admitted to himself that curiosity was not foremost in his mind as he ushered her into his study.

She noticed the papers spread out on his desk and realized she had interrupted his work. Again she was tempted to turn and leave, but she forced herself to go through with the job she had come to do.

"What is it you wanted?" he asked.

"I had the custody hearing and I won. The judge gave me legal custody of Jessica."

"Congratulations," he responded tonelessly.

"What I really came for, Alex, is to apologize. I found out from the social worker that the complaint didn't come from you," she informed him.

"Oh, really?" he asked skeptically. "I thought that kind of information was confidential?"

"Well, it is—but this wasn't the kind of complaint that was accusing me of neglect or abuse," she admitted. "She mentioned that Mrs. Thomas had requested custody of Jessica. She found out where we're living from Mrs. Cummings, my former neighbor."

Once she started trying to explain, Samantha could not seem to stop. She went on to explain about the flowers and the card with the return address. Finally she realized she had been chattering nonstop for a few minutes and was beginning to repeat herself. She stopped abruptly but avoided his intent gaze.

"I see. If you believed I could be so underhanded as to make the complaint, I wonder that, once you learned it was Mrs. Thomas, you didn't then assume that I had tracked her down and told her," he said sarcastically.

Samantha felt the heat flushing her face. "I suppose I deserved that," she murmured. "Anyway, I apologize. I hope you'll forgive me."

He looked at her a moment before replying. "Yes, I forgive you. Are you satisfied now?"

Samantha did not answer his question. She was having difficulty forcing words past the lump in her throat. It was really over. She had killed any feelings he might have had for her. She turned away quickly to hide the tears that had welled up in her eyes.

"I'm sorry I disturbed you. I'd better go and let you get back to your work."

A moment later she was gone.

Twenty-six

Alex stood there in the middle of the floor until he heard the outer door close behind her. He sank down onto the sofa, burying his head in his hands.

He should have stopped her. Why didn't he stop her? She was wrong to accuse him, but he knew how upset she had been. How could he have expected her to be thinking logically? Jessica was her whole life.

When he lost her the first time, he had hurt more than ever before in his life. When she ended their relationship, he had remembered vaguely the pain he had felt at Marci's defection. In retrospect he had realized that what he felt when Marci left was more anger and humiliation than genuine pain. Comparing that to the pain of losing Samantha was like comparing a paper cut to an amputation.

His father had once assured him that no one ever died of a broken heart. In fact, he had pointed out, there was no such thing as a broken heart. At the moment Alex was not so sure about that, and this time it was his own fault.

A week later Alex had lunch with Eloise. She had called, issuing the invitation, ostensibly to discuss the attorney's bill from Samantha's custody case. Alex insisted that she could simply mail the bill, but she had been determined to discuss it in person.

They were halfway through their meal before Eloise raised the subject that was the real reason for her invitation. She had presented the attorney's bill and had finally succeeded in getting Alex to agree to split it between them.

"I guess it's time to get down to the real reason I wanted to meet with you, Alex. You'll probably feel like calling me a meddling old woman by the time I'm finished, but your mother raised you too well for you to do it to my face."

Alex sat back in his chair and closed his eyes. "Eloise, if this has anything to do with Samantha, I think you're wasting your time. There's been too much water over the dam. I'm not sure the relationship can be salvaged at this point."

"I disagree, Alex. You're both a bit stubborn, but you're also both very much in love. I don't know everything that has transpired between you, and I'm not enough of a busybody to consider asking, but I can't believe it's anything that can't be overcome. Of course, maybe I misjudged the situation—maybe you don't care enough to try."

Alex looked her in the eye. "Stop fishing, Eloise. You haven't misjudged my feelings. I'm just not sure I can do anything about it." He paused and took a deep breath.

"I know you wouldn't ask any of the particulars, but I'll tell you this—she came to me to apologize, and I practically threw her apology back in her face. I can't imagine she'll even speak to me now."

"Well, you won't know for certain unless you try. Will you? You're not a coward, Alex. You never were." She took a sip of her coffee. "And that's all I have to say."

Eloise was glad she had talked to Alex. She'd had some misgivings about interfering—but after seeing Samantha looking so miserable, she'd had to assure herself of Alex's feelings. He'd said that Samantha had apologized. Well, now it was up to him.

Alex stewed over Eloise's advice and his own stupidity for the remainder of the week. His godmother was right. He would never be able to move on until he had settled the situation with Samantha once and for all. If she turned him away, so be it—he had to try. If there was the least chance, he would do whatever was necessary to redeem himself.

He felt no guilt about enlisting his daughter's aid by suggesting that it might be nice to have Jessica for an overnight visit on Friday. Sarah made the call and the arrangements for Fred to pick up Jessica from school.

Samantha was glad to give her permission for Jessica to visit Melanie. They had not seen each other, except in school, since her last visit to Alex. It was her fault as much as Alex's, maybe more so. The times that Jessica had raised the subject of having her friend visit, Samantha had denied the permission. She knew the excuses she gave the child were not valid, but Jessica accepted them.

Friday afternoon Samantha was preparing to leave when Amy came into her office. Her friend knew about her accusations against Alex, her subsequent apology, and his reaction.

"Since you don't have Jessica this evening, why don't we go to a movie? We can have dinner out and make a night of it."

"And what about Rob?"

"Rob knows how to cook. He won't mind."

"I don't think so, Amy. I'm not really in the mood. I'd be lousy company."

"Samantha . . ."

"Don't say it, Amy. I'll get over it eventually. I'll be fine."

"Well, I just wish there was something I could do to help."

Samantha shrugged. "There's nothing anyone can do, Amy. It's my own fault I'm in this situation. I blew it. I just hope what they say is true—that time will heal it. I'm sure I'll survive."

During the drive home, Samantha repeated those words to

herself over and over. It wasn't that she doubted them, she just wished that she could find a way to make it hurt less. A large part of her misery was due to the fact that it was her own fault.

She had given some thought to dinner but decided she did not feel like cooking or eating. *What I need is a nice soothing bubble bath,* she decided. *Isn't that supposed to be the cure-all for being down in the dumps?*

She might have been tempted to stay in the tub all night, but the water started cooling. When she started getting goose bumps, she decided it was time to get out. All she needed was to come down with pneumonia again. She wondered if Alex would be as solicitous a second time, under the circumstances.

After she slipped into her nightgown and robe, she went down the stairs to turn off the lights. She had started toward the kitchen when the doorbell rang. She was stunned to see Alex standing on her doorstep and could think of only one reason for his presence. She flung open the door.

"Jessica—" she blurted out, but he quickly put her fears to rest.

"Jessica is fine, Samantha. She's not the reason I'm here."

Her hand on her chest, Samantha closed her eyes and took a deep breath.

"May I come in?"

She stepped back and he entered, closing the door behind him. She walked into the living room and he followed her, thankful and a little surprised that she had let him in the door.

"I'm sorry," he murmured, shaking his head. "It never occurred to me that my showing up here would make you jump to that conclusion."

"It's all right. Why are you here?"

"I'm here because it's my turn to apologize."

"I don't understand. Apologize for what?"

He was elated. Not only had she let him in the door, but she appeared willing to hear him out.

"You came to me and apologized, and I threw it back in your face. I had no right to do that. Will you forgive me?"

Samantha was speechless. She could only stare at him.

"Samantha, I love you," he murmured, taking her in his arms. "I don't want to lose you. I shouldn't have let you leave that night. Please forgive me."

"I can't believe you're really here. I know you said you forgave me, but how could you still love me after what I said? I thought I had destroyed your love."

She leaned back in his arms, looking up at him. "You still love me, in spite of all the terrible things I said to you?"

"Honey, love isn't so easily destroyed, not real love. It doesn't depend on a person doing the right thing all the time either. We love someone in spite of their imperfections. We'd all be in trouble if we had to be perfect to be loved."

He gently wiped the tears that had sprung up in her eyes, then kissed each eyelid. Lifting her in his arms, he carried her into the living room and sat down with her on his lap.

"I can't believe I waited so long to come to you. I was afraid you'd never want to see me again, but I decided I had to try."

"I've been miserable, Alex. I thought I'd lost you, and I only had my temper to blame."

"Sweetheart, I told you some time ago, I've gotten used to the temper. How could you think that a few words, spoken at a time when you were under such strain, could destroy my love? Love isn't so easily destroyed, sweetheart. I still love you, maybe even more than I did before."

He kissed her, pulling her closer. When the kiss ended, she snuggled against him.

"Tell me something, Samantha. When you thought I was the one who had called the Child Welfare Agency, did you stop loving me?"

"No," she admitted with a sigh. "I was angry and hurt. I wanted to hate you . . . I tried to hate you, but I couldn't. I couldn't stop loving you."

"I think we've both learned a very valuable lesson. Hurtful words may not destroy love, but they're a waste of time and energy."

Samantha nodded against his chest. She was back where she belonged, and she never wanted to leave. She looked up at him when he spoke her name. His mouth came down on hers, and she opened to him willingly, their tongues mingling and tasting.

He held her tightly and she clung to him, never wanting to let him go. When he lifted his head, her eyes were glowing with all the love she had already confessed.

"Kitten, your eyes are getting that golden glow, and if you keep looking at me like that, I may not get home tonight."

"Well," she said smiling, "you can always set the alarm. It is rather a shame to have to sneak into your own house in the middle of the night though."

His tongue began tracing a pattern on her neck. "Some things are worth a little inconvenience," he murmured, loosening the belt of her robe. In no time her robe and gown had been tossed aside, and she lay naked in his arms.

"This seems rather unfair," she murmured hoarsely, fingering his shirt.

With a gleam in his eyes, he lifted her off his lap and stood in front of her, his hands at his sides. "Be my guest," he invited.

It was not exactly what she had in mind when she admonished him for being overdressed. She stood up and with trembling hands she pulled his shirt free of his slacks and began to undo the buttons, her knuckles grazing the mat of curls she was slowly exposing. She pushed the shirt from his shoulders, took a deep breath, and undid the button of his slacks. Her fingers moved to the zipper, the heat suffusing her body as she brushed the swollen evidence of his arousal.

"I'm not very good at this," she apologized, easing down the zipper.

He clasped her face in his hands, lowering his mouth to hers. "Baby, if you were much better I think I'd go up in flames before your very eyes," he breathed against her lips.

His kiss was her undoing. She knew her hands would never work well enough to complete her task. She could barely stand. Alex sensed her dilemma and quickly finished shedding his clothes. Samantha stared at his naked masculinity and felt as though the temperature in the room had risen about ten degrees.

Gently he lowered her to the sofa, and their lovemaking rapidly escalated to a frenzied fever pitch. The whirlpool of passion came to an end in a climax of explosive spasms unlike anything either of them had experienced before.

They lay spent and sated, absently caressing and soothing each other's heated flesh. After a while Alex stirred, raising himself on one elbow to gaze down at her with a smile that displayed the depth of his contentment.

"You and I have some unfinished business that I had intended to settle earlier. Somehow I got sidetracked. Will you marry me, Samantha?"

She smiled and could not resist asking, "For the girls' sake?"

"I said that before, thinking you might be more likely to accept my proposal for that reason. Also because until the words were out, I hadn't admitted to myself that I was in love with you."

He smiled, and the look in his eyes underscored his words. "No, my sweet Samantha, not for the girls' sake—for my sake. Because I need you to share my life and my love. Will you be my wife?"

"Yes, Alex . . . yes . . . yes," she replied, punctuating each yes with a kiss.

Dear Readers,

I hope you enjoyed reading the story of Samantha and Alex. As in my first novel, *Step by Step,* I wanted to show the importance of honesty in relationships. I also wanted to make people aware of the problems that can arise from jumping to conclusions.

Both novels also carry a message that should be taken to heart by everyone. That is, that each of us has the right to be accepted for who we are and the responsibility to accept others as they are.

I enjoyed hearing from some of you who read my first novel. It's always good to know what readers think of my work. You may write me at the address shown below. I look forward to hearing from you.

Marilyn Tyner
P.O. Box 219
Yardley, PA 19067

COMING IN JANUARY . . .

BEYOND DESIRE, by Gwynne Forster (0-7860-0607-2, $4.99/$6.50)
Amanda Ross is pregnant and single. Certainly not a role model for junior
high school students, the board of education may deny her promotion
to principal if they learn the truth. What she needs is a husband and
music engineer Marcus Hickson agrees to it. His daughter needs surgery
and Amanda will pay the huge medical bill. But love creeps in and soon
theirs is an affair of the heart.

LOVE SO TRUE, by Loure Bussey (0-7860-0608-0, $4.99/$6.50)
Janelle Sims defied her attraction to wealthy businessman Aaron Dever-
reau because he reminded Janelle of her womanizing father. Yet he is
the perfect person to back her new fashion boutique and she seeks him
out. Now they are partners, friends . . . and lovers. But a cunning
woman's lies separate them and Janelle must go to him to confirm their
love.

ALL THAT GLITTERS, by Viveca Carlysle (0-7860-0609-9, $4.99/$6.50)
After her sister's death, Leigh Barrington inherited a huge share of Cas-
siopeia Salons, a chain of exclusive beauty parlors. The business was
Leigh's idea in the first place and now she wants to run it her way. To
retain control, Leigh marries board member Caesar Montgomery who is
instantly smitten with her. When she may be the next target of her sister's
killer, Leigh learns to trust in Caesar's love.

AT LONG LAST LOVE, by Bettye Griffin (0-7860-0610-2, $4.99/$6.50)
Owner of restaurant chain Soul Food To Go, Kendall Lucas has finally
found love with her new neighbor, Spencer Barnes. Until she discovers
he owns the new restaurant that is threatening her business. They compromise, but Spencer learns Kendall has launched a secret advertising
campaign. Embittered by her own lies, Kendall loses hope in their love.
But she underestimates Spencer's devotion and his vow to make her his
partner for life.

WARMHEARTED AFRICAN-AMERICAN ROMANCES
BY *FRANCIS RAY*

FOREVER YOURS   (0-7860-0483-5, $4.99/$6.50)
Victoria Chandler must find a husband or her grandparents will call in loans that support her chain of lingerie boutiques. She fixes a mock marriage to ranch owner Kane Taggert. The marriage will only last one year, and her business will be secure. The only problem is that Kane has other plans for Victoria. He'll cast a spell that will make her his forever.

HEART OF THE FALCON   (0-7860-0483-5, $4.99/$6.50)
A passionate night with millionaire Daniel Falcon, leaves Madelyn Taggert enamored . . . and heartbroken. She never accepted that the long-time family friend would fulfill her dreams, only to see him walk away without regrets. After his parent's bitter marriage, the last thing Daniel expected was to be consumed by the need to have her for a lifetime.

INCOGNITO   (0-7860-0364-2, $4.99/$6.50)
Owner of an advertising firm, Erin Cortland witnessed an awful crime and lived to tell about it. Frightened, she runs into the arms of Jake Hunter, the man sent to protect her. He doesn't want the job. He left the police force after a similar assignment ended in tragedy. But when he learns not only one man is after her and that he is falling in love, he will risk anything to protect her.

ONLY HERS   (07860-0255-7, $4.99/$6.50)
St. Louis R.N. Shannon Johnson recently inherited a parcel of Texas land. She sought it as refuge until landowner Matt Taggart challenged her to prove she's got what it takes to work a sprawling ranch. She, on the other hand, soon challenges him to dare to love again.

SILKEN BETRAYAL   (0-7860-0426-6, $4.99/$6.50)
The only man executive secretary Lauren Bennett needed was her five-year-old son Joshua. Her only intent was to keep Joshua away from powerful in-laws. Then Jordan Hamilton entered her life. He sought her because of a personal vendetta against her father-in-law. When Jordan develops strong feelings for Lauren and Joshua, he must choose revenge or love.

UNDENIABLE   (07860-0125-9, $4.99/$6.50)
Wealthy Texas heiress Rachel Malone defied her powerful father and eloped with Logan Williams. But a trump-up assault charge set the whole town and Rachel against him and he fled Stanton with a heart full of pain. Eight years later, he's back and he wants revenge . . . and Rachel.

Available wherever paperbacks are sold, or order direct from the Publisher. Send cover price plus 50¢ per copy for mailing and handling to Kensington Publishing Corp., Consumer Orders, or call (toll free) 888-345-BOOK, to place your order using Mastercard or Visa. Residents of New York and Tennessee must include sales tax. DO NOT SEND CASH.

LOOK FOR THESE ARABESQUE ROMANCES

ROMANCES THAT SIZZLE
FROM ARABESQUE

AFTER DARK, by Bette Ford   (0-7860-0442-8, $4.99/$6.50)
Taylor Hendricks' brother is the top NBA draft choice. She wants to protect
him from the lure of fame and wealth, but meets basketball superstar Donald
Williams in an exclusive Detroit restaurant. Donald is determined to prove
that she is wrong about him. In this game all is at stake . . . including Taylor's
heart.

BEGUILED, by Eboni Snoe   (0-7860-0046-5, $4.99/$6.50)
When Raquel Mason agrees to impersonate a missing heiress for just one
night and plans go awry, a daring abduction makes her the captive of seductive
Nate Bowman. Together on a journey across exotic Caribbean seas to the
perilous wilds of Central America, desire looms in their hearts. But when the
masquerade is over, will their love end?

CONSPIRACY, by Margie Walker   (0-7860-0385-5, $4.99/$6.50)
Pauline Sinclair and Marcellus Cavanaugh had the love of a lifetime. Until
Pauline had to leave everything behind. Now she's back and their love is as
strong as ever. But when the President of Marcellus's company turns up dead
and Pauline is the prime suspect, they must risk all to their love.

FIRE AND ICE, by Carla Fredd   (0-7860-0190-9, $4.99/$6.50)
Years of being in the spotlight and a recent scandal regarding her ex-fianceé
and a supermodel, the daughter of a Georgia politician, Holly Aimes has turned
cold. But when work takes her to the home of late-night talk show host Mi-
chael Williams, his relentless determination melts her cool.

HIDDEN AGENDA, by Rochelle Alers   (0-7860-0384-7, $4.99/$6.50)
To regain her son from a vengeful father, Eve Blackwell places her trust in
dangerous and irresistible Matt Sterling to rescue her abducted son. He accepts
this last job before he turns a new leaf and becomes an honest rancher. As
they journey from Virginia to Mexico they must enter a charade of marriage.
But temptation is too strong for this to remain a sham.

INTIMATE BETRAYAL, by Donna Hill   (0-7860-0396-0, $4.99/$6.50)
Investigative reporter, Reese Delaware, and millionaire computer wizard, Maxwell Knight are both running from their pasts. When Reese is assigned to
profile Maxwell, they enter a steamy love affair. But when Reese begins to
piece her memory, she stumbles upon secrets that link her and Maxwell, and
threaten to destroy their newfound love.

*Available wherever paperbacks are sold, or order direct from the
Publisher. Send cover price plus 50¢ per copy for mailing and
handling to Kensington Publishing Corp., Consumer Orders,
or call (toll free) 888-345-BOOK, to place your order using
Mastercard or Visa. Residents of New York and Tennessee
must include sales tax. DO NOT SEND CASH.*

LOOK FOR THESE ARABESQUE ROMANCES

WHISPERED PROMISES   (0-7860-0307-3, $4.99)
by Brenda Jackson

AGAINST ALL ODDS   (0-7860-0308-1, $4.99)
by Gwynn Forster

ALL FOR LOVE   (0-7860-0309-X, $4.99)
by Raynetta Manees

ONLY HERS   (0-7860-0255-7, $4.99)
by Francis Ray

HOME SWEET HOME   (0-7860-0276-X, $4.99)
by Rochelle Alers

ENJOY THESE ARABESQUE FAVORITES!

FOREVER AFTER   (0-7860-0211-5, $4.99)
by Bette Ford

BODY AND SOUL   (0-7860-0160-7, $4.99)
by Felicia Mason

BETWEEN THE LINES   (0-7860-0267-0, $4.99)
by Angela Benson